NO MAN'S LAND

ALSO BY ROBB WHITE

For Young People

CANDY
SILENT SHIP, SILENT SEA
SURRENDER
THE SURVIVOR
DEEP DANGER
FLIGHT DECK
THE HAUNTED HOUND
THE LION'S PAW
MIDSHIPMAN LEE
MIDSHIPMAN LEE OF THE NAVAL ACADEMY
THE NUB
SAIL AWAY
SAILOR IN THE SUN
SECRET SEA
THE SMUGGLER'S SLOOP
THREE AGAINST THE SEA
TORPEDO RUN
UP PERISCOPE

Non-Fiction

OUR VIRGIN ISLAND
IN PRIVATEER'S BAY

Novel

RUN MASKED

Motion Pictures

HOMICIDAL
HOUSE ON HAUNTED HILL
MACABRE
13 GHOSTS
THE TINGLER
UP PERISCOPE
VIRGIN ISLAND

NO MAN'S LAND

by Robb White

Doubleday & Company, Inc., Garden City, New York

For
JONI

PIDGIN ENGLISH

A common language used in the Western Pacific by both natives and foreigners for neither could hope to learn many of the hundreds of different dialects. Here are a few phrases, including those used in this book:

TISPELA DOG I NOGAT TIS—This dog has no teeth.

OLOGETA MAN I HOLIM SPIA—Every man held a spear.

NO, MI NO PAITIM. EM I DAI LONG POREIT TASOL—No, I didn't hit him. He just fainted from fright.

KAITIM GRAS BOLONG MI—Cut my hair.

MI NO MOA GOT MONI, MI RABIS TASOL—I haven't got any money, I'm broke.

YUPELA SAVE TOKBOI?—Do you speak pidgin?

BOI BOLONG YU, MASTA—I am your servant, master.

WONEM SAMTING?—What do you want?

NAMBAWAN SMITH HAT WAILIS BOLONG YU—Smith has a message for you.

MASTA, LUKIM SIP—Master, look at the ship.

SAMBAI ROP BOLONG MI OLTAIM—Stand by the rope all the time.

NO KEN TINGIM—Don't worry.

HALPIM—Help!

NO MAN'S LAND

1.

It was the loneliest place on earth.

Of all the islands Garth Larson had seen in the South Pacific Ocean Molahve was the most forbidding. From the sea you first saw the island as a dark cloud resting on the surface—a dark cloud in a usually cloudless sky. You had to approach much closer before you could see that it was not just a cloud; see that there were three dead volcanoes rising from the ocean into the shroud of dark cloud concealing the peaks.

When you were close to Molahve you could make out the white sand and black lava beaches. You could now distinguish the green vegetation from the shadow of the cloud and the cloud itself. The tracks of ancient volcanic flows were wide, weirdly contorted scars streaming motionless out of the cloud, through the rain forest and down to the ocean.

Garth Larson could not explain why the sight of Molahve—whether he saw it from the deck of the schooner or merely glanced up at it as he worked in the lagoon—always gave him a feeling not exactly of fear, but of apprehension; a feeling of vague anxiety.

Molahve was not, as he had so long dreamed, a tropical

paradise. During all the years of his planning to come here he had imagined the island as a beautiful and pleasant place to work. It was not.

Perhaps, Garth thought, it was simply because Molahve always seemed to be in such deadly and silent conflict with itself.

The jungle fought the beach, but whenever its roots and vines and limbs came too far the sea roared in and tore them loose and threw them back.

The jungle also fought the slopes, smothering the earth and creeping across the volcanoes' scars and as it spread up the sides of the mountains the jungle even fought itself for there the towering trees of the rain forest formed a solid canopy which denied sunlight to the lower growing things. In this forest the light changed into a strange, dimly glowing wetness—you felt that you could touch this light and it would leave your hands damp and clammy.

Molahve was forbidding, but for Garth's purposes it was the perfect island. Molahve was one of the very few bodies of land in the world where men had never come. Men had never changed or damaged this place. Men had never polluted the water in its lagoons nor interfered with the life existing in the water and on the land. Molahve was unique because men had never interfered with nature here; for unknown thousands of years the plants and animals and fish had not been disturbed in their evolution. There were, on this island, and in the sea around it, plants and birds and animals and water creatures never seen by man, things that could be found nowhere else on earth.

Garth had heard theories explaining why men had never chosen to inhabit Molahve. It was obvious why white men had not—the island offered them practically nothing. It was far from any shipping lanes and had no flat land for plantations, no evidence of valuable minerals, and no supply of native labor.

Why the Melanesians had not established villages here was not so easy to answer. Fish were abundant, the lagoons pleasant, and enough fertile land for their small gardens could have been rescued from the jungle.

But Melanesians had never come, and if the old men of the villages on other islands knew why, they would not tell. If there were legends and superstitions about the island the old men had either forgotten them or simply would not discuss them.

Garth had a theory of his own which seemed logical. In an area where the native population was shrinking, why would anyone choose to live on such a forbidding place as Molahve when there were delightful atolls and pleasant, friendly islands all over the place?

There was a taboo on Molahve and a very strong one at that. Molahve was taboo to all natives. They were forbidden to put foot on it or, in fact, even to go near it. If it lay in their path on a journey they would sail far around it, so far that they could see of it only the cloud on the volcanoes. Although he had not been able to find out the reason, the source of the taboo, he had found out that it had been put on the island fairly recently and was not one of the ancient taboos of earlier civilizations.

Garth Larson had not come to Molahve to disturb it in any way. In fact, it was essential to his project that he not disturb it—not add any pollutants or even nonpolluting but alien substances to the water. He was there because nowhere else on earth was it possible to study marine life such as Molahve's in an absolutely pure and natural environment.

Specifically, Garth was there to discover, if he could, why some fish and shellfish feeding on essentially the same food as other fish could somehow turn that food into poison, while the other fish did not.

To find out also, if he could, why some of these poisons, although present in very large fish, were mild, causing in man a painful but not lethal illness. Whereas, some of the smallest fish and mollusks, eating a simple diet, produced poisons so powerful that a man injected with only a tiny amount died in a matter of minutes.

To find out how some inch-long sea snails could produce a venom more lethal than that of cobras and rattlesnakes. To discover, if he could, how some species of the torpid, sluglike holothurians who ate nothing but mud could produce, from mud, a venom so strong that it was not even necessary to inject it; this poison could kill without contact other than the water which the holothurian and its enemy occupied.

Molahve was the one perfect place on earth for research of this sort. In the big lagoon Garth had chosen for the project he could study the diets of his subjects knowing that the food of all these creatures was in its purest and most natural form. Unpolluted, uncontaminated, unchanged by the invasion of man.

This purity was necessary in order for chemists to be able to study the various kinds of poison Garth collected from the specimens in his lagoon. Any alien substance would confuse the scientists in their attempts to analyze the fantastically complicated make-up of these poisons created without any effort by some of the simplest animals.

To preserve this purity Garth had to be extremely careful. In order not to introduce any foreign matter into the water of his lagoon he used, first, his schooner *Uldra*. She was an old, well-built, 72-foot Marconi-rigged boat which had once belonged to his father. Every inch of her that could come in contact with the sea had been covered with sterile fiberglass. In the vicinity of Molahve, Garth never started the main engine, using only the sails to move her, and he never used the outboard available for the dinghy; only fiberglass oars.

No refuse or anything else was ever dropped overboard unless the schooner was far out to sea. Garth's instruments, diving equipment, even the mooring he had built in the lagoon were made either of plastic, stainless steel, or glass. He did not even let any part of his bare skin touch the water. When diving he wore a specially made suit of thin, but tough, surgical rubber, complete with helmet, boots, and gloves. The only thing he could not avoid putting into the water was the air he breathed exhausting from the scuba valve, but the people at Scripps were sure that this could not change the water in any way.

It was not enough simply to investigate what the organisms he was studying ate. He also had to relate them to other organisms and to the total environment in which they lived. This study of ecology, as they called it, was necessary not only to find out what produced the poisons, but what use was made of them.

Garth remembered his first long weeks at Molahve without much pleasure. The Institute for which he worked had promised from the beginning that he would be given an assistant, some young man who was as interested in marine ecology as Garth was. Only, this assistant had never showed up. Garth's appeals for help which he radioed regularly to the Institute headquarters on Guam had brought only promises.

So, alone, Garth had spent the first weeks setting up the equipment in the lagoon. Although the Institute couldn't seem to provide him with an assistant, it had certainly given him the finest tools he could ask for. These, diving alone day after day, Garth had carefully placed in the lagoon.

The first to be set up was an instrument to measure the currents below the surface, recording the speed, direction, and temperature. Next, the wave recorder was anchored to a small mound of lava he built up on the bottom.

Then he rigged the transmissometer system. By measuring the percentage of transmission of a columnated light beam through a proven path in the water, he could record how turbid such things as storms, rainfall, and high winds made the water in which his organisms lived.

The schooner, *Uldra*, was a floating laboratory. Every inch inside her hull not needed for the actual sailing of the boat was filled with beautiful equipment. Specimen tanks were mounted on gimbals, and gyroscopes could be used to steady them in case of rough weather, so that the violent movement of the schooner did not disturb the water in the tanks. The bulkheads were racks for water and sediment samplers, Phleger corers, pingers and locators, sample bags and files.

Except for the chain locker, the entire forward end of the schooner had been converted into a photographic department. Here there were the underwater still, motion picture and television cameras, a darkroom, a refrigerated compartment for film storage, cabinets for monitors and readout meters.

Aft, and separated by a solid transverse bulkhead, was the engine compartment which contained not only the ship's main propulsion engine but the air compressor for the scuba tanks and the electric generator for general lighting, laboratory, darkroom, and radio. These were air-cooled so that no exhaust pollutants went into the sea.

One night Garth had idly begun adding up the dollar value of the equipment aboard. At a quarter of a million dollars and a long way to go he gave up. For a moment he felt a little proud. Here he was, a twenty-five-year-old marine toxicologist, his diploma still very bright and curled, entrusted with a 72-foot schooner filled with hundreds of thousands of dollars worth of delicate equipment. Here he was, all alone in the most remote reach of the South Pacific Ocean, carrying on a vital experiment. They must think a lot of you, boy, Garth thought.

And then he laughed. And got back down to normal size. One day a week he spent sitting on an uncomfortable narrow bench inside a stainless-steel anti-shark cage on the bottom of the lagoon, breathing compressed air (the exhaust going past the back of his head hour after hour always sounded finally as though his head were in a gravel waterfall). Endlessly, except when he had to change film and get fresh tanks of air, he sat on the bench and photographed a marked-off area in front of him. For long periods there would be no apparent movement—no fish swimming in and out of his viewfinder, nothing moving on the bottom—but he kept the camera running, for no one could tell what was hidden below the sand, or when it would suddenly appear, sometimes to escape, sometimes to kill.

The salary of this renowned scientist, Garth Larson, entrusted with all this valuable equipment, was not enough to pay for the film the camera used in one day while the great Mr. Larson sat on the bench, hoping the sharp edges of it were not going to puncture his rubber suit.

So he was Garth Larson again, with a Master's degree (and, hopefully, a Ph.D. after a year or so at Molahve). A genuine graduate marine toxicologist whose salary was less than the janitors' who took care of the plush offices of his classmates who were really making it big in everything but oceanography. None of those big shots was sitting in a jail cell thirty feet below the surface of the Pacific Ocean.

Garth remembered the first few weeks on Molahve after the men who had helped sail the *Uldra* down from Guam had left. He remembered that time now with real embarrassment for he had, in those first weeks, just sat around sulking like a little kid. Sulking because that assistant didn't show up, sulking because who did they think he was to leave him there with all that backbreaking work to do?

Slowly, though, he had begun to work—perhaps from lack of anything else to do.

The next weeks were tough, but he remembered them now with pride for there had been no sulking—just exhausting, hard, dangerous manual labor. He didn't think he'd ever forget the weeks it took him to build the artificial reef. Since he did not want to introduce anything into the water that wasn't already there, he was forced to use whatever rocks, lava, and chunks of coral he could find, dig up, or break up. Spending hours underwater, he moved what he could lift and then, in and out of the water, he moved the heavier stuff with a jury-rigged winch in the bow of the *Uldra.*

But now there was a beautiful artificial reef on the bottom of the lagoon where literally thousands of fish and other sea animals lived.

The Institute people had been very proud of the anti-shark net they had provided and it *did* look good. The nylon rope was half an inch thick, woven so that the openings in it were not more than ten inches wide. With weights all along the bottom of it and the ends secured to boulders on the shore, the rope net screened off his entire working area. It looked fine.

Garth didn't trust it. He was glad to have it and it gave him some sense of security, but he was sure that if a really big rogue shark wanted to come through the net he could do it. That hide like a file could shred the nylon without too much difficulty, or the shark might just decide to take a bite out of the net.

So, even with the net between him and the open sea, he never dove without the combination shark-prod and tranquilizer gun (which he wasn't sure would work fast enough on a really big, hungry shark), and he was always alert.

His main consolation underwater was that, although he could not prove it, experiments he had helped make had about convinced him that sharks would not attack anything that wasn't annoying them or didn't smell good to eat. Although he saw many sharks (the small ones swam in and out of the net) he made a point of not annoying any of them and hoped that the complete diving suit he always wore prevented any body scent from entering the water.

The anti-shark net was no deterrent to barracuda who swam back and forth through it at will, but Garth had a theory about them, too. He had never heard of one attacking anything much larger than itself unless it was attracted by something bright. A shiny metal fish lure or a shiny metal belt buckle. All his gear was painted to prevent any light reflection.

He used the anti-shark cage just for his own peace of mind. He didn't want to be sitting there, his eye glued to the camera viewfinder, and have some wandering shark bite his head off. It just made him feel a little more secure to have that stainless-steel cage around him when working with the cameras.

Actually—and Garth knew this well—the greatest dangers he faced were not big voracious things like sharks but tiny animals. A cone shell, a jellyfish, a six-inch blue octopus, or the poisons he handled daily in the laboratory were far more dangerous.

After he got the project set up, his life fell into a pattern. Each day he read and recorded his instruments, took specimens of water and sediment, counted species of this or that, measured temperatures, salinity, visibility, wind, current, sea. He took care of the tanks in the lab, replacing specimens when necessary; tagged fish he wanted to study; extracted poisons; dissected; and kept what sometimes seemed endless and useless notes.

Each Friday he spent photographing the events of sea life and on Friday nights if he needed supplies he radioed Guam.

He spent all his days and nights underwater or in the *Uldra,* going ashore only to get fresh water from a little stream running beside a lava flow or for fruit and coconuts. Other than those trips he tried to ignore the gloomy island itself, confining his world to the crystal water of the lagoon and the limitless clear sky.

Although the loneliness sometimes became hard to endure, he never called Guam unless there was a good reason for it; never called just to talk with another human, although sometimes he longed to.

The only breaks in the loneliness were the rare trips to Beaufort, the nearest civilized island in the Trust Territory. It was a twenty-four-hour sail each way and he always

looked forward to it eagerly and was always disappointed
when he got there. Beaufort was a hot, dirty, ill-smelling
little island which would have been as isolated and forgotten as were those around it if it had not been for the
airstrip. Once a week an old DC-3 clattered in from the
outside world, unloaded a few pounds of cargo and some
mail and clattered away again.

Garth spent as little time there as he could. He got
his mail and any equipment the Institute had sent him,
laid in supplies of food, gas, and oil, bought all the paper-
backs he hadn't already read, and set sail again for
Molahve.

It was lonely and dangerous and forbidding, but he recognized all those things. After a few months he found that
he was talking aloud to himself and that seemed to help
the loneliness. Underwater he was never careless, never
lulled into thinking that it was not dangerous down there
alone. He was always careful, too, when working in the lab
with the poisons he knew to be more deadly than any on
earth.

2.

Garth's loneliness ended abruptly.

Surfacing after an hour in the anti-shark cage to change film and air tanks he at first did not even notice what was going on aboard the *Uldra*. He was halfway up the landing platform, just reaching for the deck edge, when he saw above the canvas windbreak the moving heads.

Garth would not soon forget that. He had seen many Melanesians on the civilized islands but these on his schooner were the wild savages of the remote islands, Stone Age men.

The dark faces were covered with lines and whorls of vivid, almost ugly, paint. Through a hole in the web of their noses they had stuck white bones or the tusks of wild boars. Their lips and an area around them were permanently stained a dull, muddy red from the chewing of betel nuts and their front teeth, which had been filed into sharp triangles, were stained black by the betel.

Even from where he was below the deck level he could see that there were a lot of these people aboard, evidently searching for something. How many were below decks he could not tell.

For a moment he was only angry and annoyed by these people stomping around on his boat, and his first impulse

was to go up there and throw them all off. But as one
of the men went by close enough for Garth to see him
clearly that impulse died in a hurry.

He recognized the paint patterns on their faces and
bodies now. These were not the patterns of celebration,
they were the patterns of war. He noticed also that the
man he had seen was carrying not only a long, primitive
spear, but a U.S.-made M-1 rifle in good condition, clean
and oiled. The fact that strips of ribbon were tied to the
shaft of the spear told Garth that the spear itself was only
a war symbol; the rifle was the weapon.

Moving slowly so as not to attract attention, he slid
back into the water and lay beside the landing platform,
almost concealed by it.

Above him he could hear them talking now, their voices
guttural and, to him, angry-sounding. Straining, he listened
but he could not understand a word of their dialect.

He suddenly wondered if this was part of the Vailulu
Madness.

If it was, he and the entire project were in trouble.

In many of the Pacific Islands the natives, both
Melanesian and Micronesian, had been radically changed
by the occupation of their land by the armies of World
War II. For the first time not only in their lives but in
their entire history they had seen a great wealth of material—food, clothing, guns, candy, liquor, chewing gum,
machines, airplanes, jewelry—things they had never seen
before and so had never known existed. But having seen
them, they wanted all these things. And to want, for these
wild people, was to take. Just reach out and take. If something tried to prevent this taking then knock down that
something. They did not understand about laws and private
property and the rights of other men.

It had started seriously with the Vailulu tribe and had
spread throughout the area. In some sections it was called
the Cargo Cult—"cargo" being the pidgin English word
for a man's belongings.

From his position beside the landing platform Garth saw a flash of sunlight off a spearhead, watched it rising as the carrier came across the deck toward him.

Garth sank silently below the surface. Angling his fins he slid downward and under the hull and then turned and swam on down to the bottom.

Down there in the shimmering light with only the sound of his breathing he was slowly overwhelmed by the seriousness of the threat aboard his boat. It gave him the same sensation he had had once when, diving near the California coast, his gear had become entangled in heavy kelp. He remembered now how his panic had made him believe that the slimy arms of the kelp were alive and wanted only to wrap around him and kill him. The kelp had overwhelmed him just as the presence of those half naked savages overwhelmed him now. He could not hope that help would come as it had in the kelp when his diving buddy had cut him loose from the slimy arms. No one was coming to aid him now.

Remembering the blind panic he had felt in the kelp, Garth tried not to let panic sweep him again. He consciously listened to, and felt, his breathing and made himself slow it down. He found that his whole body was rigid and he forced himself to relax and just lie, almost face down, in the water.

Then he made his mind stop thinking about the tortures the savages might put him through, stop thinking about the spears and guns and the ugly black teeth.

His first clear thought was to escape. By staying close to the bottom and swimming as fast as he could away from the schooner, he hoped that he could make it across the lagoon and to the beach. There, beyond accurate range of their guns, he could sneak across the beach and into the shelter of the jungle.

It was a sudden, compelling hope, and he had already moved a few feet before he looked at his compass.

And—his watch. He halted all movement, his body feel-

ing as though it were collapsing. Even his breathing stopped
for a moment.

The elapsed time dial on his watch showed him that
he had a maximum of ten more minutes of air in the tanks.
Even with minimum exertion (which would also mean
minimum distance covered) he could not get more than a
hundred yards from the schooner before the air ran out,
forcing him to surface.

Defeated, the panic again beating at him, he moved
slowly back under the hull.

Somehow the camera held back the panic. Noticing that
he still had it in his hand he held it out, staring at it, and
then swam it down a few feet and put it gently on the
sand. A little, clear thought ran straight through his mind:
this is a very valuable camera so I must take care of it.
Unsnapping the hold-down strap he released a small, yellow marker buoy attached by a nylon cord to the camera's
watertight case. Then, knowing that he should be doing
more important things, he just rested on the sand and
watched the little buoy rise up through the water, bump
gently against the hull, slide around the curve of the bilge
and reach the surface.

Only then did he begin to think again.

What were they doing up there now?

He stopped breathing for a moment as he listened in-
tently. Men with shoes on would have made small clicking
sounds as they walked about.

Stupid! They're barefooted.

What were they doing? Robbing the boat. They would
first steal everything they understood—food, clothes, his
razor.

Then, he knew from past experience and reports, they
would take everything else, whether or not they understood
it or needed it. All the instruments, the film, exposed or
not, the cameras. And, in a day or so, unable to use the
stuff, they would throw it all away.

What they couldn't steal they would ruin. All the aquariums, the radios, the gyros, the engines, the compressor. They might even scuttle the boat.

That thought jerked him rigid again. Even if they didn't scuttle it they might steal it. Then he would be absolutely helpless on the loneliest island in the world.

How long, he wondered, would it take the Institute people to come looking for him? He wasn't a very important part of that worldwide operation.

There was nothing he could do either to stop them from looting or to defend himself against them.

He had nine more minutes. *They* had nine more minutes to finish what they were doing before he would be forced to surface.

Garth was sure that when his time ran out he would not be as lucky as he had been before. The next time they would see him.

He wondered if they would even let him get out of the water alive.

His mind was full of plans and as each one came and appeared to be his salvation, it was discarded. He thought of surfacing now, while he still had some reserve air, and then, somehow, getting aboard, getting across the deck, getting down into the lab where he could find some ampuls of poison—all this without being seen by the men swarming over his boat.

Even if he reached the poison it would not save him. There were too many of them, all armed.

The tranquilizer gun clipped to his leg? He could surface under the landing platform and there, unseen, pick them off one by one. The gun made only a small *pfft* sound, and the wound of its pellet would be hardly noticeable with all that war paint.

He had only five rounds in the tranquilizer gun. There were at least a dozen men aboard.

And even if he had had enough rounds for all of them and the tranquilizer knocked them all out and left them at his mercy he would, before they became conscious again,

have to kill them, one by one, as they lay in a coma on the
deck. Garth did not think he could do a thing as cold-
blooded as that.

Eight more minutes. He prayed that by now they had
gathered up all they wanted to take and would leave—
within eight minutes.

That hope suddenly brought a new and stronger hope.
Why had they come here?

This was Molahve—the forbidden island, the accursed
island. This was Molahve—taboo to everyone. Some natives
even thought that the curse of Molahve extended for miles
out to sea and could kill them at that distance.

The savages moving around on his ship had broken
that taboo. By doing so they risked all the terrors their
superstitions gave the taboo; they risked their lives. For
them to be so daring, Garth argued, must mean that
something of tremendous importance, something so vital to
their lives that it had overcome their fear of the taboo
had forced them to come here.

His hope was that they would not break such an awesome
taboo just to rob a small schooner and kill its crew. They
had come for some other reason, much more important
than that, and so this visit to the *Uldra* was only incidental.
Perhaps in a few more minutes they would be gone; gone
about the real business that had brought them here.

They had seven more minutes to do that.

Where had they come from, Garth wondered. The nearest land—an atoll called Efrahte—was seventy-five miles to
the east. Of course, seventy-five miles was nothing to these
masters of outrigger sailing. But the natives of Efrahte
had lived closer to the curse of Molahve and thus were more
fearful of it than any others. He didn't think that these
people would under any circumstances come into one of the
taboo lagoons.

Far to the south there were wild, uncivilized tribes, but,
within a few days sailing, there were only islands like
Beaufort. There the Melanesians had lived in a modern

civilization for half a century and would not, Garth decided, be as warlike or as daring as the natives still in a state of savagery. He doubted if the Beaufort islanders even remembered their war-paint patterns.

Suddenly, feeling embarrassed and foolish, he wondered *how* they had gotten here. He did not remember seeing anything except the hull of *Uldra* above him.

He turned on his back and looked upward again. Above him there was only one black hole in the shimmering mirror of water. There was no other boat beside the *Uldra* and, as far as he could see in the clear water, no other boat lying at anchor near her.

He turned back and lay there, gazing at, but not seeing the bottom. How had they come? Dropped from the sky?

He breathed and there was no air.

Automatically he pulled the reserve valve and there was air again in his lungs.

Five more minutes. Then there would be no more valves he could pull.

If the men up there had dropped from the sky they were not going to fly back up into it. There was, he finally admitted, no way for them to leave his boat except by jumping overboard and swimming away. And if they did not leave immediately Garth would have no choice but to go up, and no hope except that perhaps they were not there to rob and kill him, but only there out of curiosity.

He came up slowly and the closer he came to the surface the more positive he became that they were not just curious. The war paint denied that and, above all, the flaunting of the Molahve taboo was not likely to be a product of idle curiosity.

Glancing up he saw the projection of the landing platform as a rectangular black shadow right above him.

He could hide under the platform, his head above water, until . . . Until when? Until they left—with everything he had? Until they sank the boat—or stole it?

Perhaps his best move was to confront them now. To threaten them or try to make friends with them.

Even as he thought about it, he knew that he could not frighten them. These were not the cowed and subservient natives of the civilized islands; the spears and war paint, the teeth, the nose bones told him that. And how could he make friends with them if he did not speak their language?

Five feet below the platform he accepted the fact that there was no solution. He could try for time by hiding under the platform but that was the best he could do.

He glanced up again at the platform to be sure that he was still directly under and concealed by it.

The platform was gone.

His air was gone, too.

For a moment after he broke the surface, the water draining from the face plate allowed him to see only the vague white side of the *Uldra*.

Then his face plate was clear.

Above him, lining the rail of the *Uldra*, were a dozen of the savages. Two of them were holding the platform up against the side of the boat.

Stripping the mask off, Garth lay for a second looking up at the painted faces above him, looking for some hint of friendliness, some sign of guilt or humility.

The faces were set in anger, the red-stained eyes glaring down at him.

"Do you speak—English?" Garth asked, not even hoping now.

No one answered, but the spears began to appear as the men pointed them down at him, the metal, barbed tips shining in the sun, the ribbons tied to them oddly gay and pretty.

"*Yupela save tokboi?*" he asked in pidgin English.

One of the men said something but it was not in any pidgin he knew, nor any dialect either.

Slowly the platform swung down and as it did four of

the men came out on it, one carrying a rifle, the others only spears.

Saying something he did not understand, but beckoning to him, the man with the rifle clearly showed that he wanted Garth to come up on the platform.

There was nothing else he could do. Stripping off the scuba and hanging it in the rack, Garth climbed up on the platform, the men, with spears leveled, backing slowly away to give him room.

Ahead of him the man with the rifle still beckoned, backing away slowly.

Garth felt foolish and helpless as he straightened up. The surgical rubber suit was almost transparent so that it gave his body the appearance of some sort of sickly worm, the matted black hairs on his chest, flattened by the rubber, looking like some other, thinner worms. The yellow fins, flapping as he walked, made his feet grotesque and, over his forehead, the yellow snorkel waved like an antenna.

Everything was ridiculous. He in his rubber suit, these savages in their stupid war paint, the dirty bones stuck through their noses. It was all ridiculous and could not be happening in this world where men were living in outer space, where, in a matter of seconds he could have been talking to civilized people around the world.

He felt a strange sadness as he walked across the familiar deck of his boat, stopping when the man in front of him held up his hand. He stood there in the sun, the heat building up in the rubber suit, and looked at the spear tips now all around him and at the angry faces of the men.

They were going to kill him. They were going to take those spears and run him through. Perhaps they would take a long time doing it, enjoying it, or perhaps not. It didn't matter. In the end they were going to kill him.

For no reason at all.

And then, as he looked at them and felt for the first time a real, grinding fear, he knew that there *was* a reason.

He, not they, had violated the Molahve taboo. They had dared to violate it now only to revenge it.

As the men moved slowly closer, the spear tips almost touching the thin rubber of the suit, Garth suddenly wondered what would happen to the fish and mollusks living in the aquariums in the laboratory. They would die if no one took care of them.

3

They tied Garth to the foremast, doing it fast and well, using the jib sheet to bind him so that he could only breathe in shallow, dry gulps. When they were done they stood around him, still silent, staring at him with those red-rimmed eyes, eyes as flat and mean as a bird's.

He had listened to them while they were tying him, hoping to hear some word or phrase he recognized, but they spoke in no Austronesian dialect he knew and when he spoke to them they seemed never to have heard any English or pidgin.

This inability to communicate with them frightened him. He felt sure, since they had not yet hurt him, that if he could only talk to them, explain to them, this whole ridiculous problem could be solved. The fact that he could not was dangerous. Whatever they were planning to do could not be stopped because of his simple lack of words.

And what were they going to do to him?

From the time they had seen him until now, they had acted with decision, all of them apparently knowing exactly what they were supposed to do and doing it. But now there seemed to be no decision. Some of the men seemed to lose interest in him, one of them even sat down with his back against the winch and went to sleep. Others drifted out of sight. They had Garth so securely bound that he could barely turn his head and so could not see what they might be doing behind his back.

In the brief time it had taken for them to herd him forward, he had looked around and had seen nothing that was out of place, no piles of loot on the decks, nothing smashed or broken.

He was getting hot. Tied to the mast, with the sun blazing down on the rubber suit, his body could not cool itself by evaporation and the rubber suit was too tight to permit any layer of insulating air between it and him. He could feel his strength draining away; he was literally being boiled alive in his own sweat. His mind was already drifting, sliding into and out of focus as the heat increased.

He was thinking about a long time ago. In some school. A professor—Garth could see him clearly for a second—was saying, "Garth, you big Swede, why do you always look for the hard way to do things? Try the obvious way sometime."

Something was very funny; he was almost laughing. Suppose they did not intend to kill him? Suppose they did not want to kill him at all? Suppose they were really his friends. Wouldn't it be funny if they did not see that they *were* killing him inside the rubber suit?

The heat in the suit was brutal now; all he could feel were the bands of rope holding him against the mast and in the sun. The jib halyard and downhaul swayed slowly with the movement of the boat and looked to him like two curving black lines against the seering sky. Sweat, hot and running, flowed down him and pooled around his feet, encased in the tough rubber boots.

The heat was making him weak and dizzy and sick. He was no longer standing on his feet but was hanging from the ropes that bound him, the rubber suit now bulging between the bindings with his sweat.

Garth knew that he was vomiting; he could feel his throat straining against the ropes that held his head back against the mast. He thought how disgusting it was but could not help it.

Garth heard himself calling out to the men and thought he saw the one asleep against the winch wake up and look at him, but nobody came near him.

At some point, perhaps just before he passed out, his mind snapped into focus again and he found that he was remembering a story he had read a long time ago.

The story was about an old-fashioned hard-hat diver who, for some reason Garth could not now remember, got washed up on a tropical island.

He was remembering the story not as words on paper but as complete images, flashing into and out of sight.

Garth could see the helpless diver rolling in the surf, see him being washed by a wave up on the sand. In the background there were natives. These were not painted, savage warriors but friendly people singing songs and throwing flowers around.

The man inside the heavy, cumbersome rubber-and-canvas suit, with the lead-weighted boots and the steel helmet bolted to the steel neck ring was found by these happy natives. They rolled him over on the sand and looked through the great Cyclops eye of the face plate and saw, inside, the man's face.

They made him a god. They hauled him up from the beach and established him on a bamboo throne and worshiped him, dancing and singing and occasionally looking through the glass face plate at the face of the man inside.

The diver pleaded with them to take the helmet off, but they could not hear him. He begged them then to cut the suit open, making gestures with his heavy-gloved hands, but they did not understand him and thought that he was being godlike so they sang and danced some more.

They worshiped the man in the diving suit for many, many years as he sat there on his throne, garlands of flowers always draped around the steel neck ring. It did not seem to bother the happy natives that, after the first few days, the man's face behind the thick glass no longer moved. It did not even bother them, as the years went by, that the man inside the suit turned into a skeleton. He was their god—if he wanted to be a skeleton that was his privilege.

Somehow Garth felt cooler. He thought: This is a dream. Or, perhaps, another story. And then he thought: It isn't really cooler, this must be the way the man in the diving suit, the god of the island, had felt; cool suddenly, and free—and dead.

Garth lunged against the ropes, but nothing restrained him. And he could open his eyes now. There was no sun blazing into his face, no red-hot sky above him. Instead there were wooden beams and varnished planks. Slowly he recognized the carlins and ceiling of his cabin aboard the *Uldra*. He was lying on his back in his own bunk and when he raised his head a little he saw that someone had unzipped the rubber suit.

Sick and terribly weak and with a stabbing headache, he turned his head slowly to one side.

A white man was half-sitting on the radio table, one bare foot on the floor, the other swinging back and forth. Garth looked at him for a long time, trying to recognize him but finally deciding that he had never seen the man before.

He was rugged-looking, fifty or so and in good shape for his age. He had on some sort of native cloth shirt open down to his navel and a native pareu wrapped around his waist.

He also had on a big white Stetson hat, pushed back on what looked like a completely bald head. This made the full, bushy, sun-bleached beard look artificial.

Garth lay there looking at him and thinking that whether the man turned out to be a friend or an enemy at least he did not chew betel and carry a spear.

He felt even more relieved and hopeful when the man noticed that he was awake and said in English, good American English, "You'll be all right. Just take it easy."

"That's good," Garth said, his mind vague again as the cold spit began to gush around his teeth.

"I'm Ord Smith, from Efrahte."

Garth pushed himself up in the bunk, the nausea and headache almost knocking him back down again.

Smith said, "You need some salt tablets. Have you got any?"

Garth nodded and managed to swing his legs out of the bunk. Pulling himself to his feet, he got the rubber suit off and let it lie, slimy, on the deck. "I'm Garth Larson," he managed to say.

The fresh air helped him as he stumbled over to the medicine chest. Pouring a few salt tablets into his hand he leaned over the washbasin and drank them down. Then he washed his face and doused his head in the running water.

Straightening, he had to hold the bulkhead to keep from swaying.

"Feel any better?" Smith asked.

Garth nodded and swallowed. He could hardly hold up the towel to wipe his face.

"You better lie down."

"I'm okay."

"I'm really sorry about this," Smith said.

The nausea was dying and he didn't feel so weak. But the air in the cabin seemed hot and thin and he went over to the porthole and put his head in it, breathing the fresher outside air.

At first the ship anchored out there didn't even register. He just saw it anchored and didn't think about it as he concentrated on trying not to throw up when he breathed.

Behind him Smith said, "I told my people that if they found anyone aboard just to hold them, not boil them in a rubber suit. I'm sorry."

"So am I," Garth said, looking at the wooden ship and at last seeing it. She was a typical old copra boat, not more than sixty feet long, squatty and wide, with a ramshackle deckhouse amidships and the helm so far aft that Garth wondered how the helmsman could see where he was going. She had the usual plank sticking out from the stern to serve as the only bathroom.

"Where's the rest of your crew?" Smith asked. "I've been all along the beach without seeing anyone."

Garth noticed that the starboard davits on the copra boat were empty, the falls hanging down almost to the water.

That explains everything, he thought, his mind still vague and fuzzy. This man had brought his savages over in a small boat, left them on the schooner and gone on searching for Garth's crew.

"Underwater?" Smith asked.

Garth turned slowly around. "What?" he asked, not connecting things.

"Your crew? I'd like to talk to all of you."

Garth was feeling better now. He knew that because this guy was beginning to make him mad. "You are."

"Are what?"

"Talking to all of them," Garth said.

The man slumped a little on the table. "I'm sorry to hear that," he said. "I hoped I'd get here in time to keep that from happening."

"What from happening?" Garth asked.

The man looked at him as though really concerned. "Are you feeling all right?"

"Fine," Garth said. "Real fine."

"What did they do? Take them? Kill them here?"

It made Garth mad and then it made him realize that he was not paying enough attention to what this man was saying. "Nobody killed anybody. I'm here alone."

Smith straightened up and stared at him. "You're here at Molahve all by yourself?"

"That's right. Why not?" Garth said and then, because people didn't seem to know what a marine toxicologist was he said, "I'm a scientist."

"You're insane!" Smith said. He sat there staring at Garth as though he were a specimen in a bottle.

That irritated Garth but as he felt his mind beginning to work again, the headache fading away, he decided that the best thing to do was to play this thing real cool until he found out what the guy wanted. After all, there were still a lot of spear-throwing people up on deck. "Could be," he said, going over to his sea chest for a shirt.

"Didn't anybody warn you that Molahve is taboo? Taboo to all hands—natives and everybody. Listen, I've heard of native fishermen being killed by their own tribes just for sailing too close to this island. Didn't anybody warn you?"

"They told me," Garth said.

"And you came here anyway? That's insane, man!"

Garth pulled on a shirt and turned to face him. "You're here, so that makes two of us."

Smith took the Stetson hat off and rubbed his head with his hands. He was bald as an egg. "Man!" he said. "I'm glad I got here first. If a war party from the South Islands had found you you wouldn't have been cooked in a rubber suit, you'd have been boiled in a pot."

"The way I heard it," Garth said, "the Molahve taboo is potent enough to kill you at a range of a hundred miles. So I don't think any war parties are coming here from anywhere." He stopped and looked at Smith. "It must have taken some powerful persuasion to get your people in here."

"Oh, it did! Believe me, it did!"

"How did you happen to know I was here?"

"Last night I picked up a transmission with Guam. The thing was so loud and strong I put the RDF on it and it zeroed in on Molahve. I couldn't believe it."

"So you made up a war party just to find out who's talking to Guam?"

For the first time Smith's voice was hard and unfriendly. "I get sick and tired of you people from the States coming out here and trampling all over the beliefs and religions of the people who live here."

"I was born and raised on Guam," Garth told him. "And you know as well as I do that these taboos are made out of nothing but superstition and myth."

"Guam is a long way from here," Smith said coldly. "A long way in miles and a longer way in history. Guam is all airplanes and automobiles and air conditioners. Out here, this is still the Stone Age, so you violate a taboo of these people and you're fresh out of superstition and myth and up to your neck in revenge. Your being here at Molahve in violation of their taboo is more than enough reason for them to kill you. In fact, they think that they *have* to kill you. That it is their duty to kill you."

The trouble was, Smith was right. On the Out Islands (and on some so-called civilized ones, too) it *was* worth your life to violate a taboo.

Garth wished the queasy feeling that he was going to throw up any second would go away so he could pay attention. The salt tablets were churning around in his stomach and he felt like slumping down on the bed again, but he stayed on his feet.

He wasn't too concerned about the taboo. He thought he knew more about that than Smith did. What bothered him was what difference did it make to this guy whether he broke a taboo or not? What difference did it make to Smith if eleven thousand painted warriors came up from the South Islands and stewed him for lunch?

Smith got off the table and went over to the companion ladder, saying, "Well, you're still alive so let's keep it that way." He yelled something in a language Garth didn't know and then turned back. "I'm going to leave a couple of my men on board to help you. They look pretty wild, but they're good sailors."

Garth studied him, wondering what this was all about. "Sailors I don't need," he said, "but if one of your wild men is a good marine biologist or even a biochemist I could use him."

Smith laughed pleasantly and went on, as casually as if

he were planning a picnic. "It'll take the better part of a day to sail clear of the taboo, so I'll stay within hailing distance. Then, if you need anything, supplies or anything, come on over to my island, Efrahte."

Who did this guy think he was, Garth thought. He was saying affable and friendly things but what he was really saying was get out, beat it, take off.

Two of the savages came down the ladder, the paint all over them glowing in the light. They stopped at the door and banged the butts of their spears down on the deck like West Point cadets.

To Garth they looked silly, like something in the late late *late* show. But he had been in the islands long enough to know that they were not silly. They could be as mean and unpredictable as sharks and just as savage.

And there was no doubt about who was the boss. Smith had more control over these people than any white man he had ever seen, with or without a badge or gun.

"*Yu save tokboi?*" Smith asked.

Garth slowly realized that he was speaking pidgin to him. "Yeah, some."

"Good," Smith said. "These two speak a little pidgin so you'll get along. Anyway, they're instinctive sailors. You can just show them what to do and they'll do it. The tall one is Sam and the wide one is Jake. Their real names you don't need."

"Glad to meet you," Garth said, going over to shake hands with them.

Who was this Smith? Just some do-gooder, some great white father going around protecting the natives' rights and taboos? Or did he have a real reason for wanting Garth to get out of here?

"I've got work to do," Garth told him. "So, if it's all the same to you, I'll just stay here. And I don't need any help."

Smith's friendliness wore a little thin. "I don't seem to be getting through to you, Larson. Because you're here and alive doesn't mean that tomorrow, or the next day, you're still going to be alive. Your life is in danger, don't you know that?"

"Thanks," Garth said, "for worrying about it. But it's a chance I'll take." He smiled to take the edge off it. "I've got a good motor in this old schooner. Good enough to outrun any outrigger I've ever seen."

"*If* you saw it," Smith said. "You didn't see me—in a copra boat. If my people had been from the South Islands, you'd be dead right now."

It was time to let this Smith know that he was backed up by something, even if he had to stretch the truth a little. "You're mistaken," he said. "But I thought you were from Guam with some assistants they're sending down."

"Assistants?" Smith said. "To do what?"

"To help me."

Smith went over to the radio and, as though he knew all about it, turned it on. "Then you'd better tell your people in Guam not to send anybody else down here. I can't be responsible for what might happen."

"You're not responsible," Garth said. "Look, I appreciate your not wanting me to get into trouble, but let's look at it my way. I've been here since July and . . ."

Smith whirled around. "*July!* You've been in this lagoon since last July?"

"That's the point," Garth said. "I've been here a long time and nobody's bothered me because the taboo keeps them away. They don't know I'm here and they won't find out unless you spread the news around."

Smith hadn't heard a word he said. Now there was no friendliness in his face as he looked at Garth, his eyes squinted a little, his lips stiff. "What are you doing here, Larson?"

"I'm a marine toxicologist."

"What—are—you—doing—here?" Smith demanded. "Why —here? Why Molahve? Why this particular lagoon?"

Garth opened the laboratory door and motioned for Smith to go in.

The lab was impressive even if you didn't know anything about it. Garth hoped, as Smith looked around at all the gear, that it was impressing him. "As I said," Garth told him, "I'm a marine toxicologist working for a big State-side Institute with headquarters in Guam. I'm not here to violate anybody's taboo. In fact the only time I set foot on the island is to get a little fresh water once in a while. All I'm interested in is what goes on in this one lagoon."

Smith's voice was still cold. "If you want to know what goes on in a lagoon then I've got a bigger one and a better one at Efrahte where you won't be breaking any taboos and nobody'll want to kill you."

"It may be bigger but it's not better."

That annoyed Smith. "Why not?"

"Because you live there," Garth said. Then he smiled. "This is one of the few places in the world where every-thing is pure, natural, where there's no pollution. Where men haven't fouled things up. Don't take offense, Smith, but your lagoon's got all sorts of impurities in it. Those would ruin my project."

"Just exactly what is your project?"

Garth got a dip net and went over to the holothurian tank. Moving the net around until the little *Fierasferidae* pearlfish disappeared into the cloaca of the sea cucumbers, where they made their home, he dipped up one of the ugly, sluglike holothurians and held it out to Smith. "You know what this is, don't you?"

Smith looked up at him. "What do you mean? Of course, I know what it is. Sea cucumber. *Bêche-de-mer*. I've eaten them."

"Perhaps you won't any more," Garth told him, putting the holothurian into a tank with some small reef fish he used to feed the other specimens.

The slug sank to the bottom without a movement. The reef fish immediately investigated it but showed no alarm at having it in the tank with them.

On the bottom, the holothurian just lay breathing slowly. In a little while the pearlfish stuck its head out of the cloaca, looked around and, deciding that all was well, swam out and joined the reef fish.

"You've seen sea cucumbers along the beach in shallow water?" Garth asked.

Smith looked at him with a bored, irritated expression as though resenting this kindergarten stuff.

"You've seen fish swimming around them?" Garth went on.

"What else? They're all in the same ocean. What I want to know is . . ."

"You've even been swimming where there were sea cucumbers, haven't you?"

"Listen, I'm not even interested in sea cucumbers. In fact, I don't even like to look at 'em. Now what I want to . . ."

"Look at that one," Garth said.

The holothurian lay on the bottom of the fish tank, its dingy colors looking slimy under the light, the pudgy, cucumber-shaped body barely moving as it breathed. In the water of the tank there was no evidence of any excretion from the thing, nor of any dye such as that of octopuses.

The little pearlfish was swimming happily around, investigating its new home.

The other fish in the tank were dead or dying.

Smith leaned over and looked. "They're dying," he said.

"That's why I'm here. I've got to find out not only what it is that killed those fish, but how it got to them and, finally, how that ugly thing makes such a poison. In your lagoon the sea cucumbers have to eat food polluted by the native population. Here they eat untainted food. Pure mud."

Smith looked at him with insulting skepticism. "Am I supposed to believe that you're risking your life for a couple of sea cucumbers?"

"It doesn't make much difference to me what you believe. I'm here to study the ecology of this lagoon."

"No," Smith said, as though talking to himself, "I can't let you stay here, Larson."

That made Garth mad all over again but he had sense enough to realize that the whole thing was getting very serious.

"I don't see where you come into it," Garth said, trying to keep his voice calm. "I've told you why I was sent to this particular place. The Institute people want me to stay here."

"You don't understand," Smith said, his voice harsh with anger. "*My* people know you're here! Yesterday, last July, a week ago, they didn't know that. But they know it now. . . ."

"You seem to have a lot of control over them. Getting them to violate their own taboo."

"Up to a point. Up to a certain point," Smith said. "No, I can't control them. Nobody can. If you've been around these islands long you know that they can't be pushed around like some people."

Garth dipped the holothurian and its pearlfish out of the tank and put them back where they belonged.

This thing was bad and he didn't know how to handle it. As he stood watching the holothurian sink to the bottom of the tank, he wished that he knew what was behind it all. Why this man was so anxious to get him away from here.

At any rate, Garth decided, he was tired of the games they had been playing. He turned to Smith and said, "Say it right out. If I don't leave here, you'll tell your people to take him and they'll take him."

"No," Smith said. "But if you insist on staying here and they decide to get up a war party and come get you—it's only seventy-five miles, you know—there's nothing I can do to stop them. I haven't got that much control over them. All I can do is ask them to leave you alone."

Garth looked straight at him. "Okay, ask them. Because I'm staying."

4.

Garth did a lot of rationalizing about why he wanted to sleep on deck that night. It was cooler than down in his cabin; he wanted to listen to the island's and the sea's sounds; it would do him good after the shock of the heat stroke. And he rationalized about the tranquilizer gun. He might see a shark attacking the net. . . .

But when he finally settled down, lying on top of his sleeping bag wearing shorts and a shirt and with the tranquilizer gun beside him, he knew that he was there on deck because he was afraid.

Garth had watched Smith and his painted crew row out to the copra boat. Looking through the binoculars he had seen them get on board and then hoist the small boat back into the davits. He had watched the ugly little ship get up anchor and get underway, her slow diesel panting across the water. He had watched her until she disappeared and even then had not gone below decks until the sun set.

For some reason he had no appetite that night, nor even any desire to turn on the radio and listen to the unattached voices of the ham operators or the GI music from Guam or Kwajalein. He didn't feel like doing much of anything except lie in his bunk with the cabin lights on and stare at the ceiling.

He could not get rid of this fear he had. It was not a shaking, tongue-drying, throat-choking fear. It was more a heavy, dark foreboding; the feeling not that something very bad was *going* to happen, but that it had already *started* happening and there was nothing, nothing at all that he could do to stop it.

Lying on deck, realizing that he was listening for any sound that was not natural to this place instead of to the real sounds around him, he decided that the cause of his fear was this not knowing.

He did not know what was going to happen to him, nor when, nor—and this was the worst—why.

Garth just could not buy the idea that Smith had any real concern for him. Why should he?

He was equally convinced that Smith didn't care about the dear, simple natives and their quaint taboos. All Smith wanted was to get him away from Molahve. Permanently.

The fact that Smith hadn't let him die tied to the mast in the rubber suit or, later, had not killed him when he had refused to go did not mean that Smith did not want to kill him, or was afraid to kill him.

No. Smith had a reason for not killing him then. Only Garth could not figure out what it was.

He had started to radio Guam the moment the ship was out of sight but then had changed his mind. Smith would be listening and it would be just Garth's luck to get one of those real dumb Trust Territory operators who would blow the whole scene. Some of those operators could make you feel like you really did not exist. He couldn't risk that because it was absolutely necessary to make Smith believe that, at the drop of a threat, the entire U. S. Navy would swoop down on Molahve to rescue their boy. No. It would be better to wait until Friday and get his regular Institute operator.

He lay there, listening, and looking at the stars which,

in that clear sky, seemed to be rubbing against the mast tops as the schooner swayed gently in a gentle swell. He did not hear the low hum of bugs over on the island, nor the louder sounds of night birds and robber crabs and all the other things moving around over there. He didn't hear the occasional fish jump, or the skitter of a school of fry running from some predator. He didn't even hear a huge ray when it slithered up out of the water and crashed back into it, the whole ton of it smacking the water. He was listening for the pant of a diesel or the creak and pull of oars, or the soft slap-slap-slap of water against the prows of outriggers.

He heard nothing and when occasionally he sat up to look he saw nothing on the empty ocean.

It was long after midnight and his mind was tired of going around and around the same old What? When? Why? when he suddenly remembered the Filipino anthropologist, José Morales.

José was only about twenty-eight but for Garth's money knew more about the Western Pacific than any of the authorities and professors from whom he had tried to get information. Now working for his doctorate in anthropology, José had been hired by the Trust Territory to study the population trends in the Territory islands and had done most of the research for Garth on the Molahve area.

José had also been one of the crew who had helped Garth sail the *Uldra* down from Guam and, although he did not weigh 120 pounds soaking wet, heaved halyards with the best of them.

Thinking about him now Garth remembered a lot of the talks they had had on the voyage down, for José had stood watches with Garth and with nothing much to do in the long night watches talk helped to keep you awake.

The Molahve taboo bothered José. "When I first started researching it," he said one night, "I didn't think I'd have any trouble with it. After all, when you strip away the bangles, baubles, and beads, all these taboos come down to the same thing—somebody trying to get all the bread."

(Garth liked to hear José talk. He had spent two years at UCLA and thought he knew American slang, but José had no idea how it sounded with his strong Spanish accent.)

"Now you're confusing me," Garth said. "I thought they started with natural disasters—volcanoes blowing up, poison fish, that sort of thing."

"A few do," José admitted, "but they're not the real taboos; they're just warnings, based on fear or common sense. The real taboos are different. And they're old, you know. Hundreds, thousands of years old."

Garth had heard about taboos all his life but had never really been interested in them. Now, with the location of his project under a strong taboo, he was very interested.

"What are they then, superstitions?" he asked.

"Well, let's take a typical Polynesian taboo because that's the kind I know the most about. It all starts with a thing called *mana*. *Mana* is an idea they had that some people have a supernatural power. Okay, here's a guy walking around with this *mana*, this power which, they think, is contagious—like measles. It's dangerous. It could rub off on somebody. So, to keep anybody from catching this *mana* they set up a barrier of taboos around the man who has it." José stopped and laughed.

"Back in the old times in Tahiti," he went on, "the big chiefs got themselves so surrounded with taboos that they were practically isolated. There was even a taboo against *looking* at them. It was taboo to breathe the same air they breathed. Taboo to walk on the same ground. And, of course, nobody could argue with them. So, if they wanted to, they could cut off everybody's head, or take anybody's house or boat or money or wife—anything."

"Nice work," Garth decided.

"It was. In Tonga, for instance, the Tui Tonga kings had it made in the shade. By a nice manipulation of taboos

they wound up owning *all* the land. Not only that, everybody had to give them just about everything they had.
Those old kings ruled the whole Western Pacific. How?
By taboos. Anything they wanted they just announced
that it was taboo for anybody else to have it. Simple."

"The people must've been pretty dumb," Garth said.

"Not dumb, scared. You see, all these taboos are tied in
with native religions. The chiefs (and they were invariably
the fattest cats you ever saw) claimed that they were really
gods or, at least, representatives of gods. If they had tried
to set up taboos just on the basis of I'll-chop-your-head-
off-if-you-don't-give-me-what-I-want it would not have
worked. The people would have said to themselves, 'Who
does old fatso think he is?' and they'd have chopped *his*
head off. But those old guys were smart. They didn't say
I will do it, they said the *gods* would do it. They worked
that superstition pitch all the way."

Something in all this had been bothering Garth and now
he knew what it was. "Then if Molahve is taboo doesn't
that shoot down the experts who say that Molahve has
never been inhabited, at least in historical time?"

"At first that was the hang-up," José said, pronouncing
it *ahng-oop*. "To make a taboo you've got to have people
and Molahve hasn't got, and never had, any people. But
it's got a taboo. Don't kid yourself about that. And it's not
one of these little don't-fish-at-Molahve or don't-cut-out-
rigger-logs-at-Molahve taboos. It's *don't-go-near-the-place*.
Nobody, no time. And for hundreds of miles around nobody
goes near there, no time."

"Maybe one of your fat kings on some other island started
it."

"That's what I thought when I first started researching it.
I figured some big shot five hundred or a thousand years
ago saw the island and thought, well, I might as well throw
that in the kitty and he laid a taboo on it, just to keep some
other fatso from moving in." José paused and looked at
him.

"That isn't the way it happened," José said. "The Mo-lahve taboo, as far as I can find out, didn't get started until the late 1930s or early 1940s. So then I figured it would be easy. Just ask the people who are so terrified by the Molahve taboo why? What are they scared of? Who started it? You know something, Garth?"

"Nothing worthwhile," Garth said.

"They don't know," José said. "They don't know why there's a taboo on Molahve. They don't know who laid it on. All they know is that they're scared to death of the place."

"Still?"

"You better believe it. Scared stiff. Because they've got it all mixed up now with demons and sea dragons and stuff. Back in the 1940s when the taboo got started, and there's one case as late as 1954, people who went near Molahve developed a bad habit of disappearing. No war parties, no storms, nothing. Just—poof—vanish. That's hairy. It's different from getting aerated by the spear of your neighbor. Disappearing scares people."

"It sounds like nothing but good for me," Garth told him. "The scareder they are the farther away they'll stay and that's just fine. I can do very well without a bunch of guys talking to me with a spear in my eye."

"I've got a theory," José said.

"Speak."

"There's something on the island somebody wants. Or is taking. Or is hiding."

"Oh ho," Garth said.

"And it must be some native, or a small group of them, because they've been smart enough to establish a taboo and smart enough to make it stick. I don't think an outsider would (a) think of a taboo as a weapon or (b) know how to start one or (c) know how to make it work. . . ."

Garth lay on the deck of the *Uldra* looking up at the stars.

". . . there's something on the island somebody wants. Or is taking. Or . . . is hiding."

Was it Smith? And if so, what was there on Molahve he wanted? Or was taking? Or was hiding?

Garth decided that for the time being he would rule out taking. Nobody had taken anything from Molahve since he'd been there.

He decided to rule out wanted, too. If Smith wanted anything from Molahve he had had a long time to get it.

That left hiding.

There was no answer to that.

There was no answer to anything. His mind was just going wearily around and around. So at last he drifted off into hoping. Hoping that Smith had only come to warn and help him and had now gone, and would not come again. Hoping that the whole episode was over and done with, and that tomorrow he could get on with his work.

He went to sleep thinking about the beautiful mechanism for injecting venom possessed by *Chironex fleckeri*.

The warmth of the sun woke him up and the sounds of his world were pleasant. Birds were making a lot of noise over on the island and there was the distant soft whoosh of small wavelets on the beach and the nearer, sharper slap-slap of waves against the *Uldra's* hull.

It was a morning like so many he had waked up to here and it made him feel good.

The tranquilizer gun lying on the deck looked a little silly now as he rolled up the sleeping bag.

He had started toward the companion, already planning his breakfast, when he saw Smith's copra boat.

She was lying at anchor a half mile away and already the small boat was in the water. He could see Smith's white hat beyond the backs of the rowing men.

Something inside him started quivering and his skin suddenly felt cold. He glanced down at the gun in his hand, then looked back at Smith and went on down the ladder. He hung the gun up in its rack and stowed the sleeping bag. As he went back topside he wished that he had had time to shave.

Smith's boat was coming straight toward him. In the bow there were several bundles of something wrapped in woven straw matting and tied with hemp.

"Good morning!" Smith called, sounding cheerful.

"Morning."

"Permission to come aboard?"

"Come ahead."

Without all the war paint and spears the natives looked very different and, as they helped Smith up to the landing platform, they were laughing and talking. Just a mighty friendly group, Garth thought.

"Well," Smith said, holding out his hand and looking happy. "I see you're still here."

Garth shook his hand, wanting to break the bones in it. "Why not?"

"Well, let's don't go into that again. Had breakfast?"

"No."

"What you need is a good cook." Smith stepped into the cockpit and sat down on one of the long seats. Garth followed him and waited, standing.

"I like this boat," Smith said. "She's seaworthy. Some of the yachts the outlanders sail around in I wouldn't take out of a lagoon in a dead calm. Handle well?"

"Very," Garth said.

Smith looked all around, at the boat, at the sea, at the island and, lastly, at Garth. "I had a bad night last night," he said. "Couldn't sleep."

Garth just looked at him.

"I was worrying about you, Larson," Smith said.

"I wish you wouldn't," Garth said.

"I can't help it, boy. You may know all about Guam and the Ladrones, but this is my territory down here and I think I know a little bit more about it than you do."

"I'm sure you do," Garth said coldly.

"The people, I mean. The folks the outlanders call savages. The trouble is, they're not savages but they can *be* savage. And they're not uncivilized the way people think. They might live in the Stone Age but they're got laws and organizations just as good as any of ours."

What was the angle, Garth wondered, knowing that eventually Smith was going to get back to the same old thing—get out, beat it, take off. He was just approaching it from a different direction this time.

Smith pushed his hat back and rubbed his bald head. "Yeah, I worried. All night. It's just the way you said it yesterday. As long as nobody knew you were here, you were safe. But now somebody knows. I know. My crew knows."

"The way I said it was that nobody else would know unless you spread the news around," Garth reminded him.

Smith looked at him with an expression of hurt surprise which Garth could not believe was genuine. "I wouldn't do a thing like that! Man, that would be signing your death warrant. No. The point is this: My people know you're here. And if they start talking about it in the Men's House and get all worked up and painted up and danced up and make a war party to come get you, I can't stop them. Believe me, I can't."

"I believe you. We went through all this yesterday, Mr. Smith."

"I know. And you want to take your chances and you think you can outrun them if they come. All right. But there's a better way."

Well, here it comes, Garth thought. A better way. Just move over to this other island that Smith knows about. An island just like Molahve, only with no taboo.

"As I said, I can't stop them. But they can be stopped."

Garth hadn't expected this and wasn't ready for it.

Smith grinned. "See? I get good ideas sometimes. It's like this. Without their head man they don't make a move. The head man decides everything. To make a new outrigger, to carve a new symbol, to build a house for so-and-so

—the head man has to decide. He decides, too, whether to make a war party and come get you."

"How do I make friends with this fellow?" Garth asked.

"You got it!" Smith said. "So here's what I'm going to do. I'm going to leave the Number One and Number Two men of my tribe over here with you. Isn't that simple?"

"Here? With me!"

"Right! That way there can't be a war party. No paint. No dancing around all night to get up a little courage. Nothing."

It made Garth so mad he couldn't talk. Then he began to laugh. When he could, he said, "You must think I'm really stupid."

Again Smith looked hurt. "How do you mean?"

"How do I mean? I mean like this. You leave your two 'savages' over here with me and you go sailing off in your little stink pot and they put a spear through me. Well, you're awfully sorry about that but, you see, judge, it wasn't my fault at all."

"Oh, no!" Smith said. "You don't understand. I told you—I can't control these people. I'm not king or anything. But I can handle one or two of them; they'll do what I ask them to—as long as they're not all worked up with *kava* beer and betel. The men I'm going to leave here are to *protect* you, Larson, not hurt you."

"And that I can count on?"

"Absolutely."

"Sounds good but I don't buy it," Garth said. "I'm breaking a big taboo over here, so you leave two men whose taboo I'm breaking over here with me, to watch me break it. What makes you think they won't just decide to do something about it? Like tying me to the mast?"

Smith looked at him a long time and then said, "You will just have to take my word for that, Larson. But, believe me, if I ask Sam and Jake to guard your life they'll die doing it. Believe me."

Garth remembered the cold, black eyes looking out at

him from the war paint and he could feel all that animosity
again.

On the other hand, he thought, what's the alternative?
Smith could drive him away if he wanted to. Or kill him
—there was no need to be so devious about it.

Garth was convinced now that his suspicions of the
previous night were correct. Smith was behind this taboo.
And for some reason, all Smith really wanted now was to
protect his secret. He could do it very easily by planting
two spies in Garth's boat.

The alternatives, Garth decided, were far worse. After
all, he argued, he was not looking for Smith's secret, and
was not going to look for it; had, in fact, no interest in it.

"Okay," Garth said, "if you think that's the only way to
protect me from your people, okay. I'll take your word
for it."

Smith seemed very relieved and that secretly amused
Garth. Poor guy, he thought, he's sure I'm just here nosing
around to find his secret.

"They're first-rate men," Smith said happily. "They'll be
a lot of help to you. And no bother. They've brought their
own sleeping mats and all the food they'll need. . . ."

"And their spears and M-1s?"

"A native wouldn't go around without his spear any more
than you'd go around without your pants. And, who knows,
you might need those guns if the South Island people
wander up here." Then Smith smiled. "That Sam is the
best cook in the world. If he thinks you like his chow
you've got it made."

Smith stood up and called down to the men in the boat.

As Garth watched Sam and Jake come aboard with their
straw-wrapped bundles, Smith went on talking happily.
"Learn some of their language. Don't just stick to pidgin.
Theirs is a beautiful language. A lot of laughs. For instance,
they think all your emotions—love, hate, fear—come out of
your liver."

Garth half listened as he studied his new shipmates. Without the war paint they did not look so fearsome and he was glad to see that, when Sam, the tall one, dropped a bundle, both of them could laugh.

When all was aboard, the two men, each wearing nothing but a short pareu and carrying a spear in one hand, the M-1 in the other, marched aft. Stopping at the cockpit coaming they bowed to Garth and Jake. The wide one, said in pidgin, *"Boi bolong yu, masta."*

Your servant, master.

Garth smiled and greeted them in pidgin and thought: my two spies.

5

If anybody needed to be spied on, Garth decided, then he highly recommended Sam and Jake. After the first few days he forgot the real reason they were on his boat and just accepted them as crew. Assistants. Friends.

They were delightful people to have around; every day to them was a brand-new miracle to be greeted with happiness and joy. Every job he gave them, from backbreaking manual labor to washing test tubes, they made into a game. At first he thought their curiosity about his tools and equipment was part of their spying mission but he soon discovered that they were just genuinely interested.

They wanted to learn and Garth found them to have a great deal of intelligence and tremendous patience. They learned slowly, but what they learned they remembered. In a little while they were a real help in the lab, doing the work carefully and well.

On the other hand he was somewhat ashamed of his slow progress in learning their language. They taught with the same patience with which they learned but Garth found it a very complex and difficult language. Things were further complicated by his having to translate everything into pidgin before he could interpret it in English.

Gradually, though, he learned a few words and phrases and could, if they talked slowly enough, get the gist of what they were saying, even if he didn't get the subtleties.

In the beginning the only pidgin Garth knew were words and phrases for getting things done, such as:

Putim long hap: Put it over there.

Kam, alivum mi long bokis hia: Come help me with this box.

Brukim giraun: Dig here.

Fasim kanu long sip: Tie the boat to the ship.

Or if he wanted to be insulting (which he didn't):

Yu samting nating: You are no account.

Sam and Jake knew pidgin much better and, in the process of trying to learn their language, Garth got a better grip on pidgin. After they taught him some of the peculiarities of pidgin he found that he could talk more or less philosophically with them. Once he accepted their idea that the mind was not in your brain but in your belly, and that emotions were not (as some people think) in your heart but in your liver, they could talk about fairly abstract things. Soon Garth no longer thought it ridiculous if one of them said, *"Em i haskim liwa bolongen."* Before he learned the language he would have translated that as: "He, he asks liver his." And been amused. But now he understood it as meaning, "I'm trying to remember."

Whenever Sam did something wrong he would grab his belly and say, *"Bel bolong me i hat!"* Which meant, literally, "Belly of me it hot." But which really meant that Sam's mistake made him mad.

Or when Garth was teaching Jake something complicated Jake would sometimes say, *"Liwa bolong mi no inap long save."* Which translated, "Liver of me not able to know." But which meant, "My mind cannot grasp such things."

They were good companions, superb cooks, courteous, proud men who seemed willing and able to take on almost any assignment.

Except diving. Garth had a hard time explaining to them

that they must not go into the sea without a complete
rubber suit—no more carefree bathing and swimming. They
were adequate swimmers but, unlike the natives of the pearl
islands, did not dive or do any underwater work.

They were absolutely adamant about the scuba. None
of his persuasion could induce either one even to put on an
Aqualung.

That disappointed Garth, for he had hoped they would
help him underwater, too, but soon he just enjoyed knowing
that they were up there, on lookout for danger. He taught
them how to use a lifeline, taught them the signals he would
use if he needed help and that they would use to warn
or inform him.

Having nothing to hide, Garth hid nothing from them
and, as they became friends, went out of his way to explain
to these Stone Age men what he, of the Space Age, was
trying to do.

He had nothing to hide from Smith, either, but since
he was sure Smith monitored his calls, he was very careful
on his Friday night talks with Guam not to phrase his
conversation so that Smith could gather that the Institute
had no intention of sending him any assistance. (Sometimes Garth wondered if they even remembered that he
was still at Molahve.) Careful not to let Smith get the
idea that he wasn't being backed up by the combined
Pacific forces of the Army, Navy, Marine Corps, and Air
Force.

Garth had been sternly told by the Navy and Trust
Territory people not to use his big transmitter for casual
conversation but that he could talk all he wanted to on
the short-range rig.

He hadn't paid much attention to the Navy radioman
who had sailed down in the *Uldra* with him and who had
tried to explain all the electronic gear he was installing. At
the time Garth couldn't see the need for most of it and
had resented the enormous amount of space the stuff took.
There was, in addition to the big 110-volt transceiver for

long-range work, a cute little battery-operated rig for short-range, and another receiver always turned on and tuned in to the Typhoon Alert frequency which could warn him not only of typhoons but also other major hazards such as erupting volcanoes, seismic sea waves, and any manmade disasters, such as wars.

All these radios could automatically turn on and off a monitoring tape recorder so that, even though Garth might be on the bottom of the lagoon when a call came in, he could (if he had remembered to rewind the tape and there was a red light to remind him to do that) when he got back aboard, replay anything that had come in.

Now, with spies aboard, he was glad to have the gear. Every other night he called Smith on the short-range set. At first the conversations were stiff and formal but soon Garth began to enjoy talking to him—about the islands, the customs, the copra business—but never a word about Mr. Ord Smith personally. Garth tried various approaches, left him many openings, but Smith would not play. All Smith ever said about himself was that he had been at Efrahte a long time. He never said where he had been before that, nor how he had come to Efrahte. He had just been there a long time—period.

Each time Garth called he would also turn the mike over to Sam and Jake. For twenty minutes or so, taking turns or yakking together, they talked to their wives and friends and Smith, all of the conversation conducted with a great deal of laughter.

Those radio sessions, Garth decided, were good for the crew's morale—and good for his, too. If they were covertly reporting to Smith what their spying had accomplished their reports must certainly be convincing Smith that Garth was in no way a threat to whatever his dark secret here was.

This, the most pleasant time Garth had spent at Molahve, ended too soon. One day, as he was watching some cone shells paralyzing their food, the lifeline from the boat began to jerk. Garth straightened and looked around. There was no sign of any danger he could see but, since he had made the lifeline so important to Sam and Jake, he decided not to undermine their confidence by ignoring their signal to come up.

When he surfaced and pushed back the mask and hood the first thing he noticed was the unusually loud sound of the surf. Looking toward the beach he was surprised to see that the usually small and gentle waves were now coming in high and heavy, blanketing sections of the beach under a fog of spray.

"*Wonem samting?*" Garth asked Sam as he hung to the gunwale of the dinghy.

"*Nambawan Smith hat wailis bolong yu,*" Sam told him.

Smith had never called him on the radio during the day and Garth wondered what was so important now as he climbed into the dinghy and Sam rowed him over to the *Uldra.*

On deck he could now see that the waves were formidable. He had never before seen them so high here. And yet they were not wind waves but came in smoothly and silently until they crashed on the beach.

Going below he found Jake sitting staring at the radio. The call on his frequency kept up a steady beep-beep.

As Garth pushed the talk button, he had an irrelevant little thought that amused him. Sam and Jake addressed him with the pidgin word *Masta* which, although it literally meant "master" actually was not much more important than "mister." However, they always called Ord Smith *Nambawan*. Number One. Governor.

Smith didn't seem very alarmed as he told Garth that the Typhoon Alert was on and that a typhoon was north of Molahve and moving southeast.

"If those guys are right, you're not in the path of it," Smith told him, "but it'll come close enough to give you some trouble. Heavy seas, at least. Being anchored close on a lee shore isn't my idea of the best place to be."

"I'll get my gear off the bottom and run for some sea room."

"I wouldn't hang around too long, Garth. The sea's already making up here. Pretty heavy."

"Here, too. But that's expensive stuff."

"How long will it take you?"

"Couple, three hours."

"You're braver than I am," Smith said. "I'd be high-tailing it out of there *now*."

"I'd have a hard time explaining that to the Institute."

"Not as hard as explaining how your schooner got way up there in the jungle. Why don't you crack on right now and come over here? I've got a safe mooring for you. A lot better place to be than riding this thing out, hove to on the open ocean."

"It doesn't look too bad here yet so I'll get the small stuff up anyway."

"Okay. When you get over here head for the southern entrance. But if you see surf breaking over the western side of the atoll forget it, you won't be able to get through."

"Okay, and thanks."

On deck again, he saw that the waves were building fast. The whole beachline was now covered by a white fog of spray which floated back over the green jungle. The roar was a series of separate explosions, for these were great swells, so smooth from the distance they had travelled that you did not really see them until they exploded against the beach.

With both Sam and Jake in the dinghy, Garth dove down through the already murky water and hooked pieces of equipment to the lifeline. He left the heavy stuff, permanently anchored in the water, and had Sam and Jake haul up only the smaller instruments.

Surfacing for a look showed him that it was past time to get off that lee shore. Sam and Jake were huddling against a hard, cold rain and staring at the fury on the beach.

Thousands of dollars worth of equipment were still in the lagoon when they got sail on the *Uldra* and left.

As Garth looked back he could only hope that those smooth, tremendously powerful waves would not tear his gear loose and bury it in the sand he could already see being built up against the green wall of the jungle.

The voyage to Efrahte was just one long, fast, hard beating. With Sam and Jake in the bow to guide him, they went through the channel like a bullet, then dropped sail and went under power to where Smith was waiting in the rain in a small boat.

After the *Uldra* was securely moored to two heavy anchors with chain instead of rope, Smith invited Garth to ride the thing out ashore, but Garth told him he'd have to stay aboard to take care of the specimens in the tanks.

He watched the boat carrying Smith, Sam, and Jake disappear toward shore in a downpour of rain.

6.

Garth spent three miserable days and nights alone on the *Uldra* as she bucked and reared against two anchors in Smith's lagoon at Efrahte. The only consolation he could find was that it would have been worse anywhere else.

It rained continuously as the typhoon, passing some hundred miles to the east, rose to its peak and gradually died away. With the rain came hard, buffeting and veering winds which gave everything topside on the *Uldra* a steady, weary beating.

Efrahte was a small atoll formed probably millions of years ago when some volcano had reared up out of the ocean, exploded and sank back into the sea. Around this almost perfectly circular crater the islands of the atoll had been slowly built up by coral over millions and millions of years, until now there was a circle of islands, like a necklace enclosing the deep lagoon. Islands made of billions upon billions of once living but now dead coral organisms.

These islands did, in great measure, protect the lagoon they formed. Except in times like this, with the typhoon howling not far away, they held the roughness of the sea at bay. But Garth doubted if there was any spot of land in the whole atoll that was more than fifteen feet above sea level and so now the entire western hemisphere looked as though underwater. All the islands were shrouded in sea foam; solid waves broke completely over them and poured into the lagoon itself.

Occasionally there would be a lull in the rain and then Garth could see a little of the village. Smith's old copra boat, apparently unattended, was moored to leeward of him and beyond her was a small concrete and wood jetty with an unloading crane sticking up like a broken arm. On shore there were forty or so thatched-roof houses built on stilts and, towering above them, a handsome Men's House. Back in the coconut grove Garth could make out the white shape of a larger building and guessed that it must be Smith's house. The whole place was ragged-looking, with thatch from the roofs hanging in bundles or strewed all over the ground and more thatch torn out of the palms blowing across the open spaces.

On the fourth day the wind began to abate and the lagoon grew calm. Squalls of rain and wind kept up all morning, sweeping in black cloud lines over the atoll, but by afternoon there were times when the sun shone and even when it rained it was gentle.

Toward evening an outrigger came alongside with a message from Smith asking him to come ashore for a hot bath and some supper.

Garth, who had been eating out of cans when he ate at all, accepted the invitation with pleasure. Getting down into the outrigger he watched as the six men in the boat began paddling toward shore.

He recognized some of the men as those he had seen aboard the *Uldra*. But now they were just ordinary men who laughed and talked as they paddled in unison toward their homes.

Smith met him on the jetty. "Noisy, wasn't it? Any of your fish get seasick?"

"Like living in a bass drum," Garth told him. "And I used up almost all the gas just keeping those gyros going.

Thanks for the anchorage. It would have been rough out-side."

As they walked through the village Smith arranged to replenish his supply of gas.

The one street through the village was still a long mud puddle. The natives who were already working to repair the damage to their little houses stopped whatever they were doing as Smith came in sight. Garth was struck by the evident friendship they had for this man, and the equally evident respect. He had never seen Melanesians so openly display affection for a foreigner.

"They seem to like you," Garth said.

"We get along."

Through the wreckage the typhoon had left, Garth could see that this was an unusual native village. The houses were all well built and although some of them had lost thatch from the roofs most of the thatch was new and still in place.

The people caught his attention but it took a little while for him to realize why. It was simple—this was the health-iest-looking bunch of natives he had ever seen. They were even healthier than the Chamorros of Guam who were looked after by all sorts of U.S. government agencies. Garth did not see a single case of elephantiasis or yaws. None of the usual open sores and boils, no children with potbellies and thin legs showing the state of their mal-nutrition. They were healthy, energetic, and happy-looking people.

As Garth and Smith neared the Men's House, Garth stopped to admire it. "That's the best-looking Men's House I've ever seen."

"They really worked on it," Smith told him.

It was a beautiful building. Although not built to look like a bird, it gave you the strong impression that it was a bird—a man-of-war, perhaps, or one of the open-ocean gulls in flight. The long, curving ridgepole supported the curving and sloping sides of the roof as though they were wings. It was about three storys high at the front end with the ridgepole swooping up even higher.

All across the front of the building there were carved panels, the carvings, though primitive, artistic and graceful. The panels, as in cartoons, told the legends and stories of the people.

The whole place was gaily and freshly painted and, in the setting sunlight, soft and glittering, the light glinting off of hundreds of bits of colored glass and seashells the natives had imbedded in the wood of their carvings.

Inside the Men's House (where no women were ever allowed) men were already cleaning up the trash blown in by the typhoon. At one end Garth could see an outrigger in the process of manufacture, the long, straight log half hollowed out by fires set all along the length of it.

At the other end was a small, raised platform on which stood a throne made of carved wood and also decorated with pieces of glass and shell.

"That your chair?" Garth asked.

Smith laughed. "Who do you think I am, the Boss? No, as a matter of fact, I don't want that throne. It belongs to the oldest man in town—until he dies."

Garth knew that except in tourist places no foreigners were ever allowed in a Men's House and so he asked innocently, "Where do you sit in there? Right or left?"

"Oh, anywhere," Smith said. Then he glanced at Garth and added, "You're trying to make me out to be some sort of god or something to these people. I'm not. I just live here and since I know how to swab iodine and wrap pretty bandages they've elected me doctor."

"Witch doctor?"

Smith smiled. "There you go, still trying to make something out of nothing. I just pull out fishhooks, barbed end first."

Smith's own house was typical of hundreds of plantation managers' houses throughout the islands: A four-room affair with dogtrot down the middle and a wide veranda all the way around it. The only thing inside the house that was at all unusual was the radio. It was a powerful and very expensive rig. "You must do a lot of talking," Garth said.

"It passes the time."

"I never could understand ham operators," Garth told him. "I listen to them sometimes and it sounds like the dullest talk I ever heard. Here you are talking to some stranger a thousand miles away. You talk until you run out of something to say and he talks until he runs out and neither of you can really say anything because the rules don't allow it. So at the end you don't know any more about each other than you did to start with."

Smith chuckled. "That's about the size of it, Garth. If you get to know somebody personally it doesn't take long before you've got all their problems."

"Or is it that you want to be nothing but a disembodied voice flying around the world?"

Smith laughed out loud. "Man, that typhoon did something to you. What do you mean?"

"I've known you for quite a while," Garth told him, "but I don't know anything about you. Now every man has parents; he's had a childhood somewhere; gone to some sort of school. He's got a birthplace and a hometown. You're an American, I think, but where do you come from?"

"All over," Smith said pleasantly. "Supper will be ready by the time you get through a bath."

"See what I mean?" Garth asked, as Sam showed him where to go for a bath.

All during a fine, hot supper Garth tried to reopen the subject of who Smith was, where he had come from, and why, in the hope that it would give him some clue to the Molahve secret. If he only had a clue, he would know what to avoid, what area to stay away from, what to do to keep Smith from being suspicious of him. Smith, however, would not discuss himself at all. He turned aside every effort Garth made.

After supper Smith set the transmitter so Garth could call Guam and then went out on the veranda.

The Institute people at Guam told him that as soon as he got back to Molahve and found out if anything was missing he was to call them back, but in any case he was to let them know when he got back.

Garth joined Smith on the veranda. The moon was high and full, the sky suddenly clear. The rain had stopped entirely and there were only the sounds of Smith's diesel generator, the faint noises from the kitchen, and the barking of a lonesome dog down in the village.

"I'm afraid I'm going to have bad news for my boss when I get back to Molahve," Garth told him.

"When do you plan to go back? You're welcome here."

"If this weather holds, tomorrow morning. But thanks."

"It'll hold."

A man came up out of the dark and reported something to Smith. As the man went away, Smith said, "They put fifty gallons of gas aboard for you."

"Oh, thanks a lot. How much do I owe you?"

Smith told him and as Garth got out the money Smith twisted around in his chair and called into the house. Sam and Jake came out and he spoke to them in their language.

Garth paid him and as Sam and Jake went back into the house, Smith said, "They'll be aboard in the morning."

Garth sat for a moment, looking at the moon and thinking, and then said, as nicely as he could, "I enjoyed having them; they're fine people. But I don't really need them."

"After all the warnings I've heard about not diving alone?"

Garth tried to keep it as light as Smith was. "You know they won't dive with me."

"But they can see a shark farther than you can."

"I work in the cage most of the time and anyway there's the net."

"I think you're just being polite and I appreciate that. But take them along with you. They want to go."

Garth had hoped that it would not get to this point. He

thought a minute and then just said, straight out, "Smith, I'm not interested in anything you may have hidden over at Molahve."

"I—*what?*" Smith straightened up. "What do you mean, hidden?"

"I'm not looking for it and I'm not going to look for it and, even if I find it, I'm still not interested. I'll leave it exactly where you put it."

Smith sat in silence for a long time just looking out over the lagoon. "So that's what you think?" he asked finally.

"What else is there to think? When you first showed up at Molahve you were going to drive me away from the island, either by persuasion or, if it came to it, with spears and guns. But when you began to think that I was just there to do some experiments—and that I was backed up by Guam—you changed your mind. You may have figured that I was only some kookie scientist who was no threat to you and your secret."

Smith laughed and looked over at him. "Tell the truth, I do think you're a kookie scientist."

"And I am. But, just to be sure, you left Sam and Jake to watch me."

"For crying out loud," Smith said. "I didn't know your mind worked that way."

"It works real simple," Garth said. "Here's a man named Smith—that's an original name—who lives on about as remote an atoll as you can find. And who's lived here a long time. . . ."

"How do you know that?"

"Because it takes a long time to learn one of these dialects as well as you speak it and it takes a much longer time to get the natives to like and respect you."

Smith didn't say anything.

"Tell me, Smith," Garth said quietly, "why is protecting the Molahve taboo so important to you?"

Smith sighed, whether bored or sad or tired Garth could not tell. "I'll tell you, Garth," he said. "It's old-fashioned and corny so you won't believe it, but that doesn't make any difference. The thing is, I haven't got any past because I don't want any. I had one and it wasn't any good so I forgot it. And no matter what you do it's going to stay forgotten."

"That doesn't explain Molahve," Garth pointed out. "So you did something back in the States—killed your wife or robbed a bank—okay, you ran away and hid out here. I'll buy that. But where does Molahve come in? As far as I can find out, you're the only one who cares that it's taboo. The rest of the people in this area just accept it and stay away from the place. But you *care*. You don't want anybody near the island. Why?"

"Because I have respect for the Melanesians. I respect the way they think and I don't want to change it. If they want to make a god out of a green coconut that's okay with me. If they want to put a taboo on Molahve I don't ask them why."

"Suppose it isn't theirs?" Garth asked. "Suppose the natives had nothing to do with putting a taboo on Molahve? Would you still try to keep everybody away?"

"As I said, I don't ask why and I don't ask who. This is their land, their ocean, not mine, so I don't know and I don't care who put the taboo on Molahve. If they believe in it then so do I."

"Look, all I want is to get on with what I'm doing over there without someone—like Sam or Jake—watching over my shoulder. And, like you, I don't know and I don't care who put the taboo on the place. I'm not going to destroy it."

Garth looked over at him as he sat with his feet up on the veranda railing. "So let's make a deal," he said.

Smith did not move nor say anything.

"You tell your people that the typhoon wrecked my experiment, ruined all the instruments, fouled up everything. Tell them I've given up and gone home. Even if they don't all believe you they won't risk their lives coming over to

Molahve to find out. That way I can work there in peace, finish my job, and go home."

"We're not the only people who believe that taboo," Smith said.

"I'll take my chances with the others. All I'm asking is that you convince *your* people that I've left Molahve."

"I don't rule these people. They believe what they want to believe, not what I tell them."

"Sam and Jake saw what the waves were like when we left. They'll believe that everything was wrecked and that I've gone home. They can convince the others."

Smith got slowly up out of the chair and stood looking down at the dark, silent village. "I'll do what I can."

"That's all I ask." Garth held out his hand and Smith shook it. "Thanks for letting me get this far, Smith."

As Garth walked down the dark path to the village he could not help feeling a little confused and a little embarrassed. He was still not quite sure what to make of Smith.

A bank of clouds moved away from the moon as he passed the Men's House, now only dimly lit by a fire burning in a ring of coral. Glancing at the building, Garth saw the broken pieces of glass imbedded all over the front shining with a soft, dull gleam in the moonlight.

On the *Uldra* he started down the companion to his cabin and then stopped. Although he was tired from the long days and nights of the battering in the lagoon he decided that his best move was to leave Efrahte now. Not wait until morning when all hands could see him leave and he would have to sail on a course directly away from Molahve just to convince them that he was never going back there. It would mean a much longer voyage and he was anxious to get back to find out how much damage had been done.

There was a good wind, a fair wind for the channel and a fair wind for Molahve.

He went out under the silence of sail alone and set her on the reach for Molahve.

He sailed all night, fighting sleep the entire way, for with the wind forward of the beam there was nothing to do but sit there and hold the boat on course.

An hour or so before dawn when he was sure that he was well out of sight of Efrahte he decided he couldn't fight fatigue any more. Heaving to he lay down on one of the cockpit benches.

He had one clear thought before he went to sleep and it made him feel good.

Ord Smith had, at last, given up, Garth thought. Whatever Sam and Jake had told him about what he was doing at Molahve must have convinced Smith that Garth was no threat to whatever his secret was.

That's the last I'll see of Ord Smith, Garth said to himself and went to sleep.

7.

He woke up at dawn and climbed up on the boom to look around. The vast blue ocean seemed empty of everything—Efrahte, ships, everything.

Hungry now, he dropped down through the forward hatch and started toward the galley. With the sun barely up and no lights on it was still dark down here.

The two bodies lay side by side in the corridor. Two dark, motionless shapes.

Garth backed away from them and hit the light switch. The automatic switch started the generator aft but it took a few seconds for the light to come on bright.

Sam and Jake lay peacefully asleep on their straw mats and now, in the light, he could see their new bundles of food and clothing neatly stowed on each side of the corridor.

For an instant he felt only a wild fury. He was outraged and insulted and if Smith had been there he would not have fared well.

And then suddenly Garth began to laugh. He leaned against the bulkhead looking at the two on the deck and laughed so loudly it woke them up. As they got to their feet, greeting him cheerfully, he kept on laughing but at last returned their greetings and said to them, in English, "Good morning, you sneaky spies."

On deck as he got sail on again and put the boat back on course he debated what to do. He could turn around and take his spies back to Efrahte and dump them in Smith's lap.

Or he could dump them overboard, right here.

He held the course to Molahve. Weighing things out it seemed evident now that Smith still believed he was at Molahve to search for that buried secret.

So it could only improve his position to have Smith watching everything he did through the eyes of Sam and Jake.

From now on, Garth decided, he would radio Smith *every* night, letting Sam and Jake report whatever they wished as before. There would be nothing suspicious to report and after a while Smith would have to be convinced. He would have to admit that Garth was not bothering him, nor threatening him, nor rooting around in his past.

And, in the meantime, he'd have Sam and Jake's good company.

Garth felt fine as he leaned back, steering with his bare toes and watching the first dark blotch of Molahve appear above the horizon.

In a little while Sam and Jake appeared with an elegant breakfast and the three of them sat in the cockpit eating and speculating on what the typhoon had done to Molahve.

They reached the island in the early afternoon. The day was hot, clear, and still, the wind having dropped to a breath as it came drifting down the flanks of the volcanoes. On the wind Garth could smell the island, a familiar smell but one he could never ignore. *Uldra* ghosted slowly along the shore, the sails only half filled.

Everything along the shore of this island was changed. The great waves created by the typhoon winds and spreading out away from them had been suddenly stopped in their run by Molahve's shore. These waves moving perhaps as fast as 600 miles an hour and rising to heights of fifty feet had been abruptly stopped by the land mass.

Tons of water, followed by more tons of water, had devastated this once-familiar shoreline so that it seemed almost strange to him. What had been sandy beaches the week before were stripped by the waves down to the bare bones of the island—the rock and lava looking naked in the sunlight.

Other bays set at different angles to the path of the waves had had their once-rocky beaches deluged by tons of sand.

Garth couldn't decide which type of wreckage he preferred to find at his lagoon. If the waves had scooped all the sand off the beach, stripping it down to rock, the sand would now be piled on the lagoon bottom. It would not only have changed the entire ecosystem of the lagoon, it would also have buried every piece of equipment he had left there.

On the other hand, if the waves had picked up the sand from the bottom and moved it to the beach, the results would be just as disastrous. The ecosystem would be equally disturbed, for the lagoon would now be much deeper, the entire bottom where so much of his marine life fed totally changed. And his equipment would be buried somewhere on the shore.

As he rounded the peninsula marking his lagoon, the only thing he was sure about was that there was going to be a lot of work to be done.

Turning in toward the beach Garth stood up in the cockpit and looked ahead.

The lagoon, which had been as familiar to him as his room at home, was no longer familiar at all. For a moment he even thought he had made a mistake and had picked the wrong lagoon entirely.

He had not.

What had been a rather shelving, narrow sand beach was now a mountain range of sand. There were peaks and foothills and valleys of sand, shaped first by the waves, then by rain and wind. Tall jungle trees had been buried so that, here and there, treetops stuck up out of the smooth sand, forlorn bare bones of branches from which every leaf had been stripped.

Salt water from the waves had been thrown for hundreds of feet back into the jungle leaving a wide fringe of dying foliage, limp and turning brown in the sun.

Defeated, Garth sat down. Sam and Jake, both silent, were staring at the lagoon.

"Stand by to anchor," Garth told them.

When he had left for Efrahte, this lagoon had been an unusually gay and cheerful place. Little bright-colored flags of different shapes and markings had bobbed and flapped on their little poles all over the surface of the lagoon. He knew what each flag marked—the reef, the wave meter, his mooring, various areas of the project, the anti-shark net. Now there were no flags and this small thing seemed to depress him the most.

With the sheets flying free and the schooner barely moving he went over to the side and looked down, knowing that the water was going to be deeper.

It was very deep. And murky. Usually the water in the lagoon was so clear that when you looked down through it it was hard to believe that there was any water at all. You could clearly make out small crabs, empty shells, tiny fish on the bottom in twenty or thirty feet of water. Now, though, the water was dark, still roiled by the wave action.

From forward Sam yelled and pointed ahead at something Garth could not see. Then Jake called that the shark net was still in place.

Maneuvering slowly until the two on the bow gave him the signal that the gate in the net was open and dead ahead, Garth worked the boat into the net's protection. As it slid past on both sides he saw that although the waves had pushed it in further toward shore they hadn't damaged it, for it had offered very little resistance.

He moved forward to the mast calling out to Sam and Jake to drop anchor. Casting off the mainsail halyard he stood and caught the sail in big folds as it slid slowly down the mast.

With the schooner anchored, the three of them got all the sail off and furled. As they worked, Garth had the feeling that none of them really wanted to face the situation; they all wanted to keep putting it off as long as they could.

But then, with the booms in the gallows frames, stops on the sails, becket on the wheel, topside shipshape, he got the lead line and went forward. As he reluctantly swung the lead-weighted rope back and forth and finally let it fly, the line paying out smoothly across the palm of his left hand, Sam and Jake joined him and the three of them stood there in silence while the line continued to pay out.

A week ago the water here had been twenty-eight feet deep.

Woven into the rope of the line were the markers for the odd fathoms. The three leather strips at Mark 3 leaped through his hand. The white rag at Mark 5, the red rag at 7, past the Deep 9.

The line went slack in his hand, the leather flap with a hole in it lying on the water. Ten fathoms deep. Sixty feet.

Garth groaned and went below. As he waited for the radio to warm up he decided not to tell Guam anything yet, except that he and the *Uldra* were safely back at Molahve.

When Guam answered, he didn't even ask for anyone from the Institute but just gave his message to the operator and signed off.

Garth found Sam and Jake still in the bow when he came back on deck. Joining them he looked down. Instead of the smooth and gently sloping sandy bottom he had known, the bottom was now like the sides of a mountain in spring with nothing of the winter snow left except small drifts and basins of it. He could make out the shapes of rocks and lava, raw and dark-looking with only small patches of white sand left.

It was discouraging, defeating, depressing. He knew that he didn't have to get a lung and go down there to discover that his whole project had been completely wiped out.

Not only wiped out but so changed that all the work he had done on the ecology of the lagoon as he had known it was now useless because this water, this bottom was an entirely new environment. Everything had been changed—depth, temperature, food, concealment, food-hunting areas —perhaps even currents and salinity.

There was only one hopeful fact to be found in it all. The lagoon had changed, yes, but it was still unpolluted. That value, he thought, was still there.

So—begin all over again.

Sam came over from the port side and politely touched his arm. "*Masta,*" he said, "*lukim sip.*"

For an instant Garth thought he meant a ship on the sea and he scanned the horizon but, finding no ship, he saw that Sam was pointing down into the water.

Leaning over the rail and looking straight down Garth could make out a long, dark shape almost directly under the schooner. As he looked he had to admit that it did resemble the hull of a ship, although it was rather long and very narrow.

It was hard to tell in that depth of water exactly what it was but he guessed that it was part of a submerged lava flow from some ancient volcanic eruption. From what he could see of the top of it—a somewhat smooth surface— he decided that it must be the type of lava the Hawaiians called Pahoehoe. The fact that it was now exposed on the bottom showed him how tremendous the sand movement had been.

Not knowing the pidgin word for lava he told Sam that he did not think it was a ship, but was only *siton*—the pidgin word for rock.

Although Sam said nothing he could tell that the man

did not agree with him. "All right," he said in pidgin, "when I go down there I will look at it and if it is a ship I will tell you it is a ship."

In his cabin, with the rubber suit half on, Garth wondered why he even bothered diving here. In the murky water there was nothing to see and he already knew how deep it was.

He zipped up the suit, got his gear and went topside.

As he hoisted the lung up and over his head he noticed that Sam and Jake were still in the bow, still looking into the water.

Usually those two had a lot to talk about in loud, cheerful voices but now they weren't talking much and then only in low tones and with no laughter.

Garth called to Jake as he coiled the yellow nylon lifeline and Jake seemed almost reluctant to come aft and help him.

Patting the coil of the lifeline down into Jake's open hands, Garth went through the ritual. "*Sambai rop bolong mi oltaim! Save,* Jake?"

As usual Jake answered, "*No ken tingim, masta.*"

As Garth backed down the platform he wondered why Jake was suddenly so serious. Usually Garth had to wonder whether Jake really understood the importance of the lifeline for his *No ken tingim* (don't worry) was always said lightly, as though it were a joke.

For the first time since he had come to Molahve, diving in the lagoon was unpleasant. Going straight down, he moved into even murkier water and when he looked below him he could see the bottom coming up. Gone was the pretty white sand, gone the cheerful clear world, full of color and, in a way, gaiety. Below him was a grim, dark world of tortured lava, broken boulders, shattered chunks and bits of coral. Even the fish seemed to have gone, for he saw none on his descent.

Before he passed forty feet he knew for certain that this was a total disaster. The lagoon was now useless to the project.

He stopped at fifty feet with the bottom still ten feet below him and swam slowly over toward the dark shape of what Sam had called a ship. The steep side of it formed a cliff rising from the ocean bottom and, when he reached it and touched it, he was surprised by the feel of it. He had thought that it was part of a lava flow but the surface was too smooth—no molten lava could have flowed into the sea and retained a surface as smooth as this.

Running his gloved hands along the surface, he decided that it must have been a huge boulder belched up from inside the volcano, possibly being split in two by the force. When his fingers found a slightly rough, raised ridge on the surface he thought it was a stratum of harder rock.

Turning on his flashlight he looked at the surface of the ridge.

In the glow of the light he saw that the surface was very smooth, uniformly gray, and slightly curved.

The ridge his fingers had felt was the metal bead of welding.

Looking closely at it he could see the tiny overlaps of metal where a welder's torch had moved steadily along joining together two steel plates.

8.

The sunken ship was resting almost on an even keel on a flat slab of stone. It was too murky for Garth to see how much damage the typhoon had done before it sank her but, as he swam slowly upward, she did not seem badly hurt topside.

He was surprised at how clean and new she looked but then reasoned that the waves, loaded as they had been with sand, had done this scouring. Her gray paint was clean, all her metal gleamed dully, he could even see the grain in some of her woodwork.

As he swam toward the deckhouse which came up from the flush deck about amidships, he wondered what had happened to her crew. There were lifeboat davits on both sides but both were empty.

They must have abandoned ship before she sank, probably even before she came this close to land. He suddenly wondered if the crew might be ashore on Molahve.

Visibility was so poor that, from above the deckhouse, he could not make out clearly either the bow or stern. But from what he could see this ship was certainly not one of the little interisland freighters or a fat-bellied copra boat like Smith's. She was too long and too narrow to serve well as a freighter. There was no room for cargo below, nor on her single deck, and no room for passengers either. If she had been a yacht, whoever owned her had been loaded because this ship was, he estimated, a good 75 feet long and must have cost a buck to buy and a buck to sail.

Swimming down to look through the windshield into the bridge he was surprised to find sand packed solidly behind the glass, the entire bridge completely filled with sand. It had, he found, come in through an open hatch on top of the bridge.

Still trying to imagine how she had been sunk—Had the great seas rolled her over and filled her? Had she ripped her bottom out on some reef?—he swam slowly forward peering down at the almost clean foredeck. Gradually, as he came closer, a curious-looking winch or some piece of deck machinery took shape.

It was a gun.

Swimming down to it he found that it was the same type he had practiced loading during his years in the NROTC, the Navy's old three-inch hand-loaded cannon.

In a way the gun made him feel better about the crew. The Navy certainly wouldn't have let a small ship like this roam around alone and so, when she got into trouble, other larger ships must have rescued her crew. She might, Garth thought, even have been in tow but broke loose and sank before anything could be done to save her.

But then the sight of the ship began to remind him of his own problems. For one thing she was polluting the water of his lagoon. For another, when he reported to Admiral Stucky that a Navy ship was lying on the bottom, Stucky would send half the Pacific Fleet out to Molahve and that would really mess things up.

He swam down past the sharp bow, looking for some identification.

The paint on her bow, too, was scoured clean by the moving sand and he noticed now that the sand had, in places, even scoured the paint off, particularly along the seam welds.

The number, in white letters, was still clear: SC 206.

SC?

Subchaser.

Subchaser? The word stirred something in his memory and he was lying there, looking at the number and trying to remember when he saw the anchor chain.

At first he didn't believe it but, going over to the hawse hole in the bow, he saw that the anchor chain was secured to a bitt on deck and led down through the hawse hole and out into the murky water.

Not understanding this at all, he swam along the chain, which dropped straight down from the bow to the bottom and then lay almost straight across the rocks. Following it for more than one hundred feet he came at last to the anchor lying flat on the bottom, no fluke engaged in holding.

Looking back at the dim shape of the ship and then along the chain and then at his compass he saw that the chain was pointing straight toward the island.

He swam slowly back to the ship. Every detail he had imagined of the sinking of this ship faded away, one by one. Everything he had thought had happened had not happened, *could* not have happened.

Swimming up and over the bow he stopped at the level of the windshield and stared vacantly at the sand packed against the glass.

This ship had been riding at anchor when she sank.

An offshore wind had been blowing at that time for the anchor lay between the ship and the shore. The waves of the typhoon could not have sunk her for they would have thrown her toward shore, thrown her against the anchor in the other direction with her bow pointing seaward, not landward.

Swimming around the deckhouse he moved on aft past the boat davits. On the stern there were depth charges looking like small barrels, still held in the racks by chains over the tops of them.

Nothing here had been disturbed by crashing waves, by capsizing, by any typhoon wind.

Both rudders were intact and set amidships, both bronze propellers, polished by the moving sand, glowed in the shadow.

Swimming close along the hull he looked at the ship's hard-bilged, flat bottom. There was no damage, no sign of collision with any rock or shoal on either side of her.

Floating upward, his mind full of questions, he began to feel now the first little tendrils of apprehension.

There were too many questions.

That old three-inch gun in the bow had been obsolete for years.

In spite of the cleanness of her paint and the shine of her brightwork this was an old ship, a relic of a long-past war.

She must have gone down years ago. Riding at anchor in a peaceful lagoon she must have filled with water through some opening in her hull and gone straight down. Peacefully.

But if she had, why hadn't the sea made a mark on her? Why hadn't barnacles and teredos destroyed her woodwork? Why was there no sea growth of any kind on her anywhere? Why was there still paint on her hull?

The sand-scouring of the typhoon waves could answer some of those questions but not all.

Baffled and annoyed, he was lying there scowling at the ship when the thing hit him like a fist in the face. Instinctively he began backing away.

This ship, this subchaser of a long-gone war, was the reason for the Molahve taboo. This ship, lying dead on the bottom of the lagoon, was the secret Smith was guarding.

He started up, swimming hard, then slowed as he remembered that he had been working at sixty feet. The eight seconds he took to reach ten feet seemed more like an hour and being forced by the threat of the bends to lie at ten feet for more long seconds annoyed him.

Through the swirl of unanswered questions one thing was now absolutely clear. Just as Smith had (for how many years?) guarded the secret of the ship, now *he* must guard it. Smith must never know that he had found the ship; Sam and Jake, the spies, must never know.

In fact, Garth realized, the ship's presence here must be kept a secret from everyone.

Checking his watch he was relieved to see that he had been down only fourteen minutes. That would look good, he decided. Just a short dive to inspect the bottom. Sam and Jake would buy that.

He would move the *Uldra* as far away from the subchaser as he could. That done, all he would have to do would be to keep Sam and Jake away from where the ship lay.

As he started up the last few feet he noticed the lifeline dangling, but at first the long loop in the yellow line had no significance. Then when he looked at it again and saw that it trailed down out of sight from his body and from the water above him it had a great deal of significance.

Lunging out of the water at the platform he looked up and saw the coil of the lifeline hanging from one of the deck stanchions. Neither Sam nor Jake was in sight.

He came up on the platform, stripping off gear as he came. On deck he finally saw Sam way up in the bow leaning over the rail and looking down into the water. Jake was not on deck at all.

Garth forced his anger down as he coiled the lifeline and put it away. "Sam," he called.

It startled Sam and he whirled around almost tripping himself. Then, seeing Garth, he came running aft, his bare feet thumping hard on the deck.

In a moment Jake appeared from below.

Garth made no mention of the abandoned lifeline. Instead, he told them to lay below and fix up a good lunch for all of them.

As soon as they were out of sight Garth went forward and got the anchor up. Then, with the engine, he got under way and moved the *Uldra* north to the far side of the shark net and as far as he could get from the subchaser. Anchoring there he went below to check on Sam and Jake.

In the galley they were oddly silent as they prepared the lunch. While they packed it, he explained to them what he wanted them to do on shore.

On purpose he did not mention the ship, waiting to see if they were still thinking about it. He had about decided that they were not, for they finished with the food and followed him aft to the gear locker.

However, as he was breaking out the ping locator, Jake asked, "What did the ship look like?"

Working with the locator and not even turning to look at him, Garth asked, "What ship?"

"The one on the bottom," Jake said.

Garth, still unable to remember the pidgin word for lava, did not turn nor seem interested as he said, "It does look like a ship from up here. But it is not. It is only rock."

"It looks very much like a ship," Jake said.

At last Garth glanced at him but could tell nothing from his flat, black eyes as he stood there chewing his betel nut much like a cow chewing her cud.

"If you want to go down in the water with me I will show you that it is not a ship," Garth told him.

Sam laughed and said something in their language and then they both laughed.

Loading the gear into the dinghy Garth rowed ashore with them.

Sand that had once covered the bottom of the lagoon lay in huge drifts and dunes, completely burying tall trees and other landmarks.

It was hot and still on the beach and the sand was hard to walk in. Climbing to the top of one of the dunes Garth rigged the locator on Jake (almost laughing with Sam at the sight of the man standing there with those big padded earphones on).

Garth had equipped the large instruments with modified

versions of Dr. Anderson's abyssal pinger beacon having an extended life of thirty days. On the smaller stuff he had used a spar buoy which transmitted a continuous modulated signal. The ping locator Jake was wearing could pick up either type of signal.

He was lucky, for as soon as he turned on the locator it began registering a steady ping from something buried in the sand.

Garth showed Jake how to determine the direction by swinging the locator dish back and forth, and they trudged across the sand until it zeroed in on something directly below them.

They had dug down only a few feet before they uncovered the base of the wave meter.

As with every job they tackled, Sam and Jake were delighted with this one; it seemed to arouse all their hunting instincts and Garth left them happily arguing about who was to wear the locator next.

Rowing alone out to the *Uldra* the problem of the subchaser fell on him like a dark, ominous net. He kept asking himself why a man would spend half his life guarding the secret of this ancient wreck. What was so important about the ship that Smith would go to all the time and trouble to set up his elaborate taboo of the entire island and the sea around it?

Threaded through all that were the other unanswered questions. How had the ship come here? Why? When? What had sunk her? Where was her crew?

Although he still had no answers, by the time he reached the *Uldra* Garth knew what he was going to do. The idea of going into the subchaser repelled him; he wasn't exactly afraid of it but it would be, he thought, like rooting around in somebody's ugly private life and he did not want to do that.

On deck he got a fresh tank pack, two spare tanks and the big lamp and then waited until Sam and Jake disappeared behind a sand dune before loading them into the

dinghy. Then, when they reappeared, he got back into the
dinghy and rowed out toward the shark net. At the net
he stopped and, allowing them to see him clearly, stood up
and heaved the anchor overboard. For a few minutes he
fiddled around the net, lifting and pulling on it but watching them and when they were out of sight again, he reached
into the dinghy and got out his gear.

Putting the dinghy between him and them he got the lung
on and submerged.

It was a long swim and tiring with the drag of the two
spare tanks, but at last the shape of the subchaser loomed
up ahead of him.

Without realizing it, he stopped moving and just lay
there, looking at the gloomy shape of the ship.

He knew that the subchaser itself was not the important
thing. There must be something inside the ship, something
so incriminating, so horrible, that Smith had had to spend
his life preventing anyone from ever finding out what it was.

He swam slowly toward the door in the low deckhouse.

What thing, what evidence, what crime could endure so
long at the bottom of the sea?

As he reached for the dull brass door knob Garth half
hoped to find that the door was locked; that all the doors
and openings were locked so that it would be impossible
for him to get inside the ship.

The knob turned easily, the door swung slowly open
against the water pressure and he lay looking through a
rectangle into a dark and gloomy room.

Getting the underwater lamp off his belt, he strapped
it to his wrist and, beaming it ahead, swam slowly until
he could see into the room.

It was a small place, the beam of the lamp moving across
a built-in metal desk with a metal chair in front of it. Along
the bulkhead were two built-in bunks with closed lockers
at one end. A lamp with a white glass globe hung from
the ceiling and he noticed gooseneck lamps at the bunks

and above the desk. A closed door was in the inboard bulk-head.

The room looked bleak and empty and nothing moved.

Not going in, Garth closed the outer door and swam on aft.

Here in the lowest part of the bridge structure was another closed door which opened as easily as the first had.

This was a larger room and as he beamed the lamp into it he guessed that it must be the crews' quarters, making the small room forward an officers' stateroom.

He hesitated again at the door and then swam slowly in, beaming the light all around the room.

Just inside the door he stopped and debated. He wanted to leave the door open but common sense argued that he'd be safer inside the ship with the door closed behind him. Common sense told him that there could be nothing as dangerous in here as there was outside. Reluctantly he closed the door, cutting off the dim light from the surface.

The room was very dark and the lamp did not seem as bright as he floated there, looking slowly around.

It was a rectangular-shaped room. Down the long sides were chain bunks. Between the built-in metal lockers on the after bulkhead was a door. There was also a door directly across the room from him.

In the center of the room was a long mess table with two attached benches.

Garth swam into the room and across to the bunks on the other side.

If there had been bedding on these bunks it had long since disappeared for the bare springs were exposed, covered only with a light, wet, gray dust.

He ran his fingers along one of the strands of metal, feeling the dust and disturbing it a little. Then he beamed the light closely on it.

Ever since discovering the ship, a part of his mind had been working on the problem of why, if this ship had been underwater for years, the sea had not made a mark on her and now, as he looked at this dust, he thought he was close to the answer.

He had no idea what sank her but he was growing more and more sure that very soon after she sank a typhoon or less probably a seismic sea wave had passed over her or at least close by. That typhoon had come from a different direction than the one last week and so had created an entirely different wave action.

Instead of scooping sand off the bottom and carrying it ashore, the waves of that typhoon—or whatever had caused them—had gathered sand from the shore and carred it seaward. In the process—and Garth knew from experience that it could be done by heavy waves in a matter of hours—the waves had simply covered this ship with sand. They had packed the sand in around her, had packed it down on top of her, and then had packed down another solid ten feet of sand on top of that.

A combination of sand and silt had completely sealed off the ship. Nothing requiring free oxygen had been able to live in anything but the top few feet of that sand. None of the sea's animals, not even aerobic bacteria, could have penetrated all the way through the ten upper feet of it and reached the ship below.

She had been encased in an oxygenless vacuum and so had remained as she had been on the day she sank, protected and preserved by the sand around her.

Only the anaerobic bacteria which required no oxygen and which were present only in animal and vegetable tissue could have survived in that coffin of sand.

Everything in the room was covered with a film of the gray wet dust so that Garth did not immediately see the eating utensils on the mess table. Coffee mugs, plates, and mess gear were in a line along the starboard fiddle.

Apparently the ship had taken a list to starboard as she sank, sliding the mess gear across the table, but the wooden rails around the edge—the fiddles—had stopped them from falling off.

On the floor a big galvanized iron bucket had apparently slid from under the table and was resting against a bench leg.

Swimming above the table, the beam of his light straight ahead, he reached the open door in the after end of the room.

The next room was the galley, with pots still on the stove, but lying in a heap against the starboard side of it.

She must have gone down very gently, he decided; so gently that she only slid coffee mugs across a table, pots across the stove top.

Opening the refrigerator he found some bottles and, here and there on the shelves, thicker piles of the gray, dustlike stuff.

The food locker was almost bare. A few cans of food were lying in a heap against the back wall.

The after door of this room was also open and he swam over to it and looked aft.

A short flight of stairs went down into the large engine room where two diesels stood side by side, so well preserved that they looked as though they would run if the ignition were turned on.

He swam into the room, his tanks just clearing the overhead as he floated above the diesels.

The sand on the floor caught his attention and he beamed the light down on it.

On the starboard side he saw the four-inch pipe and recognized it as the sea water intake for the engines. A valve was set against the hull and, he knew, on the outside of the hull there was a metal scoop which forced sea water through the valve and pipe when the ship was under way.

The four-inch pipe was attached to the valve with a round flange in which six bolt holes had been drilled for the bolts holding the two faces of the flange together.

There were no bolts in the holes and the two faces of the flange were inches apart.

He reached down and found that he could easily move the section of pipe.

Sea water had moved it too. Someone evidently intent on sinking the ship had unbolted the flange, relying on the sea pressure to push the faces apart so that water had flooded first the engine room and then the rest of the ship.

That accounted for the slight list to starboard, for water had entered on that side.

Sometime later, but not much later, sand had come through the valve, too. The same sand that had encased the ship.

Floating there he looked at the flange and pipe. Something bothered him for, with only a four-inch opening letting the sea into the ship, there would have been ample time for someone to close the valve. A simple, quick operation.

But no one had. The ship had slowly filled with water—it must have taken several hours before she at last went down—and no one had made a move to save her.

Why?

Perhaps, he thought, there had been no one aboard. Perhaps Smith had opened the valve to get rid of some evidence he wanted to conceal and had then abandoned the ship.

But where had the captain and crew been while she was sinking?

Puzzled and beginning to feel desperate for he had found no other secret than this, he swam back through the galley and into the crew's quarters again.

In that dark room he could see nothing except what lay directly in the beam of the lamp and this gave him an eerie feeling. A feeling that he was in an immense, dark and dangerous room instead of a small compartment where a few men had once eaten and slept.

Opening one of the lockers he found it coated with the gray dust. A small object on the top shelf caught his attention and he took it up, the dust dripping away from it.

Some man's shaving mirror.

A razor and small metal box for soap.

Below that shelf clothes had once hung but hung no more.

The bottom of the locker was six inches thick with the dust. As he brushed it with his hands the light caught on something metal and he saw, in two neat rows, the metal eyelets for shoe laces, the rest of the shoes long ago destroyed by the bacteria in the leather.

There must be something more than this, he thought. Even if Smith had deliberately sunk the ship, was that act alone enough to spend the rest of your life concealing?

He didn't think so. Perhaps the sinking was part of it but he was convinced that there was more to Smith's secret than that.

As he turned to leave the room he noticed in one of the bunks something other than the gray coated metal springs. Swimming over to it he beamed the light down into it.

In the bunk a man was lying on his back, his arms crossed over his chest.

Garth floated slowly away from the bunk but held the beam steady on the whitish ball of the skull.

He wished that he had not seen this; wished that the man had not been here. He even hoped in a childish way that the thing would disappear or that, if he went closer, he would find that it was not a man after all.

Because the thing lying on the bare metal springs changed Smith's secret into something sinister and serious and dangerous.

He floated slowly back to the bunk and looked down at the skeleton. The bones of everything except the skull were dingy with a thick, dark slime. In contrast, the skull seemed startlingly white.

There was a hole about half an inch in diameter and about an inch above the eye socket in the front of the skull.

Garth caught himself looking around to see if anyone was watching as he reached out to touch the skull.

Lifting it a little he could see that the whole back of the head had been shattered.

He put it down gently and swam away.

There were two more skeletons in the room. These two

lay, one across the other, against the wall at the forward end.

He swam through the room and looked down. Somehow the little heap of grayish bones looked pitiful, looked as though two men, in dying, had tried to help each other, but had fallen together.

He couldn't see what had killed them and didn't examine them carefully for he really didn't care. Enough was already clear.

Someone—Smith?—had killed three men. That was murder.

Someone—Smith?—had sunk this ship. That was barratry.

As he swam out of the room and back into the dim light of the murky water he felt sad and depressed and, as the problem took shape, afraid.

The fact that Smith could so deliberately sink a ship and, possibly, deliberately kill three men changed him in Garth's mind from a man who had been a minor threat and major nuisance into someone very dangerous, a ruthless, cold-blooded man.

Garth swam forward above the narrow lane of deck between the superstructure and the rail. There was one more door he had not opened and he hesitated outside it, wondering what good it would do to go in. Perhaps there were other skeletons behind the door. Would the number of murders—one? three? a dozen?—really matter?

Vaguely in the back of his mind Garth was searching for some weapon; some way to protect himself from Smith. As it was, Smith had all the weapons and he had none.

Garth opened the door, swam into the room and closed the door.

The room was very small and he could see at a glance that it must have been the ship's office. There were file cabinets, some clipboards on the bulkhead, a slanting navigator's table.

There was a narrow door forward and, thinking that it was a closet, he turned the knob.

The instant the bolt slipped out of the latch Garth felt a

tremendous moving, living pressure against the door. It felt as though some living thing—a very strong animal—was standing behind it and pushing with all its strength.

The force rammed Garth back through the water and against the navigator's table which fell over, hitting the lamp as it fell and knocking it out of his hand. For an instant the beam of the lamp swung crazily around the room; then it went out.

The darkness was so intense that he felt it was touching him. Getting clear of the table, his tanks slamming against something with a dull gonging sound, he reached with his free hand for the lamp which was dangling by a chord at his wrist.

As the sound made by his tanks faded, the other sound took its place and he froze where he was, hand out-stretched for the lamp.

Something was moving in the room. Between the bursts of his exhaust bubbles he could hear something moving.

He stopped moving, stopped breathing, and listened.

He had never heard a sound like this before. It was as though someone in soft shoes were sliding, not walking, across the floor. Only the sound came from everywhere, as though the room were full of those soft, sliding shoes.

Waiting, expecting something horrible to touch him, Garth took a deep breath and let his left hand reach out to the lamp, his fingers fumbling on the smooth surface searching for the switch.

The switch slid forward easily and the lamp snapped a beam across the room.

The door he had opened had been slammed back against the wall and, through the opening, sand was tumbling slowly out of the room beyond, which was two or three feet higher than this one with a little flight of steps leading up into it.

Garth floated in the beclouded water and felt like a fool.

So, stupid, open the door holding the sand in and it will run out.

The flow of sand stopped and he could now see into the bridge. The brass spokes of the wheel were not shiny but they looked as though the helmsman's hands had just turned them loose. The brass and steel cases around the instruments also looked untouched by the long submersion in sea water.

Going back to the door he scooped more sand out of the bridge until he could get in without hitting his tanks.

As he swam into the small room he heard another sound —a gentle thumping coming from above him.

At first he thought it was only his tanks striking something but when he stopped moving the thumping went on, a sound like that of a soft ball bouncing.

Twisting around slowly he looked up.

A rectangular metal box which he recognized as an ammunition box was floating against the ceiling of the room. When he moved, the currents he made caused the box to bounce against the ceiling.

Catching it by the handle he pulled it down.

The lid of the box was held down securely by two steel clamps and when he turned it upside down he could see that the gasket, made of some synthetic material like rubber, was still intact.

He started to lift one of the clamps and then stopped and held the box, looking at it. Whatever was inside might still be dry and he decided to leave it that way.

Pushing the ammo box ahead of him, he went up through the bridge skylight and swam over to where he had tied his spare tanks.

He felt as though he had been inside that dark ship for hours but when he checked his bottom time he was surprised to find that he had enough air in his original tanks to make it back to the dinghy.

Suspecting now that he was not through with this ship, that he might have to come back, he put the two spare tanks down through the skylight and then closed it.

As he pushed away from the subchaser, the ammo box

strapped to his chest, he felt as though he were coming back into the real world. Inside the sunken ship there had been the feeling of a dream, a nightmare, a feeling that in each dark room he entered there would be an evil and threatening thing. Now, in the warm openness of his lagoon, he felt at home again, safe and protected.

This amused him a little. Inside the ship, where none of the great sea creatures (nor even the tiny but venomous ones) could attack him, where only long-dead men lay peacefully in their old grave, he had been truly safe. Out here he was at the mercy of every hunger.

Surfacing on the seaward side of the dinghy he pulled the gunwale down and eased the box into it. Then, pulling himself up as high as he could, he looked over at the beach.

Sam and Jake were working diligently, sand flying from their shovels.

Stripping off his gear and stowing it in the dinghy, he climbed in over the stern and rowed back to the *Uldra*.

He doubted if they could see him clearly on deck, doubted if they were even interested, but he was careful anyway. For a minute or so he moved about the deck toying with lines or furled sails before going back to the dinghy to get the ammo box and his gear.

Stowing the lung, he carried the box down into the lab. Then, before opening it, he closed the doors.

As Garth prepared to open the box, he was plagued by a memory. Dim at first, but enough to stop him from lifting the clamps while he tried to bring the memory into clear thought.

It remained vague—perhaps only a story he had read, or a tale he had heard. But somewhere, somehow he had heard of a box—or had it been a coffin?—being opened after many years and the contents of the box dissolving at the first contact with the outside air.

Had it happened in some Egyptian tomb? Priceless records written on papyrus and preserved, airless, for thousands of years suddenly turning to dust?

There was nothing for it but to take the chance. He lifted the steel clamps and gently tugged at the top. It did not move and he found that the flanges of it were buried in the soft stuff of the gasket.

Prying it gently he at last got the top off.

He stood, looking down into the box, half expecting to see everything in it start to dissolve.

Inside the box was another box, this one made of some dark, solid-looking wood. Beside that was a black binocular case and, on end, some sort of notebook with a strong canvas cover.

He lifted out the binocular case first and found inside a pair of binoculars marked U. S. Navy.

He then lifted out the wooden box and found in that an old-fashioned sextant, all the lenses and filters still in their little velvet-lined slots. Even the mirrors were clean and bright.

At the bottom of the ammo box he saw a second box, also of wood. This one contained a small chronometer, only slightly larger than a big pocket watch but mounted in a gimbal. In the lid of the box was a piece of paper with the chronometer rate and error neatly typed in the spaces printed there.

Stamped into the canvas cover of the notebook were the words: LOG BOOK - SC 206. In ink someone had printed in very fancy, decorated letters: William S. Barrett, QM 3/c, USN.

Now, he thought, this is the time when all the writing and all the paper will dissolve. Like the papyrus of the tomb, I'll open this book and all the secrets in it will disappear before I can find out what they are.

He opened the book at about the middle and stared at the two pages, waiting for the writing on them to disappear as though written in magical ink.

Nothing disappeared. The pages were filled with mathematical equations which, when he studied them, he saw were

navigational problems—sun lines, star sights, position lines
—all worked out neatly in pencil.

It was a method of navigation he only dimly remembered
for it was old-fashioned and practically obsolete. But as he
studied the book, he thought he remembered the name of
the method—Saint Hilaire.

He flipped through the pages and found them all alike
—each one a navigator's day's work. Nothing else.

There was a copy of the Nautical Almanac and some other
things in the box but now that he knew they would not be
destroyed he left them, putting everything back he had
taken out and then putting the box behind some cartons of
supplies.

Rowing ashore the first thing he saw was the anti-shark
cage which Sam and Jake had dug out of the sand and
carried down to the water's edge.

When he joined them they showed him other things, including the wave meter, and seemed jubilant because, in
another dune, they got strong pinging from whatever was
buried there.

Marking the location in case the pinger failed, they spent
the rest of the day carrying the rescued equipment out to
the *Uldra*.

As they ate supper that night, all three of them sitting
around the open cockpit, they discussed the typhoon waves,
the search, Efrahte, the depth of the sand, but neither
Sam nor Jake made any mention of the ship. Nor did they
inquire about what Garth had been doing all day. He even
gave them openings, describing the depth of water now and
the lack of sand on the bottom of the lagoon, but they did
not ask nor seem interested in what was down there.

Believing that he had convinced them there was no ship,
he felt reassured and relaxed a little, sitting in the cockpit
just chatting while the tropical darkness plunged in and the
island grew dark and silent.

As they talked, Garth made his plans. In the morning
he would keep Sam and Jake aboard to help haul up the

shark net and move. It might take all day to find a new lagoon he could use for the project but he did not think that there was any reason to hurry.

For a moment he debated whether to call Smith now or not. He decided against it. Smith knew where he was and knew that his spies were safely aboard.

Garth smiled to himself. What Smith didn't know was that his two faithful spies had been cleverly made to believe that they had not seen what, indeed, they had very clearly seen.

He felt relaxed and confident now. Tomorrow he would leave the lagoon and its grisly secret forever. In time, perhaps even in a matter of weeks, the normal wave action and the run-off of rainwater would cover that subchaser with sand again.

Just knowing what Smith's secret was, knowing the reason for everything Smith did was reassuring. Until now he had not known anything. He had only been able to guess, to wonder.

Sam and Jake said good night and went forward, talking and quietly laughing, and he watched them disappear down the forward hatch.

Garth made himself sit there in the cockpit a little while longer for now he had a decision to make.

If he reported the wreck to the Navy in Guam Smith would have no secret, and Molahve would have no taboo, and he would have no more trouble.

It seemed an ideal solution but, since Garth's father had been a naval officer, he knew a little about the Navy way of doing things.

If he reported this wreck to the Navy they would have to come and inspect it. They would fill the lagoon with ships and the shore with men and equipment. They would send divers down. They might even send a salvage ship in here to hoist the subchaser up and tow her away.

In any case, it would result in heavy pollution of Molahve's water. Pollution that could last for months, perhaps years.

And if the taboo on Molahve were to be lifted, there would be nothing to stop the natives from coming here. They might even start to inhabit Molahve and then the island, as a pure laboratory, would be lost forever.

On the other hand Garth knew that if he did not report the ship, Smith's secret would become *his* secret and he did not want the burden of that.

Weighted by this indecision, his mind slid away into memories of the lagoon as he had first seen it. He remembered the pride he had felt in knowing that he was the only man in the world working at Molahve, the only place in the world where such work could be done.

And then he thought of the men dead in the ship, thought of their parents and the people who had loved them. They would like to know, he thought. They would like to know, positively, after all these years, what had happened. Didn't the Navy report a man "missing" for seven years and then change that to "missing, presumed dead"? Seven years. Those men in the subchaser had been there many more than seven years. Would *knowing* at last where and how they died help their loved ones now, this long time after?

Garth got up and went down into the darkness of the hatch.

He would not report this ship to the Navy, nor to anyone. It was now his secret. And Smith's. And he knew that from now on he would have to guard it with the same ruthless determination and patience Smith had.

Above all, he would have to guard it from Smith, because Garth knew that if Smith ever found out that he had seen the remnants of those murders he would be forced to commit another.

10

In the lab Garth quietly locked the doors and pulled the screen across the skylight. Then, standing at the closed galley door, he listened but heard no sound from Sam and Jake. The ship was silent except for the steady muffled sound of the electric generator aft.

He brought the ammo box over to the chart table and emptied it, lining up everything that had been in it: The log book, Nautical Almanac, sextant, chronometer, parallel rulers and binoculars. He almost overlooked a folded chart pressed against the side of the box. Unfolding it and spreading it flat on his table he found that it was a chart covering an area of forty degrees east from the Celebes Sea.

Going back to the log book he started at the first page.

He had never used the Saint Hilaire system of celestial navigation and he had to study the page full of figures carefully before he understood how the sun and star sights were worked out.

He felt a little sorry for whoever had worked the sights for it was a long, laborious way of doing it, with many opportunities for mistakes. Compared to the modern system Garth used, this was horse-and-buggy stuff.

He looked at the name on the cover of the book again:

William S. Barrett, QM 3/c, USN. Whoever he was, he had
done his job well. Each two pages of the book contained
the work for morning star sights, morning and noon sun
lines, and evening stars.

There was nothing else in the book. From the first page
to the last on which entries had been made there were only
the mathematics of the man's navigation.

Garth didn't know exactly what he had expected to find;
perhaps a diary of some sort, or at least a stiff Navy report
of the ship's progress, but there was no diary, no report,
no clue as to what had been going on aboard the subchaser
during all the time these entries were being made.

All he knew was that the entries started on May 20, 1942,
and ended on June 8, 1942.

Disappointed, he went back to the chart.

He followed the line of progress from the May 20 date
when the ship had been just south of the island of Min-
danao in the Philippine archipelago, along a course almost
due east across the South Pacific Ocean.

The neat little lines and numbers on the chart could have
been made by a machine; there was no personality in them.
And no answer.

He was folding up the chart when he noticed that the
course and distance line passed Molahve and continued
in an easterly direction. This told him nothing and he
folded the chart and closed the log book.

Where had the subchaser come from? Where was it
going? Why wasn't there any entry in the log before May
20 when the ship was already at sea?

Garth remembered then that at the end of each day's
work in the log there was a breakdown of the ship's progress. There were entries starting with course made good,
distance to point of departure, total distance made, distance to destination, distance to go.

Opening the log to the last page he studied the final
entries.

Distance to go—twenty miles.

He unfolded the chart and checked the course and distance line. Right. Twenty miles beyond the end of the penciled line was a small blue dot on the chart marking an island.

Good navigator, he thought idly and pushed the chart aside.

Suddenly he pulled it back.

The blue dot did not mark Molahve. It marked an island 300 miles southeast of Molahve.

Good navigator? To miss a landfall by 300 miles?

It bothered him. The work was too neat, too exact to allow for a gross error such as this.

And yet William Barrett, Quartermaster Third Class, had drawn his position line as precisely as he did everything else. The line ended exactly twenty miles from the island —and 300 miles from where the ship now lay sunk in the Molahve lagoon.

He got out his own dividers and began picking off the latitudes and longitudes worked out in the log book.

When he found the mistake Barrett had made it seemed, at first, a simple error, one that anyone could make and not catch. But, as he continued plotting the course in the log book on the chart, he began to see that the small error had been made each day.

Puzzled now and curious, he began to study the Saint Hilaire system carefully. Somehow Barrett's position according to his sights did not coincide with the position he had marked on the chart and his advance along the course line did not coincide with the entries of the ship's speed.

It took Garth twenty minutes before he understood the steps necessary to work out the sights but once he did, it was not hard to follow through the crowded pages of equations and logarithms, chronometer corrections, time conversions, and longitude adjustments.

There was no error in the work but Barrett had not transferred the position he had found by the stars to the chart of the ship's course.

Garth began spot checking through the book, going backward from the last recorded position.

As he checked he noticed for the first time small groups of letters scattered here and there throughout the equations and arithmetic. For instance, in calculating the hour angle in one day's work, instead of entering the secant, cosecant, cosine, sine, and haversine, Barrett had substituted meaningless letters—eayke, tdnni, etc. If this was some personal shorthand of Barrett's he hadn't been very consistent for Garth found that none of the groups were the same.

Dismissing these letters he went back to the first day's work in the book and transferred the position to the chart. The two matched.

Going then day by day he found that, until May 26, Barrett had never made an error in transfer.

On May 26, however, there was a change in the ship's course and, from then on, the positions had not been properly measured on the chart. According to the penciled line of the ship's course, the subchaser passed Molahve on June 3 at a distance of 294 miles.

Using the positions in the book he transferred them to the chart correctly, making a series of little dots along the line of the ship's actual movement from May 26 to June 8. Finished, he drew a line through the dots.

The line ended, at sea, on the 8th of June.

Running his pencil along the ruler's edge beyond the 8th of June position his pencil point crossed straight through the blue dot marking the island of Molahve.

The last entry in the log book was a dead reckoning position for 8 P.M. advanced from star sights at 6 P.M. and the advanced 3 P.M. sun line.

Knowing what he was going to find before he even started measuring, he swung the dividers from the last dead-reckoning position to Molahve and then transferred that span to the edge of the chart.

He made a note of the distance and a note of the ship's speed as given in the log book and then checked the

Nautical Almanac. The moon, on that night, would rise at 3 A.M.

That subchaser, if held on the course shown on the chart, and held at the speed of ten knots, would arrive at the island of Molahve at twenty minutes past one in the morning of June 9.

It would be a dark night, made darker by Molahve's eternal clouds. If, by chance, there were no lookouts posted on the ship, or if they were asleep on watch at that hour, no one except possibly the helmsman would have seen the pitch-black island in a pitch-black sea.

Garth, no longer tired or sleepy, could see the whole thing now. Someone, and it must have been this quartermaster, Barrett, had drawn a position line on the chart which showed anyone who was interested that the ship was well clear of all obstacles, reefs, shoals, or islands; that it could sail through the dark night without fear.

Actually the ship had been on a direct collision course ever since May 26 and on June 9 would reach and most probably strike the island of Molahve.

Barrett had done this intentionally. There was no doubt in Garth's mind that a man as precise as the one who worked the log book had made those errors of position deliberately. His purpose, too, was now clear. Barrett had wanted the ship to strike Molahve. He had plotted it that way.

Someone on that ship that night so long ago must have been alert, for Subchaser *206 had struck neither rock nor shoal nor shore. She had reached Molahve (probably at the exact time Barrett had planned for her to reach it) but she had not struck it.

Garth could imagine the bridge of the subchaser at one-twenty in the morning. It must have been, until then, a sleepy, quiet place with maybe only the helmsman on duty there.

Then—bedlam. Someone yanking the engines into full speed reverse, the gears screaming aft, the wake wave slamming into the stern as the ship slowed and stopped and backed away.

What had happened next? People, straight out of sleep, piling into the bridge? Talk, argument, accusation? Barrett backed against the wall protesting?

So they had anchored her in Garth's quiet lagoon on that night so long ago.

And there she had sunk.

For a moment he felt only helpless anger at that ship on the bottom. The more he found out about her the more unanswered questions she plagued him with.

Why had Barrett wanted her to be wrecked on the shores of a totally uninhabited island?

Why had they anchored there and not simply turned away and gone on?

Who had taken the inlet water flange apart?

And why?

Another question leaped at him. Why had no one—the commanding officer or executive officer—found Barrett's errors long before the ship reached Molahve? Why had no one checked his log book against his plotted positions on the chart?

Garth could not imagine a situation in a Navy ship in which no one ever checked the quartermaster's work. Just to estimate the consumption of fuel would require such a simple check. And yet apparently for days on end no one had checked anything.

The answer seemed to him perfectly clear and perfectly obvious. The reason was that no one else on board the ship had known anything about navigation. They hadn't checked the quartermaster's work because they didn't know how.

Garth saw that it was almost midnight. He was tired and that was why he was accepting such a simple answer and rejecting the next question—*why* wasn't there anyone else aboard who could navigate?

Garth shut the book and went up into the cockpit to lie down on one of the long seats.

He wanted to go to sleep but could not. Lying there looking at the high stars he kept seeing the neat pages of the log book, seeing the angles and logarithms, sines and cosines. He kept seeing, too, the odd little groups of letters.

Suddenly he wondered about something. On any page had those letters ever been, say, three in one group and four or five in another?

He couldn't remember and it bothered him. Getting up he went below to the lab with its friendly sounds of air pumps in the aquariums and, to him, its good smell of fish and seaweed and sediment.

No . . . there were no groups of letters with varying numbers on any one page. On one page the groups had five letters each, on another there were four letters. But there were no four-letter groups on a five-letter page.

The letters started appearing on May 21 and continued in each day's work for the rest of the time.

Picking out the letters for the twenty-first Garth wrote them down in the sequence they were in in the book. There were nine groups:

YEOOY EHXWP LPDYD HTDOP KCTNA IAOLN
LTASM EAYKE TDNNI

Knowing now that he had a code on his hands he went quickly through the book, hoping as he counted the groups on each page, that they would add up to the same thing—nine.

They did and he felt himself grinning. Barrett had apparently used the same key word for the entire code.

That, Garth thought with satisfaction, is going to make this a lot easier.

Leaning back in his chair with his eyes closed he concentrated on the key word. He could remember the first time his father, then a lieutenant in the Navy, had showed

him how codes worked, had demonstrated for him the use
of the coding and decoding boards.

Garth must have been, he thought now, about twelve or
thirteen and for the next few weeks he had lived in a
world of codes with which he amazed his friends and con-
founded his enemies.

His first key word had had eleven letters—GARTHLAR-
SON

He tilted the chair forward and grabbed a pencil.
WILLIAMBARRETT—fourteen.

No. There were no counts of fourteen.

WMBARRETT.

Nine!

Making a code block with the ruler, Garth entered:

WMBARRETT

Then, numbering the letters as they appeared in the
alphabet, and numbering the same letters in sequence as
they appeared in the key word he got:

WMBARRETT
9 4 2 1 5 6 3 7 8

Next he entered the groups of letters in the order he had
found them in the book, taking the first three groups:

WMBARRETT
9 4 2 1 5 6 3 7 8
    EY   L
    HE   P
    XO   D
    WO   Y
    PY   D

Groups 4, 5 and 6 gave him:

```
WMBARRETT
9 4 2 1 5 6 3 7 8
HEYKIL
THECAP
DXOTOD
OWONLY
PPYAND
```

In the loneliness of the laboratory Garth felt as though he had just discovered America. He almost laughed out loud. By just looking at the last line he could see that he had broken this code.

He could feel his excitement growing as he entered the groups for seven, eight, and nine. There was going to be information now, answers; no more secrets, no more helpless guessing.

```
WMBARRETT
9 4 2 1 5 6 3 7 8
THEYKILLE
DTHECAPTA
NDXOTODAY
NOWONLYSK
IPPYANDME
```

He wrote the words in horizontal sequence:

THEYKILLEDTHECAPTANDXOTODAY
NOWONLYSKIPPYANDME

And then broke them into words:

THEY KILLED THE CAPTANDXO TODAY
NOW ONLY SKIPPY AND ME

He stared at the sentence, deciding that the CAPTANDXO was a garble. But the rest was clear enough.

What had gone on aboard that little ship so long ago?
Who were "they"?

Garth could feel the questions crowding in again, the
code not solving anything, only adding questions.

1942?

June 1942? What had been happening then?

1942? 1941. December 7, 1941, was the date Pearl Harbor had been attacked.

He tried to remember. Hadn't Wake Island fallen in
June 1942? The Marines finally surrendering Wake? The
Philippines? Bataan? Corregidor? When had the Philippines
surrendered?

The first marked position on the subchaser's route was
just south of the Philippines in May of 1942.

He couldn't be sure but he thought that the Philippines
had surrendered about then—May or June of 1942. If that
was right the subchaser may have been escaping—and been
caught?

THEY KILLED THE CAPTANDXO TODAY
NOW ONLY SKIPPY AND ME

"They" meant more than one. Barrett and Skippy, whoever he was, made two more. Then why were there only
three skeletons aboard the ship now?

History was slowly coming back to him. The waters the
little ship had sailed through in those long-ago days had
been enemy waters and the big islands had been in enemy
hands. Malaya, New Guinea, New Britain, Truk, were all
enemy occupied. "They" could mean that an enemy ship
had caught the subchaser, or an enemy plane.

Then why wasn't she marked with the wounds of gun-
fire or bombs? How had she survived?

THEY KILLED THE CAPTANDXO . . .

It was an odd way to phrase an enemy attack. . . .
And why put the report of such an attack in code?

Garth felt confused and exhausted but his mind kept nagging at the thing.

Mutiny? Had there been a mutiny aboard—a mutiny Barrett wanted to conceal in this code?

CAPTANDXO . . .

Garth looked at the letters again, checked them, and then suddenly saw the sentence differently. "THEY KILLED THE CAPT *AND* XO . . ." They killed the captain and executive officer. . . .

With a ship in such desperate circumstances, running for her life through this enemy sea, why had the men aboard her mutinied against her officers?

Wearily he got the log book again and found the last entry of coded letters. As he carefully broke the message he hoped that it would, in thirty-six symbols, spell out all the answers.

The message only added more questions:

REFUELED SONSOROL THEY PAID WITH DIAMONDS

He checked the chart and found Sonsorol Island.

Paid with diamonds?

The endless questions plagued him and for the time being he gave up. Tomorrow, he thought. No more tonight.

This time before going topside he was more careful.

Instead of putting everything back into the ammo box he got the paper jacket off a book called *The Natural History of Mammals* and fitted it on the log book. Then he put both books and the chart in with his own technical books and papers. He dropped the ammo box in the waste disposal, making a mental note to make a dump trip as soon as possible. After that he destroyed every piece of paper with the key word and the key sequence numbers by burning them with the Bunsen torch.

As he settled down in the cockpit to sleep he thought: what an odd way to pay for fuel.

11.

Suddenly Garth was wide awake.

The night was marvelously clear but he had been thinking, or dreaming, of another night—a rough and stormy night . . . and of José Morales . . . "two and two makes three and a half. . . ."

He wished now that that other night had not been so rough for, if it had been calm, he might have listened more carefully.

Going back to the lab he got down the log book and sat holding it, as though the book could help him remember.

The voyage of the *Uldra* down from Guam to Molahve had been strenuous. Of all the people who had volunteered to help him sail her not one had ever been out of a bay in a sailboat and he soon began to think of them as his "motley" crew.

Admiral Bill Stucky, a big carrier man, didn't know a dolphin striker from a triatic stay but he was able and willing. The Institute people aboard were much more interested in plankton samples and transmissometer readings than they were in handling lines or steering a straight course.

José Morales, the Filipino anthropologist, was the most

useful because he paid attention. With him on the wheel
Garth felt fairly sure that the boat wouldn't be jibed all
standing, taking out a mast or two.

On the other hand, the biggest guy aboard was the most
useless and every time he appeared on deck Garth checked
the life rings just in case he decided to fall overboard.
This one, Hal King, was a comic. He made a business
of being a comic and, in such close quarters, that got to
be a little wearing. Hal seemed to forget that he had
proudly showed all hands his calling card—with PROFES-
SIONAL COWARD printed on it—and showed it to all
hands two or three times.

Hal had some vague connection with the Trust Territory government and worked (if you could call it that)
with Professor Castle, the atoll-formation expert. For as
long as Garth had known King he had never seen him
do much more than roam around Guam in an official jeep
making more or less a nuisance of himself.

Why Professor Castle chose to make the trip to Molahve
Garth never did figure out. He certainly didn't do it for
the sun, air, and exercise because he stayed below almost
the entire voyage, never lending a hand with the ship's
work, but continually griping about conditions in a flat,
harsh voice Garth found irritating. Castle did not lend a
hand at Molahve either, taking no part in the work of
setting up the project. In fact, he slowed it down because
he was forever commandeering the dinghy to go off explor-
ing the lagoons with his buddy, King.

Now, sitting in the lab with the log book in his hands,
Garth remembered that voyage which seemed to have happened long ago, and remembered the people aboard the
ship.

He was thinking particularly about the only really rough
night they had had. With a strong, veering wind making
a confused sea, Garth had double-reefed the fore and main
sails at dusk and had only the storm jib up forward. It
was a pay-attention sort of time, rough and wet and poten-

tially dangerous so Garth had asked all hands except José Morales to stay below unless he needed help.

The appearance of Hal King in the cockpit had annoyed Garth and he started to send him below again but King had said, "I know you don't want anyone on deck, skipper, but if I stay down there I'll die."

"That would be thoughtless," Garth said, motioning for him to sit down and get a lifeline around himself.

"I've upchucked meals I had in San Francisco two years ago," King said, slumping on the seat and letting Morales get a rope around his waist. "Any cure short of death for seasickness?"

"Yeah," Garth said. "Get a flat plate and put six raw oysters on it."

"I don't want to die like that, just shoot me," King said and stretched out, face down, on the seat.

Garth forgot him as he hunched against a sudden squall of wind which put the lee scuppers under and had solid water running down the deck.

After the squall the weather eased a little and he went on talking with José.

They talked about the project at Molahve and Garth described some of the ridiculous things he had been asked to do. "The State Department guy wants me to watch out for any U.S. farm machinery I see and report to him what type, who's operating it, what they're doing with it, and so forth and so on. Now what would a John Deere tractor be doing on Molahve?"

They had thought King was asleep but he turned over on his back, groaning, and said, "You can report to me any bending maidens or dusky palms. Let me know the latitude and longitude of them."

"I'll do that," Garth said, "because you'll look good with a spear going in one ear and out the other." Then he turned to José. "This one's for you, José. The CIA man asked me to report to him any subversive activities I observe among the natives, and the Office of Naval Intelligence wants me to report any and all combatant vessels or aircraft I see."

"If you really want to get famous," King said, rolling back on his stomach, "find Amelia Earhart."

"Who?"

"The girl aviator, the lady *pilote*. She was flying around the world and all of a sudden she disappeared. Out here somewhere. There're all sorts of stories, like the Japanese captured her, or the natives ate her, or she just forgot and landed in the ocean."

"When?"

King had gotten the rope off and now slid off the seat and began crawling toward the companionway. "A million years ago," he said, "so move over, Amelia, I'm going to die too."

They watched him make his way to the hatch and disappear down it.

"When I first saw King and found out what he did around Guam wasn't very important I thought of asking Castle to let me have him as an assistant," Garth told José. "All that beef and muscle. I'm glad I didn't. I wouldn't go diving in a bathtub with him."

"I've never understood why Professor Castle bothers with him," José said.

"I've never understood Professor Castle," Garth said. "When I was doing the terrain research with him all he seemed to want me to do at Molahve was bore holes in the bottom. He loaded me down with a Phleger corer you could drill oil wells with."

"Absent-minded professor he ain't," José said. "He's got more dope on lagoons in the Molahve area than any man alive." José stopped and thought a minute. "I hadn't thought of it that way," he said, "but I don't understand him either. I'll bet he's visited every island and atoll between New Guinea and Nagasaki—but what *for*? What's his field?"

"Hold the fort!" Garth warned as a new blast of wet wind struck them, whistling out of the darkness. He strained at the wheel, yelling above the wind, "Maybe he's looking for that lady aviator."

When it calmed a little, José said, "People get really hung up on these disappearing acts. They sit around all their lives wondering where did the Aztecs and the Mayans go? What happened to Atlantis? Where's the crew of the *Marie Celeste*? Or the lady aviator. They don't really want to find the lady avaitor, all they want is the *answer*." He laughed and said something in Spanish and then said, "I've got a little hang-up myself."

"Looking for the fountain of youth?" Garth asked, not paying much attention.

José got up and went over to the hatch. He stood there a moment in silence, looking down the dark stairway and listening, and then came back.

José sat down close to Garth at the wheel and said quietly, "Garth, my father wants you to know something. But only if you'll keep it to yourself. I sort of agree with him. It isn't something everybody should know."

"Who am I going to tell it to? The Molahve fish?"

José chuckled and said, "Not even them. There're only a few people who know this. My father is one and some other people in our government, but that's all."

"Why include me then?" Garth asked, realizing now that José was very serious about this.

"Because, if my theory is right—and there's no guarantee on that—you might be able to solve the case of the vanishing washtub."

When Garth didn't answer José looked at him, smiling, and said, "This isn't another chore, another John Deere tractor to look for. It's nothing but a myth. Like Atlantis."

"Okay," Garth said.

José leaned back against the thin cushion and looked at the stormy sky. "I don't remember it and neither do you but back in 1942 my country surrendered. May 8th, 1942. . . . It was a bad time."

"Must've been," Garth said, feeling but not seeing another squall sweeping down on him.

"My father says so. They defeated us everywhere—and that was the U. S. Army and Navy too—just driving us like cattle until finally the only place left to go was Corregidor. You ever been to Corregidor?"

"Just past it," Garth said, wondering whether it would be a good idea to heave to until dawn.

"It's a fairly large island with mountains," José said. "The Malinta Mountains. You can't see them from Manila Bay but there's a series of tunnels dug into the mountains on Corregidor. Big deal. They had hospital tunnels and supply tunnels, tunnels all over the place. So, during the last days before the surrender, all the Americans—Army, Navy, and Marines—were in the tunnels. The Philippine Government was in there too. Altogether there were about 12,000 people crowded into those little tunnels."

"Must've been pleasant," Garth said, deciding to ride out a few more squalls in the hope that things would calm down a little.

"Real neighborly, I guess," José said. "Anyway, all the money was in the tunnels, too. All the gold that belonged to the Philippine Government and all the American money for the troops and like that. All in one part of the tunnels. My father says he never saw so much money in his life. There were bales and bales of paper money—dollars and pesos—and they didn't mean a thing. Just obstacles in a tunnel. You couldn't buy a pound of rice with all the money there, and you couldn't buy freedom either."

"I would have just carried some around. About a million dollars would have looked nice," Garth said.

"That wasn't all," José told him. "All the Philippine jewels were in there, too. All the church jewels, the museum and palace jewels, bushels of jewels." José laughed. "My father used to break me up about those jewels. He says that because there wasn't anything else to put them in they had them in ordinary GI washtubs. You dig? Three or

four million dollars worth of jewels in some buck-fifty galvanized washtubs?"

"I dig," Garth said, feeling in front of the wind the
lull he knew was coming.

"When they knew they were going to have to surrender
—my father said the bombs and shells came down like
rain, day and night, just pouring down on them—they had
to get rid of all that loot to keep it from falling into, shall
we say, the wrong hands."

"I should have been standing around," Garth declared,
not really paying much attention to the story.

"Maybe somebody was. You know what the problem was,
Garth? The money wouldn't burn. The tunnels were full
of people and junk and all the air vents had been shot
up so that there wasn't any draft and all that paper money
did was lie there and smolder." José laughed. "Imagine.
Everybody choking and crying and sneezing the most expensive smog anybody ever made."

"That offends me. Burning money."

"There must have been some pretty gutsy people in
there," José said, "because they got all that gold and all
those jewels buried *outside the tunnels*. Which means that
somebody had to risk his life to bury the stuff.

"They did a good job, too, because after the war when
things got back to normal my government went back to
Corregidor and dug it all up again."

"Don't tell me nobody went over there in the middle
of the night and did a little fishing-worm digging?" Garth
asked, bracing his legs for the blow he could hear coming
out of the darkness.

"A lot of people did a lot of digging, but they didn't
find anything. But this is the funny part. There's a little
village on Corregidor—it was just a *barrio* then—just a
couple of buildings, some *nipa* huts, and a little fishing
wharf. Well, anyway, the day before the surrender there
was one Navy ship left afloat and that was at the village,
all covered up with tree branches and fishnets so even

the people in the tunnels couldn't see it. They knew it was there though."

José paused and looked at him. "The next day, when all the shooting stopped and everybody surrendered, they went down to tell the folks on that ship about it and the ship was gone."

"Good thinking," Garth said.

"Could be," José admitted, "because, after the war when they dug up all those washtubs full of jewels what do you think they found?"

"Beer bottles."

"Close, but no cigar. One washtub, complete with contents, missing. One ship missing. One washtub missing. Two and two makes . . ."

"Three and a half. . . ." It was Hal King coming up the companion ladder. "Mr. Larson," he said in a pained voice, "I must ask you to stop making this ship jump up and down. I am at death's door. . . ."

Garth looked at the book in his hand and thought about what José Morales had said that night.

For the rest of the voyage they had never been alone, so José had never been able to finish the story.

On the last day of the voyage, when Molahve lay ahead of them like a dark mushroom growing from the blue ocean, José had passed Garth at the wheel and said in a low voice, "Two and two doesn't make three and a half, it makes a myth in a washtub."

Garth had wondered for a moment what he was talking about and had then forgotten it.

Now, in the lab, with Sam and Jake asleep forward and the subchaser lying on the bottom of the lagoon, he thought about it again hard and long.

Wasn't there a bucket or something like that under the mess table? Was it larger than a bucket? The size of a . . . washtub?

REFUELED SONSOROL THEY PAID WITH
DIAMONDS . . .

In the Malinta tunnel that night the smoke of paper money not really burning but only smoldering must have been thick and irritating. Men moving in that smoke must have been just indistinct figures. . . .

Some men carrying a washtub through the smoke . . . out of the tunnel . . . down to the camouflaged ship. . . .

Had they been brave men, to risk that shellfire, or just thieves?

Twelve days after the surrender the Navy subchaser 206 had been sailing south of the Philippine archipelago, heading east. . . .

It was three o'clock in the morning. Looking out the porthole Garth could see that the night had turned gloomy, clouds all across the sky, the moon down. The lagoon would be black.

Putting the book away he turned off the light and went aft to the storage locker. He got the metal detector Professor Castle had insisted he bring along and then picked out one of the large underwater lights he used for the TV camera, and a readout meter for the detector. Moving silently, he took these on deck and stowed them in the dinghy which was tied up alongside the landing platform.

Picking a back pack with two filled tanks, he attached the regulator and stowed them in the dinghy.

He pushed off cautiously, making sure he did not let the oars thump against the gunwale as he fitted them into the oarlocks.

For some distance he rowed slowly and carefully; then as he headed south through the lagoon he picked up the stroke.

When he was well clear of the *Uldra* he streamed the metal detector on a fifty-foot line and attached the wires to the readout meter. Holding a small penlight between his knees, the tiny beam just covering the face of the meter, he began to row slowly, watching the meter and feeling the heavy drag of the detector, gliding along through the water fifty feet below him.

It seemed hours before he got any reading on the meter and, for a time, there was a break in the clouds which let starlight flood the dinghy. Looking back at the *Uldra* he could not tell for sure whether the dark shadows were men standing motionless and watching him or not.

At the maximum reading of the meter he dropped anchor and hauled in the detector.

The clouds were across the stars again and as he worked he saw that the surface of the lagoon was black.

Ready to go at last, he sat on the gunwale with his back to the water, the big lamp cradled in his arms.

Garth did not like night diving under any circumstances and now it took a great deal of willpower to push with his feet and feel himself falling backward into that black water.

He had not thought it would be so completely dark under the water and he wanted to turn the lamp on just for solace, but did not, reasoning that his enemies down there could not see him any better than he could see them and that the light would only attract them.

Swimming absolutely blind he found the anchor rope and holding it lightly in one hand headed downward.

It seemed much, much deeper than he remembered and for a while he was afraid that the detector had been picking up some metal in an abyssal depth.

His hand on the anchor rope touched the ship first and he suddenly felt a panic to hurry; to get into the safety of the ship with the doors closed and steel walls around him.

He went directly to the crew's compartment door, entered, the light still off, and closed the door.

The light gave him a great feeling of security and he floated for a moment beaming the strong floodlight all around the room.

Nothing had changed. The skeletons lay as he had first seen them.

Swimming over to the mess table he beamed the light down beside the bench.

It was not a bucket as he had thought when he first saw it. It was a small, round washtub.

It seemed to be filled to the brim with gray dust and when he pushed his fingers slowly into it they sank without any resistance for an inch or two and then touched what felt like gravel.

Scooping up a small handful he lifted it into the beam of the light, the dust washing off his hand in slow, gray swirls, leaving in his hand glints and gleams of light—red, blue, green, and hard, colorless flashes.

Tipping his hand slowly he let the jewels fall, a cascade of colors, back into the washtub where they stirred up a smoke of dust.

There were diamonds, rubies, emeralds, sapphires. . . .

12.

Garth was reacting childishly and he knew it, but could not stop the feeling of resentment against these rocks. It was the same resentment he felt about the ship, about Smith.

Why didn't they all disappear and leave him alone so he could get on with what he had come to Molahve to do?

Slowly the significance of the jewels pushed up through all that and he began to recognize the tremendous threat they now were to him.

Until now he had been simply sharing a secret with Smith. First Smith and then Garth had been intent on hiding the presence of the ship from the rest of the world.

Now he realized that Smith was not just hiding an ancient crime. Smith's secret was not the sinking of this ship and the murder of the men in her. No. Smith wanted to keep this ship a secret only because of these small rocks, this little pile of bright gravel lying in a washtub. These rocks were what Smith wanted.

For a moment Garth had a stream of small, warning thoughts. In a few more hours this water would be glass clear again, every detail of the ship would be easily visible from the surface. . . . Smith would surely come to Molahve to inspect the results of the typhoon's wave action. . . . He had probably been waiting for years, hoping that some typhoon would do exactly what this one had done . . .

Knowing now how imperative it was for him to hide this dive from Sam and Jake he turned off the light before going forward for the two spare tanks he had left in the bridge.

Swimming these back to the engine room, he wedged them down between the engine beds and then began looking for a wrench.

As he came around the port engine he saw the skeleton. This one was not complete, some of the grayish bones lying on the gear box, some lying on the deck.

After the first shock of surprise he felt again what he had before—a sort of pity for these remains of men.

Skippy? he wondered.

Barrett?

The man must have been standing beside the gear box when someone had killed him. From the position, the skull face down on the gear box, it looked as though he had fallen forward when the bullet struck him in the back.

Garth swam on above the bones until he found a tool locker and a wrench.

Opening the valve on one of the spare tanks he moved back as an explosion of escaping air poured around the engine. Then it died and he adjusted the wrench around the valve base.

Fortunately the valve was one of the sealing-ring types, not screw-thread sealing or he would not have been able to get it out.

Taking out both valves he put the wrench back and swam the empty tanks forward to the crew's quarters.

Working hurriedly he scooped up the jewels and, making a funnel with one hand, poured them into one of the empty tanks.

They filled the tank almost to the top and as he put the

valve back in and turned it hand tight he idly wondered how much the tank was worth now.

The tank, plus the valve, probably cost thirty-five dollars. . . .

He left the empty washtub beside the bench leg and then for a moment longer lay still, beaming the light slowly around. He could not see any sign of his movements in the room. The silent skeletons lay as before, the wet dust from the jewels had settled again in the washtub.

Pushing the tanks ahead of him he went out and closed the door.

Then he tied the tanks to the dinghy's anchor rope and began his ascent.

When he could see the even darker outline of the dinghy's bottom in the black water he stopped and, using the penlight for a second, checked the time and depth.

The two minutes he lay there in the black, silent water were long and frightening. Occasionally some invisible fish would move close to him, leaving a pale, fading swathe of phosphorescence.

He also worried about Sam and Jake. They were early risers and it was close to dawn.

Surfacing at last he was relieved to find the sky still overcast, the night dark.

Dumping his gear into the dinghy, he got in and took in most of the anchor rope before rowing over to the anti-shark net.

By the time he reached the net he could clearly see the *Uldra* but there was no sign of Sam or Jake. Rowing over the top of the net he paid out all the anchor rope, letting the anchor and the two tanks sink to the bottom. Then he tied the bitter end to the top strand of the net.

Finally, rowing hard but easily, he returned to the *Uldra*.

There was no one on deck as he silently tied up the boat and climbed aboard. Racking his gear he got a mop and went to work.

There was nothing suspicious about what he was doing;

every morning at dawn it was his custom to sponge the dew off all the brightwork. The fact that he was also sponging away his wet tracks across the deck and drying the scuba gear was hardly noticeable.

The sun had been above the horizon for five minutes before he heard Sam and Jake talking and laughing below. He called a good morning to them from on deck and then went below himself.

If they had seen him during the night hours they did not give him any hint of it. Nor, as they made their plans for the day, did they mention the ship on the bottom.

After breakfast Sam and Jake with the locator and shovels shoved off in the dinghy to continue their search ashore. Garth had told them that while they were doing that he would begin taking in the anti-shark net.

Not even waiting for them to reach shore he suited up and swam over to the net with a coil of rope.

The water was so much clearer now that he could see the two tanks and the anchor lying on the rocky bottom.

On shore Sam and Jake cast off the heavy line securing the net as Garth tied the end of the coil of rope to the top strand of the net and began swimming the rest of the rope back to the schooner.

On board he attached the rope to the deck winch. Sam and Jake turned to look when the sound of the winch gears reached them but then went back to work.

With the net alongside, Garth waited until they were out of sight before he started hauling in the anchor rope.

They were still out of sight behind a dune as he got the tanks aboard, put them in the To-be-filled rack and tightened the valves before tying on the red flags.

Leaving the winch running to cover the sound, he started the compressor and pumped enough air into the tank with the jewels and its mate to make it convincing if anyone opened the valves to test them.

That done he stood a moment at the companion hatch looking at Molahve. Now, even with Sam and Jake working over there, the island seemed to him more lonely than ever. Lonely, ominous, forbidding—dangerous.

And he felt lonely and threatened. If Smith ever found the subchaser Garth knew that his life would be in danger. And if he was alone here Smith could destroy him, leaving no evidence, no witnesses.

Almost in a panic Garth went below and turned on the transmitter. As he sat waiting for it to warm up he had no idea what he was going to say; all he could think was that he needed help, needed protection from Smith.

Waiting, he began to think a little more clearly. A panic call to Admiral Stucky would bring a lot of Navy steaming in here. He'd have all the protection he needed but the moment Stucky saw that subchaser it would be the end of Molahve's unique ecosystem.

I'm alone, Garth thought, but I'm not helpless.

It was possible, he slowly realized, to keep Smith from ever seeing the subchaser. If he moved to another location Smith might never come into this lagoon again.

He knew that that was wishful thinking but he still had a weapon—the jewels.

Garth tried to put himself in Smith's position. What did Smith really want? To conceal the murders he had committed so long ago?

Garth suddenly realized that only a one-in-a-million coincidence of wind and current and sand had left any trace of those murders. And Smith could not possibly know that the skeletons were there. He was no doubt convinced that they had long since disappeared.

Now he doubted whether Smith felt any guilt for, or fear of, those ancient murders. The jewels were all he wanted.

Smith might murder again to get them but—he would not murder the only man who could lead him to them. Not until he had them.

Simple. Get rid of them. Get rid of them without exposing Smith's past.

Garth almost smiled. That would leave Smith with no reason to kill anybody; leave him just an old, broken man who had wasted his life for some pretty rocks.

All Garth had to do was tell José Morales that he had them. The government of the Philippines would take care of the situation then and no one except he and Smith would ever know that the USS 206 lay wrecked in the Molahve lagoon.

Smith would no doubt monitor any call he made so Garth began to phrase his message to José in his mind as he started calling Guam. When there was no answer Garth noticed that the ready light was not on, nor were the dial lights.

The Navy radioman who had been one of the crew on the voyage down to Molahve had spent a lot of time setting up what Garth had then thought was overly elaborate (and expensive) equipment. But now he suddenly remembered the radioman explaining the tape recorders. These were mounted in a cabinet under the radios and one was actuated either by the receivers or transmitters and always by the Danger Alert set. This one ran at a speed of one and seven-eighths inches per second and, the radioman had said, the 3600 feet of tape was enough to record six hours of conversation.

The Danger Alert set was wired into the second recorder which, in case he wanted a permanent record, could record whatever he wanted off the tape of the Alert set.

The radioman had advised him that, if he did not want to make a permanent record of his calls, he should, after each conversation, push the rewind button on the monitoring recorder so that he would always have a full reel of tape.

Garth recalled now rewinding the tape after the typhoon alert.

He opened the cabinet door and looked helplessly at the two recorders, set side by side on the shelf. None of the reels was moving but there was tape on both the supply and take-up reels of the monitor.

Calling Guam again he saw that the reels did not move.

Then why was there tape on the take-up reel if nothing worked?

Garth pushed the rewind button and watched the reels whirl. When they stopped, he pushed the manual play switch.

After a short period of quiet he heard his own voice calling Guam. Startled and hopeful he listened but it turned out to be only his first call to Guam on the day he returned from Efrahte.

He was about to turn off the recorder when, loud and clear, another voice began speaking.

He listened for some seconds before he realized that the language wasn't English.

He was wondering if the thing had picked up someone else's transmission when he heard a second voice begin.

This was Smith's.

And then he recognized the first voice—Jake.

Speaking to each other in their language.

The transmission went on for more than three minutes, first Jake then Smith. Garth stood there, his anger rising, but could not understand any of it. Toward the end it sounded as though Smith was annoyed. He kept repeating one phrase over and over, almost shouting. Finally, at the end of the conversation, Smith's voice grew calm again and sounded almost pleased about something.

Garth was too stunned and too angry to turn the machine off and it went on, hissing softly.

Suddenly he found himself staring at the open door as though expecting an enemy to walk in, found himself listening to every sound outside the boat.

He stopped the machine, rewound the tape, and during his Guam call, sat waiting nervously for those two voices to begin again.

This time, as the voices of Jake and Smith began, Garth listened more carefully.

They were talking too fast! He caught a word here, one there, but no meaning came with them.

He slammed the rewind switch again and watched the reels. Then he hit the play switch and waited, his own voice irritating him.

Waiting, not listening to himself, he began to put things together. Sometime after he had called Guam yesterday, Jake had called Smith. Probably on the short-range set for it was all set up on Smith's frequency.

When had he done it?

Not before Garth had gone down to see the ship. And not after he had put Sam and Jake ashore or after he had brought them back and they had eaten and gone to bed.

The only times Jake could have done it were while Garth was actually in the water on the first dive or—in the water on the dive in the night. . . .

Now, perhaps because he almost knew what Jake was going to say, the conversation on the tape became clearer.

"A ship." "Bottom." "Molested." Could that mean ruined? Wrecked?

He rewound the tape and played it again and this time half a sentence leaped out of the meaningless sound.

"The English"—there was a phrase or word he didn't understand—". . . is stone. . . ."

He played the tape again and this time caught more words and the sentence became: "The English estimates the canoe is only stone."

In pidgin, "English" could mean either "British" or "stranger," "foreigner." Perhaps it was the same in Jake's language. And in many dialects "canoe" meant any kind of ship from an outrigger to a battlewagon.

Putting it into English it came out: "Larson thinks the subchaser is only a rock."

Garth felt as though something had struck him from behind.

He watched his hand go slowly down and push the rewind button and then just lie there as the reels whirled.

Smith would be here soon. He was probably on his way now.

And this time there would be no effort to persuade, no easy relationship.

Garth stood there feeling alone and defenseless; he was unable even to talk to a living soul except his enemies.

As he started to close the cabinet door he suddenly wondered why it had taken so long for Jake to give his simple message. Why three minutes—some of it angry talk?

He pushed the play button.

Smith talked too fast. His angry shouting still had no meaning.

Then, as the conversation ended and the reels only hissed quietly, Garth knew without hearing any words what Smith must have been saying.

Now more than at any time in all the years Smith had been waiting, the secret of that ship must be guarded. The news that it was lying there exposed on the bottom must not go any farther.

How could he stop it?

The answer was so simple.

Jake knew enough about the big transmitter to turn it on and talk. But that was probably as much as Jake did know.

Garth stared at the transmitter. What would I do? he asked himself, whispering. What would I tell a Stone Age man to do to wreck this thing?

The fact that he knew little more about it than Jake frustrated him and made him angry.

He glared at the radio. . . .

The antenna!

He ran aft and up the ladder. The radio antenna was mounted on top of the mainmast with the lead-in stapled to the forward side.

There was nothing wrong that he could see, no break

in the lead-in from the antenna to the waterproof grommet
in the deck.

Disappointed, he went aft, glancing over at the beach as
he went.

Sam and Jake were no longer shoveling but were standing
on top of one of the highest sand dunes, doing nothing.

Garth took the binoculars out of the case and trained
them on the dune.

The two men were laughing and talking. Sam raised his
arm and pointed seaward and both of them seemed very
pleased about something.

Garth swung the glasses seaward.

A little copra boat was just above the horizon and heading
straight toward the island.

Garth was surprised to see the binoculars shaking in his
hands. He put them in the case and went slowly down the
ladder.

He knew now that he had not really been thinking. Just
fooling around, panicked, wishing, hoping, guessing. Wasting
time. The antenna had nothing to do with the indicator
lights.

Something was wrong with the electricity. It was not
doing what it was supposed to do; not getting where it was
supposed to get.

Jake must have gotten into the box and done something
to it.

He had not. The radio was secured to the bulkhead by
a formed metal strap. The screws holding the strap had
been painted over and the paint seal had not been broken.

Power was flowing *to* the gray metal box. No one had
opened the box to disturb the flow. Therefore Jake had
done something on the outside of the box.

Garth searched the front of the radio as though seeing
it for the first time.

He remembered now how impressed he had been on
the voyage down from Guam by the radioman's swift
and knowledgeable setting of the controls, zipping from

switch to switch and dial to dial. Then, patiently, showing
Garth where each control should be set and warning him
after they were properly set not to fiddle with them.

Now he studied each gadget on the front of the box,
and he was sure they were set exactly as the radioman had
shown him.

His breathing was tight and he was sweating as he
stepped over to the porthole.

The copra boat was coming straight at him, men in the
bow already getting the anchor ready.

Going back to the radio he sat down and forced himself
to think only about that.

Then, as though the radioman were right there in the
room with him, Garth heard him saying, "Now if anything
goes wrong you've got this fuse. The only reason for that to
burn out is if your line voltage from the generator goes
too high, or something shorts out in the set. If it blows
you'll know it because none of the pretty lights will wink at
you. Put in another fuse. If that one blows there's something wrong with it you can't fix. Just turn it off and
forget it."

Garth unscrewed the black knob marked FUSE and
looked inside the little round black tunnel.

There was nothing in there.

The radioman had left him some spare fuses in a plastic
box and Garth got one, shoved it into the tunnel and re-
placed the knob.

When he turned on the radio, red, green, and yellow
lights lit up all over the thing.

He stood away from it, wondering if it was now going
to explode or something, but nothing happened.

Not knowing whether the radio sent out a signal even
if no one was talking on it, he turned it off just to be
sure and went back to the porthole.

Smith's copra boat was at anchor in the lagoon.

Garth could see people moving around on deck, a party
of them standing by the boat davits.

He stood watching as the boat was lowered and four men pushed it around to the gangplank. Smith, wearing his big hat, came down and got into the stern.

Garth hit the ON switch and then stood over it scowling as though that would make the ready light come on sooner.

Impatient, nervous—and afraid, he suddenly realized that it was only six o'clock in the morning in Guam. No one would be awake. As the ready light came on Garth prayed for an alert and intelligent operator on the other end of this radio hook-up.

At least he was alert for he answered after Garth's second call.

"This is Garth Larson of the Institute at Molahve," he said. "Please record this because I haven't got time for repeats and it is important."

"Everything on this frequency is supposed to be important —official business." The voice reminded Garth of a mean and petty little piano teacher he had had when he was a kid.

"It *is* official business. This is a message for José Morales. Tell him . . ."

"Do you wish to speak to Mr. Morales?" the voice asked.

"No! I haven't got time!"

"He isn't here."

"*Please*, just tape this. For José Morales from Garth Larson . . ."

"Is this an official message?"

"I told you it was!"

"This frequency cannot be utilized for person-to-person messages."

"This is not personal," Garth yelled at him. "This is from Larson of the Institute to José Morales of the Admiral's staff, now take this message. . . ."

"Mr. Morales is on a field trip now and I don't know when he will get back."

"Well, be sure he gets the message when he gets back.

The message is . . ." Garth paused a moment and then slowly said, "I have his washtub and his—myth."

"You mean bathtub?"

Garth had to take a deep breath and hold it for a second. Then, as quietly and in as friendly a way as he could, he said, "Just take what I say down on tape, please. For Morales: I—have—his—washtub."

Garth turned so he could see out the porthole.

Smith's boat was close aboard, the men rowing well, the boat surging toward him.

The voice in Guam said monotonously, "For José Morales: I have his washtub. Is that all?"

To Garth the voice seemed to boom around the cabin. "Yes," he said, whispering, "that's all."

He flicked the switch off, took the fuse out and dropped it in a drawer and then ran forward. In the chain locker he grabbed the lead line off the peg and went up through the hatch. Without looking aft he walked on into the bow of the boat. Standing there with his back to Smith and the natives, he began swinging the line with the lead weight on the end.

He watched the lead fly out over the water and splash into it as the coils of the line spun off his hand. Aft he could hear people moving and, through his bare feet, feel them on his boat.

They were silent, no talking, no greetings to him.

He remained standing with his back to them as the line moved, slowly now, through his hand.

People had told him that you did not feel the bullet that killed you. He wondered how they knew a thing like that.

He waited, the line motionless in his hands, the ten fathom marker lying on the still water. The nerves in his back began to feel like tiny, hot wires just under the skin as they, too, waited for the bullet, or the poisoned spear, or the hands. . . .

13

"Ahoy, Larson," Smith called.

Garth turned half around, holding up the remaining coils of the lead line. "Good morning."

As he hauled in the line his throat was tight and his heart felt as though his chest wasn't big enough for it.

Taking in the last fathom, the salt water dripping from his hands, he turned around.

Smith, in shirt and shorts, the big hat shading his face, was standing near the landing platform. Behind him were two of his men.

Two other men in Smith's boat were rowing toward shore. As Garth walked aft he saw Sam and Jake running down to the beach. He was not sure at that distance but it didn't look as though they were carrying anything, even the locator.

Laying the lead line carefully on the main cabin skylight, Garth walked slowly aft. "Good morning," he said again.

"Morning," Smith said curtly and turned to say something to the men behind him.

Now Garth could see Smith's face in the deep shadow under the hat.

The man looked as though he had aged ten years since

Garth had last seen him on Efrahte. His face looked old and worn, his eyes were flecked with the red of weariness, his lips were pressed together, giving him a grim, wary expression. As Garth looked at him the only word he could think of was haunted. Smith looked haunted.

"We've got a problem, Larson," Smith said.

He must have left Efrahte within minutes after Jake's message about the ship. He must have run that old diesel with the throttle bent over the stop to get here so soon.

"Have we?" Garth said.

Smith raised himself on his toes to look over the deckhouse. Garth did too and saw Sam and Jake wading out to meet the small boat.

"There's some coffee below," Garth said.

Smith nodded and moved toward the companionway. He stopped, said something to the men, and went below.

Garth took one last look at the silent, ominous men and one last look at the small boat, now with Sam and Jake aboard and towing his dinghy. Six men in all. No. Seven, counting Smith.

He dropped down the ladder.

Smith was standing in the after cabin watching him.

Garth went over to the thermos and set out two cups on the little shelf. "I've got sugar, but no cream."

"I don't want anything—coffee, nothing."

Garth didn't want any coffee either. Slowly and carefully he put the two cups back behind the fiddle and pushed the thermos into the spring clip that kept it from turning over in heavy weather. As he moved, doing these things, he knew that he was only trying to postpone something that could no longer be postponed.

At last he turned around and said, "Okay, what's the problem?"

Smith said, "I can't control my people. They know you're here. They know you're breaking their taboo. They don't like it, Larson. Already they are beginning to work themselves up, chewing a lot of betel, mixing body paint, talking war."

He seemed to want Garth to say something but Garth just stood looking at him.

"All right," Smith said, "this is the way it is. You've got to go, Larson. I'm sorry about it, but there's nothing I can do to stop them now. If you don't go they will kill you."

Garth's hands were sticky from the salt water and he dipped them into a tub of fresh water he kept for washing out the rubber suits and then slowly dried them with a towel.

He didn't have to look at Smith to know that this was the end of the line. The only reason Smith had not killed him long ago was simply because he had not made up his mind to do it. Now he had.

"The English estimates the canoe is only stone."

With Smith thinking that, wouldn't it be possible for Garth just to pack up and go? To stay away long enough for Smith to find the jewels gone and to get rid of the evidence lying pitifully in the ship? And then, when Smith had nothing to hide, come back—in peace?

No. If the jewels were not in the ship Smith would know that he had taken them.

But, Garth argued, if he proved to Smith that he had returned the jewels to the Philippines?

No. How could Smith ever trust him after he knew that he had seen the evidence of his murders and so could accuse him of them at any time?

Smith would *have* to trust him—or Garth could never work here in peace again. He would become like Smith, forever wary and forever afraid.

Garth looked at Smith's haunted face and made up his mind. This man would have to be *made* to understand. If I have to break his bald head, Garth thought, I'll make him understand. He looked straight at Smith and said, "There's a ship on the bottom of the lagoon."

Smith seemed not to have heard him. "Just get out of here, Garth."

"It's a Navy subchaser."

He heard that. "I know," he said.

"The number is two zero six."

"How do you know that?"

"It's painted on the bow."

Smith gazed slowly around the cabin and then walked over and sat down in a chair. Without looking up he said in a vague, low voice, "You've been down to look at her?"

"Yes, and she's in beautiful condition." Garth looked directly at him. "She's exactly the way she was the day she went down because she's been buried in sand and silt so thick that nothing in the sea could get to her. Not even aerobic bacteria."

In the same low voice, Smith said, "You went inside her?"

"Yes, the whole story's there. As though it happened yesterday."

"What story?" Smith asked in the dull voice.

"You'd know more about that than I would. The bodies of four men are still in her."

Smith raised his head slowly and looked at him. "Bodies?"

"Four."

"Bodies?"

"Skeletons now. One of them looks as though he had been shot through the head. I don't know what killed the other three."

"Four skeletons . . . ?" Smith asked. "How could that be?"

"If they had been exposed to the sea they wouldn't have lasted long but under the sand only the anaerobic bacteria which were there all the time and need no oxygen could work on them. So there they are, four dead men."

"Just bones?" Smith asked.

"Bones are calcium phosphate which bacteria don't like." Garth paused and looked at him. "Now that they're exposed to the sea they won't last long. Worms will bore holes in them, sponges and clams will root in them, and crustacea will take them apart. In a little while they'll disappear. There'll be nothing at all left, Smith. *Nothing!*"

Smith did not seem to understand what Garth was telling him. He looked up, frowning, puzzled, and said, "Where are these—people?"

"Where you left them," Garth said. "Three in the crew's compartment and one in the engine room."

There was still no reaction from him. Garth leaned close to him and said in a low voice, "Smith, I don't care what you did years ago. I don't care how many people you killed nor what sort of barratry you pulled. . . ."

"Barratry?" Smith asked, at last seeming to listen to him. "What's barratry?"

"Someone deliberately sunk that ship. That's barratry."

"Oh," Smith said and slumped back, his head forward, his hands hanging down between his knees.

Garth wanted to grab him and shake him and make him listen. "Listen to me, Smith! If you did it, I don't *care!* Don't you understand? I don't want anybody to know about that ship any more than you do. I don't want the Navy sailing in here with salvage equipment to foul up this water." He stopped and waited for Smith to look up, to pay attention, but the man didn't move. Slowly Garth reached out and touched his shoulder. "Believe me, Smith, keeping this place pure is far more important to me, and to science— and maybe to everybody in the world—than nailing you for some forgotten murder." He took his hand away. "I am not your enemy," he said. "Don't be mine."

For some reason Smith raised his hands and laid them on his legs, palms up. Then he sat there studying them until he finally looked up and said, "Could one man be different from another? Could one man have different bacteria from another man?"

For a second Garth felt like reaching out and strangling this man, but then he looked at the tired, haunted face. "Are you all right, Smith?"

Suddenly Smith's eyes flamed with anger and his lips quivered, "I just asked you a simple question!" he yelled.

Garth backed away from him. "Ease off. One man different from another? Not basically. Maybe you've got more disease germs of one sort or another than I have, or vice versa, but we're pretty much alike."

Smith pushed himself up to his feet and started walking slowly toward the door. Garth watched him for a moment and then said, "I don't want to hurt anybody, Smith, but if you threaten me I can. I've got poisons here which can kill you in a matter of seconds, poisons that can wipe out the entire population of Efrahte." Garth walked across the cabin and faced him. "Let's make it so you don't have to hurt anybody and neither do I."

At last Smith looked directly at him. The vagueness was gone and his face was somber. "I had to once," he said. "And now I think I will have to do it again." He walked on toward the door.

Garth let him go, saying, "I'm sorry you think that way."

Smith didn't answer as he walked into the main cabin, picked up his hat, and started up the ladder. Halfway up he stopped and looked back. "Garth—don't ever go near that subchaser again." Then he disappeared up the ladder.

Garth heard him call out something and then heard bare feet running on the deck above his head.

Listening, he backed slowly toward the lab, watching the hatch opening as he wondered if there was anything in the cabin he could use as a weapon against them when they came down the ladder.

For a moment longer there was the sound of movement on deck but no shadow appeared in the hatch and after a little while there was silence topside.

He went cautiously up until he could see out.

Smith's boat was a hundred feet away, the four oarsmen rowing steadily. Smith sat in the stern; Sam and Jake sat on their grass sleeping mats in the bow.

14.

As Garth worked, getting the *Uldra* ready for sea, he kept an eye on Smith's copra boat. Two oarsmen were still sitting in the rowboat, evidently waiting to go somewhere, but Smith had gone below.

In the chain locker Garth rigged the mooring pennant with a pelican hook so he could cast off without wasting any time going back and forth. Then, on deck, he took the stops off the sails, keeping his movements small, and rove the halyards around the power winches.

Smith had come on deck and was moving some scuba gear around.

For a little while, Garth thought, this is going to be a stand-off. Smith wouldn't move against him until he found that the jewels were gone and, until then, Garth had a little time.

Perhaps enough. Once out of the lee of the island and under the strong sea wind he could make nearly eight knots, using sail and all the power of the diesel. Smith's old boat could make ten, perhaps eleven.

Suppose, Garth thought, it takes one hour after Smith starts his dive to convince him that the jewels are gone. That would give him an eight-mile head start.

Not enough. Smith could overtake him with two hours of daylight left.

But, Garth thought, if it takes him much longer than an hour it would be dark before that old copra boat could catch him and in the dark with as little as a mile between them Garth thought that he could lose him.

Smith, in a wet suit and carrying his tanks, got down into the rowboat.

As the men rowed out into the lagoon Garth dropped down into the cabin, slipped the fuse in and switched on the radio. Waiting, he wondered if Smith had a tape recorder-monitor such as his but then decided that it made no difference. He couldn't hear this transmission *now*. Whether he heard it later on tape didn't matter.

Looking through the porthole Garth saw the rowboat going in a wide circle, evidently looking for the subchaser.

Gaum answered on his first call and immediately told him to stand by, that Professor Castle had a message for him.

Just the sound of the voice, so secure, so unworried coming from a nice air-conditioned room made Garth feel better. In a moment Castle came on.

"Hello, Garth. This is Castle."

"Yes, sir. How can I get in touch with José Morales?"

"José? I'm not sure just where he is, but I'll find out for you. In the meantime I've got some good news."

"I could use some."

"First, though, Dr. Jenkins wants to know how much equipment was ruined by the typhoon."

The rowboat was very close to where the ship lay. "Tell him I'll call him later," Garth said. "I'm heading out for Beaufort in a few minutes and I'd like . . ."

"Beaufort? No, not Beaufort," Castle told him. "That got wiped out by the typhoon. You're supposed to go to Monique Island."

"*Monique?* Why there?"

"Some people from Scripps are going to meet you there. How long do you think it'll take you?"

It worried Garth. "That island isn't even in the Trust Territory; it's foreign. I haven't even got an entry permit."

"It's all arranged. How long will it take you?"

Garth looked up at the chart. "Monday morning at the earliest."

"That'll be perfect. We'll meet you there. And here's the good part. Your assistant is coming with us."

A man in the rowboat dropped anchor. "Okay, I'm on my way," Garth said and switched off.

On deck he watched Smith go over the side. The minute his head slid under the water Garth hit the ignition switch and pulled the lanyard on the pelican hook.

He passed within a hundred yards of the rowboat but the men watching seemed uninterested. He noticed no sign of excitement, nor any signaling on a lifeline he could see on the gunwale.

Smith must not have expected this, he thought, and so had not warned them to signal him if the *Uldra* moved.

It was too easy. Clear of the peninsula the trade wind caught him and he got up every piece of canvas he could fly. The old boat really moved with the wind abaft the beam and the diesel going four bells and a jingle down below. Only fifteen minutes had passed since Smith had disappeared under the water and already the lagoon was fading into the distance.

An hour passed. Smith had probably finished searching the boat by now, Garth decided, looking nervously astern. In a few minutes more he would be starting the long stern chase.

Two hours. Only the clouds clinging to the volcanoes showed above the horizon now and still the sea was empty.

Even from up on the gooseneck he could see nothing behind him.

Three hours . . . four . . .

Slipping the beckets on, Garth climbed the belly of the

sail and scanned the whole horizon with binoculars. From that height he could see for twenty miles and there was nothing marking the blue sea.

Coming down he set a course westward toward Monique and got the ship ready for the night.

Suddenly he wondered if, perhaps, Smith had run into trouble below. The shark net was no longer there to protect him; or, perhaps, something had gone wrong inside the ship. Garth could think of no other reason for Smith not following him. The washtub was there, empty. It could not have taken Smith much more than an hour to convince him that the jewels were gone. And no time at all to know who had taken them.

Puzzled, but glad it had worked out this way, Garth got his sextant and chronometer out of the rack and prepared for the evening star sights.

15.

It was a pleasant trip upon an empty sea. The wind, though light, was steady so that for hours at a time he could use the automatic tiller while he caught up on much-needed work both for the ship and in the lab.

By the second night he knew that he was not going to reach Monique until late Monday afternoon and so radioed this information to Guam.

His only worry was that if Smith did have a monitor like his he would know where he was heading. If it had been Beaufort or almost any of the islands in the Trust Territory Garth would have been safe from attack, but Monique was a foreign island with a bad reputation as a base for smuggling narcotics and other contraband and Garth was not sure that the authorities there would stop Smith from molesting him.

By now, Garth reasoned, Smith would have gotten rid of any evidence of murder and so could go after the jewels without the threat of exposure.

All during the daylight hours he had kept watching for Smith's boat but now, almost at the end of the voyage, he realized that by simply running before the wind on that first day out of Molahve he had lost a lot of time. If Smith took a direct course to Monique he could actually be ahead of Garth now and could beat him to Monique by as much as a day.

Garth thought how good it would be if, when he got to Monique, José Morales was waiting for him. Thinking of this he realized suddenly that José's jewels—and his only weapon—weren't very well concealed. The jewels stashed in the scuba tank might be well hidden from some searchers, but not from Smith. That would be the first place he would look.

They were not even safe from a good customs inspector. He had a bad moment as he thought of what could happen to him if he did not declare this fortune in gems at a foreign island like Monique and customs found them. . . .

He sat there, seeing the whole ship in his mind, space by space, trying to imagine himself a customs inspector —or Smith.

The jewels would not be safe in any space or compartment, box, bilge, locker, lazaret, or diesel fuel, water, oil, or gas tanks. A determined man might even take the heads off the engines to be sure nothing was in the cylinders. . . . And then he thought of the one perfect place.

He secured the wheel and took the tank down into the lab.

It was the first time he really looked at the jewels out of the water and in a good light. As he poured them into the sterilizer the stream of brilliant colors, some hard some soft, was beautiful. For the first time Garth, who had never had a jewel, nor wanted one, could understand why other people could have such a desperate desire to own these beautiful rocks.

While they were being sterilized he began preparing the aquariums, working only on those containing the most venomous species—the stone and scorpion fish, the sea dragons, and the *Hydrophiidae* family of sea snakes. He also chose the tanks containing specimens of the genera of jellyfish *Chiropsalmus*, *Chironex*, and *Carybdea*, and the tank with his collection of venomous mollusks, including the two most venomous cone shells, *Conus geographus* and *Conus textile*.

The stainless-steel aquariums had thick, clear plastic panes only in the front and each had a layer of sand on the bottom, the depth depending on the size of the tank. Wearing heavy, sterile, arm-length rubber gloves he moved the layer of sand in each tank to one side, piling it up against the end wall.

When the tanks were ready he scooped the jewels out of the sterilizer and spread some of them over the bottom of each tank. Once they had all been put into the tanks and leveled he carefully pushed the sand back over them, making sure to have a thick layer of sand between the plastic panel and the layer of gems. That done, he read-justed the filters and sea-water pumps and arranged whatever rocks or sea growth were needed for the various species, and checked for any damage he might have done to the specimens.

He then carefully checked to see that no gem was visible through the plastic and that none had been left in the sterilizer or dropped on the deck.

As he was about to take the scuba tank topside again he suddenly remembered some useless signs the Institute had provided him with and had asked him to use at all times. He had never used them and it took him a little while to find where he had stowed them.

They were very impressive signs, each one being lettered in fluorescent, quivering red on a black background.

DANGER

DANGEROUS ANIMALS

If poisoned by specimens
inject anti-venom at once

For a moment he hesitated, wondering if the signs would be a giveaway but decided that they would not.

He hung a sign on every tank in the lab, including the ones with perfectly harmless little reef fish.

Finished with that job he went forward and cleared the photographic supplies out of the forward cabin, let the chain bunk down, and got the place shipshape for the assistant Castle had promised. As he worked he wondered who the assistant would be. Maybe someone he had gone to school with or had met at Scripps. At any rate Garth hoped that the man would be physically—and mentally —up to life as it was at Molahve. There was plenty of hard physical labor and plenty of painstaking, tedious, and fin-icky lab work. There were also the loneliness and the risks. Carelessness in the lagoon could be dangerous; carelessness in the lab could be fatal.

But at least there would be someone to talk to, Garth thought with pleasure. He hoped the guy had a sense of humor and, if it were not asking too much, liked to cook.

Life with someone to talk to could be good at Molahve after he got rid of those rocks—and Smith *knew* that he had done it.

He did not begin to worry about Monique until he could see the mountains of the island like small, dark clouds on the horizon.

He had heard a lot of disturbing things about the gov-ernment of Monique. A friend of Garth's had had his yacht impounded there only because he didn't have a rhinoceros beetle clearance—although he had been nowhere near a beetle menace.

There seemed to be a lot of animosity toward outsiders. Monique, he had heard, was a good place to stay away from and, as he sailed into the harbor, it looked as though most shipping had. There was a long concrete wharf, the outboard Tee end of it long ago broken off in some storm. He could see the usual collection of small fishing boats and outriggers, and a few interisland deep-bellied sloops, but there was only one real ship—an ancient Liberian freighter —tied up to the wharf.

The town of Roseau spread out along the beach and up a small slope until it met the jungle and stopped. In the dying light the town seemed pretty, the houses might once have been painted in vivid colors but these had long since faded to pastels, blending with the soft brown of rusting galvanized roofing. An imposing, two-story building facing the end of the wharf held, Garth knew by experience, the Government offices and the highest, largest house on the slope would be Government House where some civil servant, having reached the end of a sorry career, ruled this pitiful domain.

The whole place looked like trouble and he expected it as he came smartly alongside the wharf under the critical eyes of half a dozen Malays who lazily threw him a bow and stern line. But, as he secured the lines and got his fenders in place, he noticed the small airfield. If Castle and Dr. Jenkins were already here he should have no trouble with the authorities.

He had none. A tall, rather sinister-looking customs inspector drove out on the wharf and was polite enough to ask permission to come aboard.

The inspector seemed bored and did not even go below. After charging Garth a pilot's fee (for a pilot Garth never saw) he gave him his clearance and offered to take him anywhere in town he wanted to go.

Garth declined, wanting to get the boat shipshape, but did ask where he could find Professor Castle. The inspector did not know Professor Castle.

Garth put a Sunday furl in the sails, flemished down his lines, secured the halyards and then went below. He tidied up a little there and changed out of his shorts into shore clothes—shirt, pants, and shoes—then closed the hatches, put rain baffles on the skylights and went up the steps to the wharf.

There was no sign of Castle or any Institute people; in fact, there was no sign of anyone except a few hands on the old freighter. Disappointed and wondering what had gone wrong, Garth strolled down the wharf which was hardly lit at all by feeble lamps mounted in ornate, wrought-iron standards.

At the end of the wharf a Hindu noticed him, jumped out of an old World War II jeep, and came running over to him. "Are you Mr. Larson?"

"What's left of him."

"Sir?"

"Yes, I'm Larson."

"Very well, sir. I am to drive you to Professor Castle."

The Hindu drove like most people in these islands. It was a simple system: start the engine, shift into high, let the machine buck until it got rolling and then, as soon as it had gained speed, lean on the horn and drive straight down the middle of the road. The one rule was: Never take your thumb off the horn.

Moving at much too high a speed the jeep went through the town and up a long, curving road, turning off finally at a small hotel set among some trees.

"The hotel of Professor Castle," the Hindu said and waited only long enough to let Garth get out before taking off, the horn blowing.

Professor Castle was sitting in one of the rocking chairs on the hotel veranda. As Garth came up the stairs Castle pushed himself to his feet and came to greet him.

Castle seemed much more amiable than he had on the initial voyage down to Molahve and, as they stood chatting, Garth decided that perhaps Castle was a real human after all.

He looked a little like one, but one who had been assembled from a lot of spare parts. He had a very large, heavy head covered with stiff gray hair. His face was large too, with an overhanging forehead, a big pudgy nose, and fat lips. His eyes, in all this bigness, were small and the color of diluted milk.

Garth had not particularly liked Castle either during the voyage down or the talks he had had with him in Guam.

Now, however, Castle seemed affable and even a little interested in what Garth had accomplished at Molahve. Over a good dinner, French cooking and French wine, they talked about the project and about a world Garth had almost forgotten. It was rumored, Castle told him, that Admiral Stucky was being transferred to a bigger job; that the Institute was moving into a larger headquarters building; that José Morales was being sent back to the Philippines as soon as he finished his study of the people who had been moved off the Bikini atoll for the atomic bomb tests. They talked of other islands and atolls and Garth was impressed again by Castle's encyclopedic knowledge of the southwestern Pacific.

It was only after dinner when they had moved out on the veranda that Castle changed, going back to the way Garth remembered him—coldly sarcastic and seeming to take pleasure ridiculing the efforts of others.

It started when Castle told him about the new oceanographic ship the Institute was having built in the Trust's shipyards at Palau. Garth couldn't help feeling a little envious as Castle described the ship. Larger than *Uldra* by thirty feet, she had been designed from the keel up for just such projects as his at Molahve and was to be equipped with the latest models of everything.

"I'd love to swap with them," Garth said. "I could use twice as much lab space as I've got."

Castle said it pleasantly, "What for, Garth?"

"For . . . ?"

"Forgive me, but I've never known *why* you're doing what you're doing. I know it's an interesting new area of oceanography and you've no doubt discovered strange things about sea shells. But what's the end product? What's it good for?"

Garth laughed. "I have no idea," he confessed. "But you've got to admit that it's worth looking into when you consider that we've studied less than one percent of the marine organisms known to have biotoxic substances—actually we've only studied and evaluated about half a dozen. But in that half dozen we've found chemicals that are fungicidal, growth-inhibitory, antibiotic, antiviral—maybe some little fish has the cure for the common cold—or cancer. We've found chemicals that are anti-tumor, analgesic like aspirin, hemolytic, cardioinhibitory (and you know that the best heart medicine we've got comes from a weed called foxglove)."

"But can't we make such chemicals synthetically?" Castle asked. "Must we spend, if you'll pardon me, millions of the taxpayers' dollars gathering sea cucumbers and jellyfish?"

This was the Castle Garth had known before—the put-down expert. "We haven't been able to make any biotoxins yet which can compare to the potency found in marine organisms," Garth said stiffly. "For instance one of our most powerful synthetic poisons is diisopropylfluorphosphate. The MLD of that . . ."

"The what?"

"MLD—minimum lethal dose. The MLD of that is 3000 units. Compare that to the saxitoxin produced by dinoflagellates. The MLD of saxitoxin is only nine units—in other words, it's almost 3000 times as potent."

"Potent, perhaps, but important?" Castle said.

"That's only the beginning," Garth told him. "Saxitoxin takes nine units but when you get up into the neurotoxins you're talking about three-tenths of a unit, which is about thirty thousand times as potent as our best synthetic. And if you go on to *Ricinus* and *Clostridium* you're into an MLD range of two one-hundredths down to three one-hundred-thousandths of a unit."

Through a yawn Castle said, "Most interesting."

"It doesn't seem to apply to anything, does it?" Garth admitted. "But when you begin to think of those poisons as a weapon—a national weapon—it does get interesting. And I can assure you that the Russians have been studying marine biotoxins in the role of national weapons for a long time. For instance, in the United States we eat sixty-three pounds of fish per year per person. Suppose an enemy could suddenly poison our fish supply with a substance we couldn't detect before or after we ate it? It would not only kill millions of people but it would greatly reduce our supply of protein. And, if this enemy had developed only the ability to poison fish but not the ability to control the spread of that poison he could wipe out the world's population."

Garth stood up and held out his hand. "*That's* where the taxpayers' money is going," he said pleasantly. "So good night, professor. Thanks for dinner and I'll see you in the morning."

"I thought you were a man of action, Garth, not a daydreamer," Castle said. "I'll have the hotel drive you down."

"A walk would do me good," Garth said. "Good night."

16

Walking down the middle of the dirt road with the dark jungle on both sides of it Garth wished that he had not gone on so about his pet subject. People like Castle were not interested and were not going to get interested.

The town did not smell good. The widely spaced street lamps looked like small dirty yellow moons dripping a dim glow down on the muddy ruts in the road. Most of the houses which had looked so pretty and pastel from the bay were now dark, unlit places, the wooden walls rotting and sagging so that the jalousied windows were askew.

The only building of any consequence was the two-story Government building made of concrete blocks with wide concrete steps leading up to the door. A few of its windows were lighted and two black American-made limousines were parked in front of it. A uniformed guard armed with a rifle stood lazily on watch at the door.

Turning away from the building Garth walked along what someone had once planned to be a beautiful, wide avenue but was now only an overgrown strip of land with a narrow muddy road running down the middle of it. At the far end he could see the dim wharf lights on the ornate standards and the even dimmer lights from the sloops and the freighter. The spars of his own ship stood straight and aloof against the sky.

The wharf was deserted although there was a dim tinkle of music coming from the freighter and, as he walked past her, he could see a few lonely-looking men leaning on the lifelines. He waved to them and they waved back.

The smell of the town seemed to be in his clothes as he walked on toward the *Uldra* and he decided to take her out into the harbor where the air would be cleaner and anchor her for the night.

He could not explain why he had not noticed it before but he was halfway down the wharf steps leading to the deck before he noticed the light coming from the ports and skylights of the main cabin.

The assistant!

Happily he jumped over to the deck and dropped down the companion ladder.

The lab door was open, light from it streaming across the floor of his cabin.

A tall man in military uniform walked past the open door.

Garth hesitated for a moment and then turned to go back up the ladder.

A man had moved in behind him and stood halfway down the ladder, a rifle across his chest, completely blocking the companionway. "*Non*," he said, and then called over Garth's head, "*Commandante!*"

The tall man came to the lab door and felt around until he found the light switch. Garth stepped down off the ladder and turned.

It was the customs inspector. "Ah, we meet again, Mr. Larson."

"Yes . . . why?" Garth asked.

"Why?"

"As I understand it, Inspector, you have the right to come aboard my ship to make your inspection but after you've done that and cleared the ship you don't have that right any more."

"Let's not discuss 'rights.' I assume that you are the master of this vessel?"

"I'm the master, but the ship itself is sponsored by the U. S. Government."

"I'm only concerned with you."

"I'm also concerned. Under international law you have no right to break and enter this ship."

"We are rapidly coming to another discussion of international law. Would you step in here a moment, please?"

Garth didn't know what to do. His first anger had cooled a little and he was more cautious now, wondering what complaint the customs man was going to make. No beetle clearance? The chemicals aboard? Importing fish without a license?

Suddenly he felt cold all over . . . the jewels?

There were two more uniformed men in the lab. Garth noticed that both of them were wearing low-slung shoulder holsters, the holsters made of very shiny hard-looking leather. The handguns in them had the biggest grips he had ever seen.

He glanced at the aquariums and almost sighed out loud when he saw that the sand looked undisturbed.

"There's a Professor Castle in the hotel," Garth told the inspector. "If there's a real problem we'd better get him down here as a representative of my government."

"That will not be necessary. . . . Your port of departure was Molahve?"

"Yes."

"Where did you stop en route from Molahve?"

"Nowhere."

"Then where were you before you arrived at Molahve?"

"I've been there since last July."

"July? So. How many in your crew, Mr. Larson."

"One. Me."

"You Americans are very brave. Or—foolish." The inspector nodded to the two armed men.

Garth watched as they got down on their knees and took small daggers out of scabbards. With the points of the daggers they pried up a 32-inch-long piece of deck planking which served as an inspection plate for the limbers.

Wondering what this was all about, but feeling more and more at ease about it, Garth watched as one of the men reached down into the bilges of the *Uldra* and brought out a small box which appeared either to be wrapped in brown paper or to have been dipped in brown wax.

As they carried it to the lab bench and put it down Garth looked at it and realized that he had never seen it before.

The inspector picked it up and Garth noticed that it had been opened.

The man held it in both hands for a moment as he stood looking at Garth and then, with his two thumbs, he pushed up the wooden lid of the box.

Inside there was something wrapped in heavy brown paper which appeared to have been soaked in oil.

The man unfolded the paper slowly and held the box out for Garth to see.

It was a brownish-yellow brick of something, like spoiled butter. "Recognize that?" the inspector asked.

"No"

"Smell it."

It had a faint, sweetish smell.

Garth had never seen any before, even in a laboratory, but as he slowly straightened he had a sick feeling that that was what it was. "Whatever it is," Garth said, "I've never seen it before and don't know how it got here."

"It is, of course, pure opium."

"I know nothing about it."

"Of course not. Now, please, you understand that I must search you."

"Not without a warrant."

The inspector held the box out. "This is all the warrant I need. We consider smuggling opium a very serious matter."

"So do I. That's why I don't smuggle opium," Garth said. "Before we go any further, I want to get in touch with my government here."

"Your government is not represented here."

"Then my government in Guam."

The man looked at him coldly. "I am quite sure that your government dislikes an opium smuggler as much as mine does."

"I am not an opium smuggler. Somebody put that box here to get me in trouble."

"Why do they always say that?" the inspector asked, grinning. "Now, Mr. Larson, oblige me by standing against the wall there with your hands above your head."

"I don't mind being searched," Garth told him, "but after that I want to get Professor Castle down here. It won't take fifteen minutes."

The inspector said something in French to the other two and they moved over beside Garth as though ready to shove him against the wall.

Garth moved without having to be shoved and faced the wall, his arms up, his hands flat against the wood.

As the men searched him, his fingers felt the side of the rack where he kept the tranquilizer bullets.

Slowly his fingers moved into the wooden rack. He could feel the two men searching him but had no idea what the inspector was looking at.

Expecting to get hit in the back any second, he teased one of the bullets up and out of the rack so that he could roll it down into the palm of his hand.

The search ended and the inspector said, "Very well, Mr. Larson, turn around."

Garth turned, thinking: Now he'll demand the bullet.

"Hold out your hands," the inspector ordered.

Garth held his arms out, both hands lightly closed, the tranquilizer bullet lying in his fingers.

The speed of the inspector surprised him. It seemed to be one swift, smooth movement but at the end of it he was securely handcuffed, the smooth steel bands tight around his wrists. "Don't be alarmed," the inspector said, "I will see to it that your boat is carefully guarded while you are gone."

"Where am I going?"

"We must hold you for the authorities."

"Hold me? Where? For what authorities?"

The inspector ignored that. "And I must apologize for the meagerness of the accommodations I can offer you. We have tried for years to obtain more fitting quarters."

Garth lowered his hands, liking the feel of the smooth bullet along his fingers. Without the gun to shoot it the bullet was as useless as any bullet without a gun, but he liked the feel of it.

17.

Garth had never seen the inside of a real jail before but the one they put him in didn't resemble any he had ever seen in the movies. It was a dank, windowless concrete room at the end of a dank, dimly lit corridor in the town's Government building. Except for a pile of thatch in the corner the room was empty. No bed or furniture of any sort, no sanitary facilities—just a narrow, high-ceilinged room. A door of rusty steel bars on rusty hinges closed the room off from the corridor.

Garth watched as the inspector unlocked the door with a big, old-fashioned key and then unlocked his handcuffs and took them off. Pushing him into the room he closed the door behind him and locked it.

The three men strolled down the corridor and disappeared through a door at the end.

As soon as they were gone Garth tried the door of his cell. It looked old and feeble and rusted away but it was not. It was solid.

As he walked around hitting the walls with the outside of his fist but not expecting to find anything but solid wall he consoled himself with the knowledge that Dr. Jenkins and the Scripps people would arrive tomorrow. But, even before they got here, he would get in touch with Castle and see what could be done. The whole thing was ridiculous and evidently a mistake. If this was a plot to get somebody in trouble the dope had been planted in the wrong boat.

Then, as the cell and the dim light and the sharp odor of the place depressed him, he began to wonder if it really was a mistake.

He thought of Smith. Could he be involved somehow? But Smith didn't even know where he was.

It had to be just a mistake. Wrong man, wrong schooner —wrong everything.

He was about to examine the tranquilizer bullet when someone came in from the far end of the corridor. Hoping that it was Castle, Garth went to the door.

It was a casual-looking young man dressed in civilian clothes but wearing one of the shiny leather shoulder holsters with the big-handled gun. As he came under the only light in the place Garth felt strange—he had seen about a million young men like this one on the California beaches. Sun-tanned, long-haired, affecting a swinging, slouching walk but, all in all, good-looking, healthy people. As he came on to the door Garth noticed that he had a key ring on his belt with a key which looked exactly like the one the inspector had used to lock him in.

"Greetings, friend. And what brings you here?" the man asked, and laughed, saying, "As if I didn't know."

He spoke good plain American. "Who're you?" Garth asked.

"Just call me Steve."

"There're a couple of other things I'd like to call you," Garth said as he vaguely remembered an organization to control drug traffic run by the United Nations. "Who do you work for, the UN?"

"No, the ME. Me. They fed you yet?"

"Not yet."

"They might." Steve came over to the bars and stood

looking in at him. "Tell me something, is all that equipment, the tanks and fish just a front for your smuggling or are you a marine biologist or something?"

"Toxicologist. Look, there's a Professor Castle staying at the hotel. Could you get a message to him?"

"What's it worth to you?"

Garth stared at him. "Nothing. I haven't got anything."

The man laughed at him. "That's not what I heard."

Garth was about to answer when Steve turned away. The door at the far end of the corridor opened and some Malays came in. Two of them were carrying an iron cot with a mattress on it, another a tray of food.

Steve showed them where to put the bed and watched them make it up and hang the mosquito net. Then he unlocked a small metal panel in the bottom of the cell door and pushed the tray of food in to Garth.

"What's this?" Garth asked. "My last meal?"

"Oh no, you're going to get a fair trial. Of course, if you don't cooperate you'll be convicted. And that will make you feel depressed."

Garth looked at him as he sat down on the bed and started taking his shoes off.

"Yeah, you'll be so depressed you'll hang yourself."

"In here?"

"Yeh."

Garth looked up at the high, plain ceiling. "How? With what?"

"Don't worry. That'll all be arranged for you so the inspector can just come in one morning and there you've gone and committed suicide. You better eat, buddy, that stuff's bad enough when it's lukewarm. . . ."

"Who are you anyway?" Garth asked. "Why are you working for a crook like the inspector?"

"Me? I'm a TTT," Steve said, hanging the belt with the holster from a nail in the wall. "Typical tropical tramp. And I work for that crook—or any crook—for loot, bread, *argent*, money." He stretched out on the bed, propping the

pillow so he could look in at Garth. "So you're a marine
—what? Toxicologist?"

Garth nodded. "If you could get a message to Professor
Castle maybe we could make a deal."

Steve ignored him as he lay back, looking up at the
ceiling. "That's what I wanted to be when I was a kid.
A marine biologist, or something in oceanography. I really
dug that biology in school and I used to have some pretty
good specimens. For a kid, you know. Is that a real *Chironex fleckeri* you've got in that tank?"

It surprised Garth. "Your Latin's good."

"I really dug it. I didn't have any equipment, just some
old bottles and battery cases, but I had some pretty good
specimens. I wonder what happened to 'em?"

"When?"

Steve turned and grinned at him. "I changed educational
institutions. Where they didn't teach biology." He suddenly
laughed. "They had a real fancy name for the place but
the kids in it just called it jail. . . . Hey, you ever been
to Fiji?"

"No."

"You ought to go. There's more stuff in the ocean around
Fiji than any island I ever saw. When I was there I got
really hung-up on *Medusa*."

"*Scyphozoan* or *Trachyline?*"

Steve looked into the cell. "*Scyphozoan*. You really know
your stuff, don't you?"

"I know I'm in a lot of trouble. How much do you want
to get a message to Professor Castle?"

"I could hang you out for a couple of hundred but I'm
telling you now it won't do any good." Steve got up, arranged the mosquito net, turned out the light and got back
on the bed again. "I'm going to sleep now," he said. "You
can't get out of there, so don't try because it'll wake me
up and I don't like that."

Garth stood where he was looking out. Dim light from
the other end of the corridor made the mosquito net look

like a small gray cloud. The belt, with the keys, hanging from the nail was a black loop.

There was no way he could reach the belt.

Steve's voice startled him. "You'd better make a deal with the inspector, fella. He might take it all, but it's the only way you'll ever get out of here alive."

"What sort of deal?"

Steve sounded angry. "I've got all the problems I need without any of yours."

"If I make a deal, what guarantee . . ."

Steve yelled, "I said I was going to sleep! Now shut up!"

Garth looked up from the dim shape on the bed to the belt but gave up hoping. There wasn't anything he could do.

He found the tray with a tin plate of food and a tin mug but in the dim light couldn't tell what it was. Smelling it didn't help either. But it did not smell good so he put the tray down and walked over to the pile of thatch.

Lovely place for a recluse spider or a fine specimen of scorpion.

Moving away from the thatch as far as he could he sat down on the filthy floor with his back against the wall. Now in the dark Garth was truly afraid. Perhaps it was the unreality of the whole affair that left him defenseless against this flooding fear. That, and his absolute helplessness.

Smith was behind this; Smith was the cause of it. Garth didn't know how; didn't know the mechanics of it, but he was becoming sure that Smith had engineered this whole thing. That old copra boat could have beaten the *Uldra* to Monique by a day. Was it here now, at anchor in some other harbor?

Garth thought of the coded diary . . . of the cold-blooded, deliberate murders. . . .

He slept a little during the long night but was awake when Steve came pushing out of the mosquito net.

"Morning," Garth said.

Steve sat on the edge of the bed stretching and yawning. Then he peered in at Garth. "You look horrid. When did you shave last?"

"Was the guy who planted that opium in my boat bald-headed with a red beard? About fifty?"

"Don't ask me things like that before breakfast."

"Do you know?"

Steve started putting his shoes on, his head down as he tied the laces. Suddenly he looked up and his face was serious. "Look, I can't help you, buddy. I could be your brother and I couldn't help you."

"Did he come in just ahead of me in an old copra boat?"

"All this time I thought I was talking English." Steve stood and got the belt. As he buckled it on he looked at Garth. "I feel for you, fella, but I can't reach you." He started away and then turned. "What do you want for breakfast?"

"Out."

As Steve walked on he said, "One out, sunny side up. Ham, but hold the hash browns."

Ve-ry funny. Garth watched him until the door closed.

The morning dragged on, the sun shining hotter and hotter down the long, empty corridor. Somewhere in the building he could hear noises—the murmur of people, even the ringing of phones—and faintly from outside came other sounds. But he could not see beyond the wall of the cell and the corridor.

He had no way to find out what time it was as one of the soldiers (or whatever they were) who had searched him had stolen his watch, but he knew by the slant of the sunlight that it was nearly noon. No one had brought him anything to eat or drink; no one had even come to help him commit suicide.

Garth glanced at the tray on the floor. Some sort of gray, now-stiff gravy covered some lumps and ants covered everything. He brushed live ants off the tin mug, scooped the dead ones out and took a sip of the stuff in it. It was wine and tasted like warm wet rust. He could not drink it.

As time dragged on Garth's resentment grew deep and bitter. Where was Castle? Where were the Scripps people and that mythical assistant? Was anybody doing anything about him?

Garth didn't believe the Monique authorities could conceal the fact that they had jailed him. Professor Castle must surely have heard about a thing as serious as that.

So where was he? What was he doing?

The door at the far end opened and a man came in. With the sun behind him Garth did not recognize Castle until he had almost reached the cell.

Garth had a funny little tag end of resentment as he greeted Castle. The man had strolled down the long corridor as though nothing at all were wrong; as though he were merely strolling in a park somewhere with all the time in the world.

"Man, am I glad to see you!" Garth said. "This is a real fouled-up situation. Have you told Guam?"

"Told Guam what?"

Garth stared at him. "Told them that I'm in jail! On an opium-smuggling charge. Didn't they tell you? This is serious, professor. We've got to get some authority down here."

"I'm not sure Guam will want to get involved in this," Castle said.

Garth looked at him, not believing what he had heard. Then the ridiculousness of it made him laugh. "Professor, I didn't smuggle anything. You know that. The stuff was planted in my boat. They've as much as admitted that."

"Have they?" Castle said, that faint tone of sarcasm in his voice. "Why would anyone want to do a thing like that?"

Garth hesitated and then said, "There's a man named Smith who lives on Efrahte. He's been trying to drive me away from Molahve for a long time and it looks like he's done it . . . unless you help me get out of this jail."

Castle's eyes were distant. "Why would anyone want to drive you away from Molahve?"

Garth tried to make it sound both casual and serious. "Oh, there was a taboo on Molahve and Smith was pretty sore about my breaking it. He's one of those back-to-nature boys, all gung ho for keeping the native traditions. He's a nut, but he's dangerous and he's smart."

"Very smart. To be able to plant a packet of raw opium in your boat at a distance of several hundred miles," Castle said.

Garth could feel his anger beginning to shake him and he stood a moment controlling it. "If you want to think I'm an opium smuggler, I can't help that. So all I ask of you is that you call Guam and tell Admiral Stucky and Dr. Grigg that I am in jail on this island. Will you do that much for me?"

For a long time Castle stood there looking at him with those washed-out blue eyes and then said, "I consider a narcotics peddler the most reprehensible person on earth. Good day, Mr. Larson."

Garth had never before felt a desire to reach out to a person with his hands and really damage him.

18

Streams of ants moved across the floor to do battle with the cockroaches clustered around the tray of food. As the light faded out of the cell the whole tray seemed to become a writhing black mass.

Gradually the sounds of people in the building died away and, when it was totally dark, even the sounds from outside faded.

Garth, on his feet now since he couldn't see to fend off the insects, could no longer think except in small bits. Would the guard, Steve, come back? Would they ever bring him some decent water to drink? Would they turn on the light so he could see what was on the floor? He was filthy, his clothes dank and bad smelling, his unshaven face sticky.

If they didn't turn on the light he would have to stand like this with his back against the bars (for fewer bugs crawled up and down them than on the damp walls) all night. Could he do it? He was very thirsty, very hungry, weak; weak mostly from the strain of the long hours of confusion, helplessness, and fear.

He had looked at the mug of wine again. A pretty sight. Live cockroaches walking around on the dead ones.

Suddenly he thought of the tranquilizer cartridge in his pocket.

They had told him at Scripps that there was enough tranquilizer to knock out a one-ton shark but Garth had always wondered what the swimmer did until the stuff took effect. It didn't take a shark long to bite your legs off.

He knew that what he was thinking and doing were absurd but he went on, taking the cartridge out of his pocket and unscrewing the metal case. Tipping the thin glass ampul of tranquilizer out into his hand he stood and felt it with his fingers.

The Scripps people had said a one-ton shark. Not just a "big" shark, a one-ton shark. Two thousand pounds. All right. He weighed 185 pounds. Or did he? This worried him. He hadn't eaten for . . . how long? Oh, well, say less than a tenth of two thousand. . . .

He felt the shape of the ampul. Two inches long? One tenth of two inches . . .

He could measure out one tenth of the fluid and drink it and lie down on the floor and sleep and it wouldn't make any difference what crawled on, under, or around him. Thirst and hunger and even fear would no longer bother him.

He was standing there thinking how absurd all this was when, suddenly, the lights came on.

Dropping the ampul in his shirt pocket he turned and saw the inspector coming alone down the corridor. As he passed under the light Garth saw that he was carrying a tray with dishes on it which shone like silver. At the prospect of food and drink saliva began to run in Garth's mouth and he began to tremble.

The inspector's immaculate uniform looked out of place here as he put the tray down on the little table and came on to the door of the cell. Garth stood back from it watching and suddenly wondering where the Monique authorities had found pistols with such huge, shiny butts.

"Good evening, Mr. Larson," the inspector said.

He was blocking the view so Garth leaned a little and looked past him at the tray on the table. He could see a silver pitcher and a deep silver bowl, and two glasses. There was no smell of food.

"Evening," Garth said. "Are you through with your little games?"

The inspector smiled at him and said, "Not quite. A detail or two to be cleared up."

"Such as who planted the opium in my boat?"

The inspector laughed. "Oh, we know who did that."

"So do I," Garth said. "So why am I still in here?"

"There are other matters," the inspector said and turned to the table. "Would you care for a drink?"

"Of water," Garth said.

Garth watched as the inspector poured two stiff jolts of whisky into the two glasses. Then, as he took the top off the deep silver bowl, Garth felt oddly hurt and insulted. There was nothing in the bowl except ice.

And then he felt outraged. The inspector had seen to it that he had not been fed nor given anything to drink. "Real smart," he said angrily.

"Sir?"

"I don't know what you want to find out," Garth told him, "but feeding me a lot of booze on an empty stomach isn't going to help you any."

"I am simply trying to be hospitable, Mr. Larson," the inspector said, holding the drink for him but not reaching inside the bars. Garth reached out for it.

"There is no reason for you to stay in this filthy place," the inspector said. "So let's have a drink and talk a little. In your honor I've brought good American whisky. Bourbon, which I'm not very fond of." He sat down and put his feet up on the bed and then reached inside his tunic and took out a big, old-fashioned iron key. "If you don't mind a little pun, Mr. Larson, this"—he held the key up and turned it back and forth—"is the key to the whole situation." He looked at the key, holding it out under the light. "Isn't it odd how such a small, inanimate thing like this can represent so much? Your freedom, for instance. . . ." He looked directly at Garth. "Your life."

The fumes of whisky coming up from his glass seemed inescapable.

"You are apparently not impressed by my philosophy," the inspector said. "So let's discuss more practical things. Drink up, my friend, for I think I have a solution to your problems."

The whisky in the glass had a thick, sweetish smell and it was making Garth a little dizzy. He looked down into the glass, at the ice floating in the brown liquid, and felt the cool wet surface.

"You see," the inspector said, holding the key by the end and waving it slowly back and forth. "I have something you want and you have something I want. It's as simple as that."

As simple as that. Plant the opium to give him an excuse for jailing Garth and then find the jewels and take them.

Smith and this man were working together; there was no doubt of that. And to get the inspector's cooperation Smith had been forced to tell him what his reward would be.

Only they had not found the jewels yet.

Garth wondered what the inspector would do if, instead of the whisky making him talk, it only put him to sleep or made him sick?

"You aren't very talkative," the inspector said.

"What's to talk about?"

The inspector held the key out toward him. "This . . . What's it worth to you?"

"A drink of water."

The inspector looked at him coldly. "I'll tell you. To make it very clear to you, this key can prevent any accidents happening to you. Fatal accidents."

Garth held his glass in both hands and walked slowly along beside the bars. At the corner he turned and walked along the wall, his back to the door.

Holding the glass in front of him he took the ampul out of his shirt pocket, pressed his thumbnail against the slim neck, and felt the glass break. Then, still walking slowly, he tipped the ampul and watched the clear fluid running into the glass.

He walked on, going completely around the cell and coming back to the bars.

He watched the inspector's face closely as he said, "How much did Ord Smith say he'd give you to plant that opium in my boat?"

The man was a good actor. He looked genuinely puzzled by the name. "Ord Smith?" he asked. "I don't think I know anyone by that name."

Garth raised his glass to drink but stopped it before it touched his mouth. He could smell only the whisky. "It won't work," he said.

"Pardon?"

Garth held the glass out to him. "I thought for a while that you were going to rely on booze to make me talk. But you're too intelligent."

"I don't understand you," the inspector said.

"And you've wasted enough time not to waste any more on a scientific study of the effects of whisky on an empty stomach." Garth held out the glass. "I don't know what you put in this drink—truth serum, LSD—who knows? But, thanks, I'm not having any."

The inspector took his feet off the bed and leaned closer to the bars, his eyes studying Garth. Then he began to laugh. "Oh, you Americans amuse me. So melodramatic! Do you think I'm a child playing silly little games?"

"You're playing games."

"Ridiculous! How much. . . ." He stopped suddenly and began to laugh again. "You've seen too many motion pictures, Mr. Larson."

Garth stood looking at him.

The inspector got up. "We should go through the entire

scene properly, should we not? We must swap these drinks we have. . . ." He held his drink out to Garth.

Garth was afraid his hands would shake as he handed his drink through the bars.

"Now," the inspector said, "let's drink to the end of this childishness."

The inspector raised the glass. "And to the good life—yours. Because if you do not tell me where the jewels are you haven't got much life of any sort left."

And then he drank, looking at Garth above the rim of the glass.

Garth had reasoned that if the tranquilizer was intended to knock out a one-ton shark within range of a spear gun before the shark could cover that short distance and devour you, then the drug must act almost instantaneously.

He waited, ice burning against his lips, the fluid in his mouth tasteless, as he held the glass and looked at the inspector, who was now lowering his glass.

He waited for the glass to fall out of the man's hand, waited for the man himself to fall. . . .

The inspector swirled the ice around in the glass and said, "I want you to realize, Mr. Larson, that you are in serious trouble. Your only friend, Professor Castle, is convinced that you are an opium smuggler and I am not going to disabuse him of that idea. We have evidence against you to account for your being in this jail and we will have evidence that you hanged yourself here."

Garth stood near the bars looking at him. There was no trace of slurring in his voice, no loss of grip on the glass, no evidence of any effect from the drug.

Enough to stop a one-ton shark. . . . When? Garth thought bitterly. Which week?

From a spear gun the drug would be injected intravenously if it hit an artery or large vein, or interveinally if it struck between veins; either way it would go into the bloodstream. Drinking it as the inspector had done apparently had no effect.

"What's this key worth to you, Mr. Larson?"

Garth watched the key fall and when he looked up again the inspector was staring in horror at his fingers.

The glass fell out of his hand and broke on the floor as the inspector's hand moved up his side toward the holster.

The gun came out slowly and steadily and swung around toward him.

The inspector fell forward, his face sliding down between the bars, the gun falling out of his hand.

Garth reached out and got the key and then had to twist awkwardly around to the front of the door and feel around with the end of the key for the slot.

He swung the door open, pulled the inspector into the cell and covered him with thatch. Leaving the cell he locked the door and then turned to the table. He drank from the edge of the pitcher, gulping down the water as some of it ran down his chin and down his chest.

He put the pitcher and his glass on the tray and then shoved it under the bed. Using his hands carefully he scooped the wet, broken glass under the bed also, and then turned and ran down the corridor toward the window in the far end.

He was halfway there when he suddenly swung around and ran back to pick up the gun.

When he opened the window, cold rain swept against him. Crawling out on the ledge, he closed the window and dropped to the soft, muddy ground.

19

Running through the rain Garth noticed the muddy glow of sheet lightning and it worried him. This was not going to be a passing squall lashing the island for half an hour and then leaving. This was building up into a true Pacific storm packing gale winds which would work the sea up into a gray mess.

With sea room between the *Uldra* and any land Garth would not have worried. She was a good old boat, built for a stormy sea. But now she lay in a landlocked harbor and, as the storm bore down on the island, there would be violent and unpredictable blasts of wind sweeping through the canyons and pouring over the high mountains. The *Uldra* was no motorboat with the power and rudder area to handle that kind of thing. She was long and narrow and her tophamper made her unwieldy under power in any sort of wind.

As Garth ran out on the wharf he was thinking that he should have been at sea an hour ago—two hours.

Suddenly, still running, he looked around. The old freighter, dim yellow lights glowing from her portholes in rainy blobs, was still there but *Uldra*'s berth was empty.

She was gone. He ran on until he could see the end of the wharf. The *Uldra* was not there.

She was riding at anchor in the harbor. In a glow of sheet lightning he saw her spars and when the lightning faded he could see the gray indistinct shape of her.

Cargoes were stacked along the sides of the wharf. Piles of copra smelling sour in the rain, logs bound with heavy hemp, crates under ragged tarpaulins which flapped and cracked in the wind. Running between them he searched along the wharf until he saw some small native fishing boats tied up to a floating platform.

He chose the one that seemed the most seaworthy and swore at the water in her as he got in and felt around under the thwarts for the bailing gourds. Bailing with both hands he got the water down to a few inches in the bilges and then broke out the two long, heavy oars and shipped them in the thole pins. Casting off he settled down and began to row.

Until now Garth had only been moving—running, searching, rowing. But as he swung into the rhythm of the long oars he began to have for the first time the good feel of freedom. He was out of that jail, off this island, moving, going—gone. As he rowed he thought of the schooner and could even feel her moving under sail with the strong wind against her.

Occasionally looking over his shoulder to pick out the gray mass of her, he rowed through the rain, sheet lightning sometimes lighting up the whole harbor with a dirty, misty glow.

And there was another light.

This was so disturbing that he did not want to believe he had seen it but when he rested on the oars and turned he could see the dim glow of light coming up through the skylights of the laboratory.

For a moment he sat staring at this light as the rowboat, heavy with water in her, wallowed in the sea.

There was no other explanation. Someone was aboard.

His sense of freedom drained away as he rowed on.

Secured to the stern of the *Uldra* and swinging slowly from side to side was a motorboat, the forward end equipped with a canvas top. Somehow the fringe of ropework flapping in the wind infuriated him.

Garth swung in under the starboard counter so that his boat was almost concealed by the stern overhang and then climbed aboard and tied his boat in close.

In the rain he could see no one on deck between him and the glow coming up through the skylight but he kept low as he went forward to the aft end of the deckhouse.

Rain running down the glass made the scene in the lab wavery, as though underwater. The light was coming from a Coleman gas lantern hanging just above a lab table. Four men, in uniform, were playing cards at the table. All of them had on the cross-chest harness with the big-butted pistols in the holsters.

Garth moved along the deckhouse looking down through the glass but could make out no one else in the room and there was no light coming in from the main cabin or the galley.

He felt the big pistol under his belt and thought for a moment of taking it out, shooting a hole in the skylight glass with it and killing the men, one by one, as they sat there.

He couldn't do that. Furthermore, with the weather he was going to have to take the ship into he did not want a jury-rigged patched and weakened area in the topside.

He squatted in the rain watching the men playing inside the small cone of white light. His mind offered and discarded a dozen ways to get rid of them until at last he turned and moved aft to the davits where the ship's dinghy hung, shrouded in a tarpaulin.

The rope lashings were stiff, the knots tight with water, slowing him down as he untied all the knots on the tarpaulin except one forward and one aft.

Reaching under the tarp he set the control lever on the

outboard to start and turned the petcock in the gasline to
on. Then he felt around in the bottom of the boat until
he found the brass drain plug. This was a two-inch plug
screwed into a ferrule through the bottom of the boat. He
unscrewed it and wondered a little at himself as he carefully
stowed the plug. If his plan worked he'd never need that
plug again. If it didn't work he'd never need anything again.

Not knowing whether the men below were soldiers, police-
men, or sailors, he decided to make lowering the dinghy as
simple as possible, hoping that in the time he was going
to give them, the boat wouldn't be damaged by the increas-
ingly violent movement of the schooner.

He tripped the pelican hooks in the gripes which held
the boat against the strongback and let her swing free in
the davits. Then, just in case they were sailors playing cards
in his lab, he rigged the frapping lines and travelling lizards
and checked to see that the falls were rove through the
davit heads. The coils were triced to the davit beckets and
toggles so he took these off and, in the rainy darkness, made
them clear for running.

There was nothing more he could do. The dinghy swung
wildly in the davits, the tarpaulin flapping in the wind,
but she was not being hurt.

Moving aft he cast off the fishing boat he had borrowed
and watched it disappear over the choppy sea. Then he
hauled in the Monique powerboat and dropped down into
it. The engine started on the first try and he throttled it
back until he was under way with no way on, being pushed
stern first by the crest of the waves then making up the
distance in the troughs.

The chance that they would hear the sound of the engine
made him nervous as he rigged a length of mooring rope
into beckets and experimented, tightening one rope, slack-
ing the other, until he thought that he had the wheel lashed
so that the rudder was amidships. That way, unless a very
heavy wave caused her to broach to, she would hold a
fairly good course without anyone manning the helm.

Fending off with his hands and knees he worked the boat forward along the starboard side of the *Uldra* until she was abeam of the lab. Holding her there he switched on all the lights and, at last, opened the throttle, the boat surging hard against the rope holding her.

Now he moved fast, climbing over the *Uldra's* rail and, still holding the rope, got out the pistol with his free hand.

The four men were still playing cards.

The fresh air vent for the lab had a hood on deck which was set in a swivel so that it could swing easily and the hood was faired so that the opening for fresh air was always to leeward thus keeping out the rain and spray. Garth used his knees to stop this swinging and then, holding the pistol across the opening but aimed seaward, he fired once.

Looking down through the skylight he saw them react to the shot. They sat there suddenly motionless, evidently listening.

It couldn't have worked out better. As he was watching them a wave slammed the powerboat hard against the hull of the schooner. The impact shook the Coleman lamp.

Garth fired across the ventilator again.

Now they moved, grabbing up their foul-weather gear, checking their pistols, moving.

Garth watched them leave the lab, crowding each other in the doorway.

No longer able to see them he physically felt them as they ran through the main cabin and up the companion ladder.

Watching the powerboat moving in the sea he waited until it was in a trough and on a fairly even keel and then let the pennant fly. The end of the rope whipped around the shroud and the powerboat, free, and with the engine at half speed, surged forward along the side of the *Uldra*, past her bow and, still on a steady course, moved away, her lights bright watery blobs in the darkness.

As Garth slipped down onto the forward ladder, keeping

only his eyes above the hatch coaming, he saw the men reach the deck, their drawn guns glimmering in the rain.

For a second they did not see the powerboat but when they did they ran forward, yelling and gesturing.

The boat continued to move away, the sound of its exhaust fading.

Garth could have reached out and touched the foot of one of the men as they stood there shouting and arguing. One of them began firing his gun up into the air.

The boat went on, the glow of its lights growing dim.

It seemed to Garth that it took them forever to make a decision for they stood in the bow now arguing in their language so that he could not understand what they were saying.

But he could guess. They were debating whether someone had stolen their boat. "Someone" would be him. A matter to be reported to the inspector. And such a report required transportation.

At last they made up their minds and ran aft to the dinghy.

They were seamen. They moved smartly, taking off the tarpaulin, embarking and lowering away together.

In a moment he heard the hard, flat sound of the outboard and then the dinghy came into view, heading straight for the wharf.

Coming on deck and closing the hatch Garth leaned against the foremast and watched the dinghy as it plowed steadily toward the wharf.

Good. Good, he thought, as a flash of bolt lightning showed him the dinghy almost awash now, sunk to the gunwales, only the flotation keeping her from going down. He could not see the men in the water as the boat was at least a hundred yards away but he was sure that they would swim toward the wharf.

Good. So far.

He debated whether to go below and search the boat to see if there were any other people aboard but decided against it. The storm was growing more violent and he could tell by the change in the lightning that he had very little time left to get out of this difficult harbor. He argued, too, that any guards the inspector had put aboard would stay together, playing cards, and would leave together.

In the bow he was glad to find that the inspector's men had anchored her with a hawser rather than a chain.

Reaching down into the forecastle he got the fire ax and laid it handy before going aft to the wheel.

In such rain Garth was sure that no one on shore could see if he turned on every light aboard but he took no chances, flipping on only the binnacle light over the compass.

It did not come on.

Pushing the companion hatch open he listened but there was no sound from the generator motor.

Grimly Garth felt for the main engine ignition switch and then let his breath out as the starter motor whined for a second or two and then the diesel caught and ran.

As he stepped out of the cockpit on his way forward to the anchor he heard the diesel slow down, run rough for a few seconds, and then die.

Leaping back to the switch he started it again.

He knew by the emptiness of the sound that no fuel was available for the compressed air to ignite.

Reaching into the companionway he got the emergency lamp. He shielded it against the rain as he scanned the instrument panel. The fuel gauges of both the main and generator engines read Empty, the needles right down against the pegs.

For a moment Garth could feel fear all around him as though stalking him but he fought it off.

If he stayed, the inspector would take him.

If he tried to beat his way out of this harbor under sail alone, it would be a most perilous voyage. There was, however, a chance. With the inspector there was none.

Grabbing for handholds as he ran forward he noticed for

the first time that the sails were no longer furled as he had left them but were lying in great, gray soggy folds all over the deck.

It took all his strength to get the jib up. Leaving it luffing furiously in the wind, the canvas cracking like a gun as it slashed back and forth, he ran to the mainmast, cleared the halyards from the now useless power winch, and started manhandling the sail.

It was backbreaking. Every fold of the heavy sail was full of water so that the only way he could get the canvas up was to loop the halyard around a belaying pin in the pinrail and then, holding the free end with one hand, the fall taut with the other, leap up to jam his feet against the mast and use his body's weight to hoist the sail a few inches, take in the slack he gained, and do it again—and again and again.

The sail rose slowly up the mast and as some of it was freed from the weight of the water and was caught in the wind it began to flail him as he struggled to haul it up the tall mast.

The rough, wet canvas tore his shirt off and bloodied his back and shoulders before he at last peaked the sail, took one final sway before securing the halyard and then had to slump down against the mast as above him the wind slammed the heavy boom from side to side, the running rigging wild in the wind, ropes and blocks lashing around in the dark.

Crawling so as not to get killed by the stuff hurtling above him he checked the jib sheets to see that they were properly in the fairleads and then, in the cockpit, took them off the power winches and rove them through a burton so as to get the purchase he knew he was going to need.

He did the same with the mainsheet and when all was ready, he slipped beckets on the wheel and went forward, still crawling.

Finding the ax he swung it down on the anchor rope which exploded into a bush of fibers and disappeared.

As he crawled aft he felt the schooner falling off fast under the weight of the wind but all he could do was pray that she would not broach to before he could reach the cockpit.

Solid water was coming over the side and he could feel the ship being knocked down as he got the jib sheet and threw his weight against it.

Forward, the sail filled with a cannonlike boom and as he secured the sheet he felt the sail taking charge.

It seemed to him that he hauled in fathoms of rope before at last he felt the tug of the boom against the sheet and then the real weight of it as the sail filled.

Throwing off the beckets he took a firm grip on the wheel and braced his legs.

For a long, long moment the ship felt dead, as lifeless as a downed tree, helpless under the wind and waves as they drove her backward and laid her over on her side.

Slowly, slowly the power of the sails began to take over and he could feel life coming into the boat little by little as she fought, staggering, to right herself and move.

Suddenly she was fully alive, leaping forward, the sails driving hard. No longer knocked down but heeling hard so that solid water flowed from her bow and over the skylights and raced past the cockpit, she began to move ahead.

Rain and spray lashed him, blinding and choking him, so that he could only sail her by the feel of her hull under his feet, the feel of the rudder through the spokes of the wheel, the sound of the wind in her sails.

He had to beat her to windward for there was no other way out of that harbor and he knew that he was hurting her, an old boat, masts and spars and shrouds no longer able to endure this.

He had too much sail on her and there was nothing he could do about that except pray that neither the jib nor mainsail blew out on him, leaving the boat helpless. With no power to give him delicate control of the sheets he could only set them where they were and hope.

Lightning showed him high mountains and white water

boiling over the reefs on both sides of the channel but it showed him gray water, too, and he worked her toward it as best he could, measuring his distance on this tack only by feel and a sense of time.

He sailed her on the starboard tack, driving toward the land until he could hear the sound of heavy surf pounding against steep cliffs and then, when he could see the high, gray cloud of broken water against the black land he brought her about, slamming her head into the wind and through it and then, by feel alone, waiting to clamp her on the other tack.

As the wind drained from the mainsail and left it limp and snapping the boom rose high, like a broken arm, and slammed down across the deck, screaming just above his head.

The weight of the boom and soaking sail and wind and sea struck down through the mainsheet, through the blocks of the burton and on down the ropes until it was finally checked by the traveler block racing across the iron horse set in the deck. For a second he thought the horse had been yanked clean out of the heavy timbers to which it was bolted but at last he felt the heavy boom stop, felt the sail fill and drive the schooner down on her other side.

He stood for a lifetime with the boat going at incredible speed, the roar of surf over reefs on both sides of her, solid water rushing down her deck and pouring against him. Although he could see nothing he could feel the sheer stone cliffs on both sides of him and, with his whole body, feel the fragile hull of the ship racing over the coral bottom with coral reefs as sharp as axes on both sides of her.

He waited for that sudden, sickening jerk and plowing and slowing and stopping of a ship going aground, knowing that when he felt it the coral would be tearing away the whole bottom of the old schooner while momentum and wind would take the masts out of her.

The *Uldra* drove on, racing, and struck savagely into the high, steep waves of the open ocean, buried her bow under them and then struggled up again and fell steeply into the trough, staggered and drove on again.

Garth had to hammer her thus until he was sure that he had sea room but, the instant he felt he had it, he eased the poor old boat, slacked her sheets and let her off the wind so that she could coast along the wave fronts and down their backs and ride without her beam ends in the water.

Lightning struck jaggedly down into the sea and he turned for that instant and looked back to see Monique as a huge, black monster rising from the white surf.

Once out of sight of that baleful island he could reef her down and let her take it a little easy until the storm blew out.

He could just sit, then, and sail her. . . .

To where?

20

For the rest of the night the storm did not allow Garth to think much beyond how to steer through the next wave, how much to ease her, when to turn his back when a wave came aboard, but toward dawn there was a short lull.

For the first time he sat down on the wheelbox and eased his aching legs. His back and shoulders felt as though bound by iron bands and he was extremely thirsty.

He had no idea where he was nor what course and distance he had covered during the black night. Under such wild winds he might have sailed around in a circle so that when daylight came he would find himself looking straight at Monique again.

Or straight at the Monique ship he had seen moored across the harbor. From that distance she had looked exactly like the U. S. Coast Guard's 75-foot cutters—fast and seaworthy boats. This one was armed with at least a one-pounder in the bow and what looked like heavy machine guns.

He stood up again, uneasy and apprehensive, knowing that he could make no decision until this storm passed, until he could get some star sights to tell him where he was, some daylight to show him the condition of his ship.

He knew that the sun was up only because the light around him turned from black to deep gray and the crests of waves speeding toward him looked whiter and cleaner.

He took another long look around the gray and empty horizon and then sat down on the wheelbox to wait. He was sitting there wondering what had happened to the four guards after the dinghy swamped when he thought he heard a sound that he could not possibly have heard.

A human sound. A low, tortured groaning that could only come from some human in dreadful pain.

Mentally he shut out every other sound around him and sat forward listening.

Someone was aboard. The sound seemed to be coming from the after cabin and there was no doubt of it. Someone was down there hurt and moaning.

Garth thought of the pistol and wondered what he had done with it and then forgot it, knowing that it had been washed overboard long since.

Holding the wheel with one hand he reached into the locker and felt around until he touched the butt end of the marlinespike he used for rope splicing. The steel spike was pointed at one end and weighted at the other so he could use it either as a dagger or short club.

The sound from below seemed closer as he stuffed the marlinespike down in his belt and stood up listening. It seemed to be coming up the companion ladder.

And then he heard a man's voice crying, "I'm dying! I'm dying!"

Garth hove the boat to and moved forward to the hatch. The voice was close now as he stood to one side of the door, the marlinespike in his hands, and waited.

The lower hatch doors opened slowly and he could hear someone just behind them breathing heavily and moaning.

A hand appeared, sliding out on the cockpit deck. Then the other hand and at last the head and shoulders of a man.

Garth stood ready as the man crawled in apparent agony out into the cockpit.

On his hands and knees he crawled toward the little skiff lashed on the fantail. He pulled himself up over the seat and started up the side.

He didn't make it. Garth watched as his whole body collapsed, head and shoulders out on the deck, the rest of him dangling down into the cockpit.

He vomited, crying all the while, and Garth could tell that this was not the first nor, perhaps, the hundredth time he had vomited for only a little slime came up and he lay there retching, his face lying on the deck.

Garth put the marlinespike back in his belt and walked over beside the man. Leaning, he looked at the face, the mouth wide open, the moaning broken by the dry retching in his throat.

It was Steve, the prison guard.

Garth picked him up and held him by his shirt, his feet dangling just above the deck. Pulling him close Garth whispered, "Who else is aboard? And don't lie to me."

As Steve recognized him he cringed away, his hands working feebly at Garth's arm.

"*Who else?*"

"Nobody. You don't understand. Nobody!" Steve cried.

"Keep quiet!" Garth hissed at him and dropped him on the seat. As he tied him up with the beckets, he said, "You make one sound and I'll throw you overboard."

With the marlinespike in one hand Garth went cautiously to the hatch. Reaching in he got the battery-powered lantern out of the bracket but did not turn it on as he went slowly down into the pitch darkness of the main cabin.

At the bottom of the ladder he listened for any unusual sound and looked around for any movement but saw and heard nothing.

Stepping forward into the cabin his foot found empty space where the deck should have been. It threw him off balance and he fell across some bare timbers, his hands plunging into several inches of water.

He didn't move for a second but listened and waited. Nothing moved nor made any sound, nothing struck him.

Garth felt around with his hand, feeling rough wood under the layer of water.

Finding the marlinespike where he had dropped it, he got it ready and moved, so that he was crouched and ready, before he switched on the lantern.

The sight made him sick. And angry and hurt and sad. He wanted to cry and hit somebody.

The main cabin had been wrecked. The mattresses in the bunks had been slashed open and lay soaking in the bilge water. Every locker and compartment had been torn open. The sink had been ripped off the wall. The radios and tape recorders lay shattered in the bilge.

The paneling on the walls had been pried off, stripping the walls down to the bare frame and outside planking of the ship. The deck planking had also been ripped up, exposing the keelson and frames. Even the ceiling had been torn from the carlings.

Furious, he walked across the frames into the laboratory.

The Coleman lamp, long since burned out, swung from the ceiling. The cards they had been playing with floated in the bilge water.

Devastation was everywhere. Cabinets, emptied of everything, stood wide open, their doors swinging idly with the motion of the ship. Lab benches had been overturned, supplies emptied. Here too the wall paneling, decking, and ceiling had been ripped off.

When the beam of the lantern struck the aquariums the sight startled him. There they were, row after row, untouched, intact, the fish and other animals living as contentedly as though nothing had happened.

He played the beam of light down the rows, the red warning signs glowing.

Garth turned and went aft to the engine room, knowing before he got there what he would find.

The fuel tanks, both gas and diesel, had been emptied.

The steel deck plates had been lifted and lay at all angles, every locker and tool chest had been opened, drawers pulled out and emptied, every container opened and dumped.

Going forward to the galley he found nothing but wreckage. All the food not in sealed cans floated in the bilge water, the stove had been upset and lay on its side, the refrigerator doors swung back and forth.

He tried to open the fresh-water tap. It was already open, the tank empty.

Raging, sick, he closed the tap and went on into the forecastle, also a shambles. Coming out the fore hatch he stood a moment, totally defeated, then walked slowly aft and into the cockpit.

Steve had fallen off the seat and lay huddled, retching and shivering on the deck.

Garth went aft to him with a length of the mainsheet. When he touched him to untie the becket Steve tried to crawl away. "I didn't do it! Honest." Then his whole body doubled up in a spasm and he cried, "I want to die!"

"Go ahead," Garth said, reaving the mainsheet around his waist, across his chest and under his arms.

"I'm sick."

"That's news. Get up."

"No, I can't. What are you going to do to me. I . . ."

Garth jerked him up and threw him out of the cockpit. Using the mainsheet and the seat of his pants Garth duck-walked him to the side.

"Wait a minute!" Steve said in a strangled voice. "Wait a minute!"

As Garth hoisted him up over the lifeline Steve began to struggle. He got his arms around Garth's neck, crying, "Don't kill me. Please. . . ."

"Oh, shut up!" Garth said and heaved him over the side.

Screaming and twisting in the air Steve fell, landing face down in the sea. Garth stood at the rail paying out the line as he saw him sink slowly into the gray water. A wave sweeping by lifted the body up, then dropped it down again and then Steve began to struggle.

Garth watched him as he desperately tried to keep his head above the water and held the mainsheet taut so that Steve was not swept away.

When the man got over his panic and really began to swim Garth hauled him up out of the water and dragged him back aboard. Steve lay on his back, spouting water, as Garth untied him. Then he picked him up and dumped him back into the cockpit.

As Garth got some ratline and started tying Steve's wrists and ankles Steve strained around to look at him. "What are you going to do, kill me?" he asked in a small, terrified voice.

"I'm debating it," Garth said. He got out a tarpaulin and threw it over him and then went forward.

In the wreckage of the forecastle he found the six-foot collapsible nylon funnel and took it topside, rigging it so that any rain falling into it would drain down into the fresh-water tank.

Then he stood in the bow of his ship, cold rain spattering on his back and looked down the length of her.

She was wallowing in the heavy seas, sails luffing, her booms swinging and crashing around, her tall masts sway-ing across the gray-black sky.

Below decks he had been ridden by fear and helplessness; he had wanted to sit down and weep and his rage against Smith and the inspector had been futile and childish.

He looked out at the ocean around him—a no-man's-land of dark troughs and gray crests, the spray torn loose from them and blowing across him.

They knew, Smith and that inspector, that he now had no water, no fuel, and almost no food. They knew that if he ran for help to one of the nearby islands the authorities on any of them would arrest and hold him. They knew that he could never survive the thousand miles of stormy sea to the north and the friendly islands in the Marianas, or even Palau.

The lagoon at Molahve was a trap; the jail waited for him at Monique.

They would be searching for him now.

Where could he run to? How could he escape them?

Garth's hot outrage had cooled. His trembling anger was still and calm—and deeper.

He thought of Smith's slick, wet-looking bald head.

They would be talking to each other now, radioing back and forth. If he goes east or south I'll take him, the inspector would be saying. And if he comes west, I'm waiting, Smith would say. So he can't escape us because he can't go north. To go north would be a dead beat to windward and he won't try that; not in a wrecked ship with no food or water to sustain him. To the north there is nothing but the empty sea. . . .

Garth went to the rail and leaned over to examine the chainplates and then inspected each of the shrouds which held the foremast erect.

Going forward he stood in the eyes of the ship and studied the martingale but could see no wobbling of the dolphin striker as it stabbed into the waves and hauled itself clear again.

There was a lot more storm coming with heavy, rain-laden winds.

It was going to be cruel and he knew it but he hoped that with careful, tender handling he and the old boat could somehow survive it. They could, with all sail, drive straight ahead into the storm, hammering their way north where no one believed they could go.

Hating to punish the old boat, he hauled up the fore staysail, the canvas clattering in the wind, and then dragged the foresail off the deck and up the mast and peaked it.

When the sheets were clear in the fairleads, Garth rolled the reefs out of the mainsail and the *Uldra* wallowed under a cloud of wet, gray sail.

Running aft he dropped down into the cockpit and took the wheel, ignoring Steve who had gotten up on the seat and was sitting huddled under the tarpaulin.

For a moment longer he spared her and then let her fall off and the heavy wind flowed into her sails and almost knocked her down with its weight. Garth fought her back up and felt her begin to move, pounding into the seas. As she gathered speed he brought her up higher and higher, trimming her sheets until she was close hauled and driving.

Now the pain began, every line and shroud and through-bolt and frame and carling of the old boat feeling the lashes of the wind and the pounding of the seas as she moved ahead almost on her beam ends.

Let them search the whole ocean—to east and west and south, he thought. I'm going north. Close hauled and a beat to windward into an empty sea—but north.

He reached over to Steve and jerked the tarpaulin off him. Steve's body didn't move but his head slowly turned and his eyes were terrified.

"What were you doing in my boat?"

"Listen! Listen, Garth—that's your name isn't it?—listen, I didn't have anything to do with it. I didn't do it!"

Garth felt like putting the flat of his hand against the terrified face and just pushing it.

Steve, still staring at him, said, "How'd you get out? And the guards . . . there were four of them. . . ."

"Stand up," Garth said.

Steve cringed away. "I didn't do it. You've got to believe me!"

Garth reached over and yanked him along the seat. "Now, stand up."

"Wait a minute! Please . . ."

Garth pulled him around until, using one hand he could untie the ratline. As soon as Steve's hands were free he raised them, palms outward as though fending off something. "Please listen to me. . . ."

"You listen to me," Garth said. "I can sail this boat alone —*forever*. I don't think you can."

"You don't understand. . . ."

"Shut up," Garth said, "and listen. I can drop you overboard right now and never miss you. But—without me—this boat could kill you. Do you understand that?"

"Garth, look, you've got to believe me. . . ."

"You're not listening," Garth said. "Without me you're in trouble. So we're going to keep it just the way it is. You and I are going to work this boat together and you're going to do it the way I tell you. If you try a move against me, any sort of trick, just remember this—if it works, you're dead. If it doesn't work, you're dead. Because, buster, I don't need you, but you need me. Have you ever sailed a boat?"

"Oh, yeah!" Steve said eagerly. "All over." Then he said quietly, "Only a little. When I was a kid. But I can learn. . . ."

"All right, you'll learn. . . . Right now there's no drinking water but if it rains and we can keep the salt spray out of the funnel we'll have some. There's a little food, not much. . . . We can live."

"Where are we going?"

"That's another thing for you to remember. You don't know where we are, nor where we're going. I do."

Steve looked at him with empty, scared eyes and said in an almost childish voice, "If you take me back to Monique I'll be in trouble."

Garth stared at him and then had to laugh. "*Be* in trouble! Man, you're in trouble *now*."

"I know." Steve raised his head and looked out at the angry gray sea. "But you don't have to worry about me. I'll help, I'll do anything you say, work, sail. . . . But if the inspector catches us . . ." His voice trailed off and he looked helplessly at Garth.

"What's he got? What sort of boat?"

"It used to be a Coast Guard cutter. And it's fast. I've seen him outrun some pretty fast stuff."

"He's got to find us first. What's it got? Radar?"

"No. He's been trying to promote a radar set but he hasn't swung it. He's got a radio direction finder and some sort of sonar, too, because sometimes they'll drop whatever they're smuggling overboard to hide it but if it's in shallow water he's got something aboard that can locate it."

"None of that will help him," Garth said. "My radio's soaking up water in the bilges and I haven't dropped anything overboard. Not even you."

Steve looked surprised. "You've still got 'em? Aboard this boat? I thought . . ."

"Got what?"

Steve looked afraid again. "If you've still got 'em then he'll be here. You can count on that."

"Got *what?*"

"Oh, come on," Steve said, worried, "the jewels you stole from the Philippines."

Garth tried to make his laugh sound casual. "Who told you that?"

Steve was thinking about something else as he said, "Nobody told me. . . . He'll never stop—he'll catch us."

"So that's what you were doing aboard."

"We've got to do something," Steve said hopelessly and then looked at Garth, alarmed. "Wait a minute! I didn't do anything to your boat. They'd already done it. It was torn up when I got here. . . ."

"Who?"

"I don't know."

"Then how do you know so much about those jewels?"

"I overheard them talking. They . . ."

"Overheard who talking?"

"I don't know who it was."

"Ord Smith?"

"Who?"

"Ord Smith," Garth said. "A bald-headed man, about fifty, with a beard."

"They were in the office so I didn't see him, just heard

him. That was Sunday." He looked over at Garth. "We'd been waiting for you and I was surprised he didn't kill you as soon as you got here. He's done that before—some guy hangs himself in that cell. Without any rope. But there he is next morning hanging by a rope."

"The man was here before I got here?"

"Yes, we'd been waiting. So I figured the reason he didn't kill you was because he wasn't sure where you'd hid 'em."

"So you tore the boat apart looking?"

"Honest, Garth, I *told* you. I helped the inspector search the boat the first time but we didn't wreck anything. We just emptied stuff out, looked around, cut up some mattresses. He got pretty sore when he didn't find anything. Somebody was crossing him up, he said."

"Ord Smith? Did he ever mention that name?"

"He didn't mention anybody; he was just sore. Then he asked me how long it had been since you'd been fed and I told him and he said he was going to pour the booze to you and see if you'd tell him anything."

"And while he was doing that you were doing a little looking all by yourself," Garth told him. "Tearing the walls off."

"I was a little late," Steve said. "They were here."

"Who?"

"I don't know. I wasn't exactly invited to that party."

"So you just hung around?"

"I tried to get off the boat but the cops came. There was a good deal of argument going on and the next thing I knew the boat was moving. When I finally took a look there were four cops still on board and we were anchored way out in the ocean and I was beginning to get sick. In a little while I wasn't sick, I was *dying*. . . . Tell me something, Garth, how did you manage to hide a washtub full of jewels from that gang?"

Only Smith would know a detail like that.

"By not having one," he said.

Steve thought that over for a moment and then said hopelessly, "As long as he *thinks* you've got it. . . . How'd you get out of that jail, Garth?"

"I tranquilized your buddy."

"Tranquil . . . Some sort of drug?"

"Some sort."

Steve shook his head sadly. "That tears it," he said. "Now if he catches us he'll accuse me of giving it to you. Oh, man, am I in trouble."

Garth saw the bow slam into a wall of water which rushed down the port side, sizzling around the handholds and deckhouse. "Duck!" he yelled.

The wall struck the cockpit, washing Steve against the lockers and then ramming into Garth, almost tearing him away from the wheel.

Coming up out of the water he said angrily to himself, Stop yakking and pay attention.

Steve, scared, pulled himself out of the water and got back on the seat. He sat there looking at Garth with wide, frightened eyes, water dripping down from his hair.

"By yourself," Garth said, "this boat can kill you. Remember that."

Steve didn't answer, just sat, his arms hugging his body. At last he said, "I'm cold. Can I go below?"

Garth studied his face. "Go below. But remember, *you* need me. I don't need you."

"I'll remember," Steve said in a small voice.

Alone Garth stood braced at the wheel, watching the waves, watching the sails. He, too, was wet and cold and miserable, his mouth parched, his lips cracked open and bleeding, his skin burning under the lash of spray.

But he was free and moving, the ship clawing her way out of the trap being set for her.

21

In the scudding black sky a hole opened and sunlight shot down through it, forming a golden column from sky to sea. The *Uldra* moved into the warm light, her sails glowing in it, her wet decks shining, the sea around her which had been gray and ugly all day long was suddenly a deep, soft, and beautiful blue.

Garth eased his aching body down on the wheelbox, the iron bands across his back now red hot. He was so tired, so sick from lack of food and water that he even prayed for the sun to keep on shining, for the storm to end, although he knew that the black clouds and gray sea gave him the concealment he needed from his stalking enemies.

Just ease up for a little while, he thought. Just let me and this old boat rest for a little while.

Steve came up out of the hatch, the dried salt on him looking like some sort of powder. "You look bushed," he said, sitting down.

"But we moved. We put a lot of miles between us and them."

"I hope so."

"How do you feel?"

"Fine!" Steve grinned at him. "Did that dunking you gave me cure it, or what?"

"Larson's Instant Seasick Remedy. I don't know why it works but just getting in the water cures it every time. I guess it restores your balance."

"I don't know about my balance but my stomach's okay."

"Good. Let's put something in it. There're some cans of food in the galley. We can afford—one. You take your choice. And bring a little water."

It didn't take long for Steve to get back with a pound can of roast beef hash, a small pot half full of water and two spoons. "Okay?" he asked, showing Garth the can.

"Just right." Garth took the pot. "You drink any?"

"It's all yours."

Garth drank, the water tasting a little salty. "Is this all there is?"

"No, I think there's a lot more. Hard to tell."

As they ate Steve said, without looking at him, "What chance have we got?"

Garth chewed awhile and then said, "Fair. If they don't spot us in the next few hours we'll have the whole night to run in and every mile we make gives them a lot more miles they have to search. With no radar they'll have to get within ten, eleven miles of us before they can see us."

Steve looked away. "He'll catch us," he said quietly. "I've seen him operate for a long time. He never gives up and he's smart."

Garth shrugged. "It's a big ocean."

"Even if he doesn't what can we do? Go on like this—to nowhere?"

There was a small, almost landlocked bay on the northern end of Molahve with jungle-covered cliffs so close around it that even the masts of the *Uldra* could not be seen above them. Garth had already decided to keep going north until he was well clear of the inspector and Smith and then turn east until he was abeam of Molahve, then south to the bay.

Ashore on Molahve there was plenty of fresh water and emergency supplies of food and fuel.

"We're going somewhere," he said to Steve.

"Where?"

"You've never been there."

Steve turned slowly and looked at him. "You don't trust me, do you?"

"No," Garth said. "Not yet."

"Don't you see that I'm in this just as deep as you are?" Steve asked. "If the inspector catches me aboard this boat he'll know exactly why I happened to be here." Steve sat looking at the spoon in his hands. "He won't get rid of you until he finds out where you've hidden the stuff. He's got no reason to waste any time with me."

"That's your problem."

"No, it's our problem . . ." Steve suddenly looked up, his eyes no longer dull and defeated. "And there's a way to solve it! How much does a washtub hold? How many jewels? How big is a washtub? Was it full? Maybe he doesn't know. . . . It's the only way to get out of this alive. So here's what we've got to do, Garth. And we'd better do it now while we've got time to do it right. Get the washtub out from wherever you've got it hid. Take out some of the jewels— maybe as much as half, to make it look good—and hide them where, this time, the inspector can find them. Put the rest back because, man, that's a good place.

"You see, what I'm counting on is that he doesn't know exactly what was in the tub so when he finds what we let him find he'll think he's got it all! That way we get off the hook—and end up with half the loot. That's *smart!*"

"That's dumb," Garth said.

Steve leaped up, his face suddenly tight with anger.

As he came aft Garth didn't move nor take his hands off the wheel. "Sit down, buster."

Steve hesitated a moment and then slowly sat down, glaring at Garth. "I dig," he said slowly. "You think I'm just a plant, don't you? You think I'm in this with the inspector, don't you? You think all I want is for you to show me where they are so I can show him when he gets here."

Garth said quietly, "Steve, you, the inspector, the jewels, are not important. I'm running from a man named Ord Smith. It wouldn't matter to him if we gave him one jewel or half of them or all of them. If he finds us that's the end of it."

Steve sat there slowly tracing with his fingernail the lines in the palm of his hand. Finally he said, "It's the same with the inspector, I guess. Once he finds the stuff he wouldn't need us. No, he'd get rid of us."

They were silent for a while. Finally Garth moved to one side. "We're going to sail all night. Let's see what sort of helmsman you are."

As Steve moved to the wheel he grinned at Garth. "I thought you didn't need me."

"It's a Mexican stand-off," Garth said, smiling.

As soon as Steve stopped oversteering and settled down he handled the ship well. "You've done more than drive around a harbor," Garth told him.

"I used to sail a lot when I was a kid—just small stuff. But the action's the same, isn't it?"

"Slower, so don't let her get knocked down. Look, I'm going to catch some sleep. Wake me up well before sunset."

"Okay, boss."

Garth glanced at him. "I've been sailing a long time. Any little thing—a change in the wind or—a change in the course —wakes me up."

Steve looked up for a second and then laughed. "You still think I want to turn around and go back into that snakepit, don't you? Well, you're wrong, friend."

"Good," Garth said, lying down and pulling the dank tarpaulin over himself. "Before sunset."

The sun was warm and although the motion of the ship was hard and choppy she was not under too much strain. Garth, knowing that rest was now important, pushed everything out of his mind and went to sleep.

He woke up to see the sheepskin chafing gear on the main crosstree streaming in the wind like a flag.

Raising his head he looked aft at Steve who was sitting relaxed on the wheelbox steering with one hand and one foot. At first this irritated him but the ship was going well, the sails filled to the luffs, so if that was the way he wanted to do it . . .

Steve noticed him and said, "We've been beating our brains out. You sleep good?"

Garth nodded. "And as soon as I sew up that Irish pennant it'll be your turn," he said, rooting around in the locker for the awl, palm and needle. Putting them in his pocket he stepped on deck, saying, "The only thing that makes me seasick is climbing the mast so don't be surprised if I miss my hat."

"And you ain't even *got* a hat."

Garth climbed the mast to the crosstree where he could swing a leg over and sit down. He had never liked being at the top of the masts even with the ship in dry dock. The height bothered him and the long, pendulum-like swaying of the mast scared him.

Looking down, the topside of the *Uldra* seemed tiny, a little model of a boat with a tiny man sitting at the wheel looking up at him.

The ship below swung out from under him and he looked down at the sea, already losing its color as the sun hung low on the horizon.

Feeling nauseous, Garth caught the flapping piece of sheepskin and began sewing it back around the steel crosstree. By looking only at what he was doing, at the palm in his hand pushing new holes through the sheepskin with the awl, he could forget that he was swaying back and forth high above the ocean.

With the sheepskin back in place so that the rigging and sail could not rub directly against the steel crosstree he put his gear away and, before going down, took one long last look all the way around the horizon.

On deck he walked slowly aft and, in silence, put away the sewing gear and took the wheel. "There's a ship astern," he said quietly.

Steve jerked around, staring. "Where? I don't see it."

"She's hull down. All they could see is our topmasts." He looked at Steve.

"What did it look like?"

"Big. Fast. And directly on our course. I couldn't tell whether she was gaining on us or just holding her distance."

Steve looked scared. "Could she be just sitting back there, tailing us? If they couldn't find the stuff aboard maybe they think you'll lead them to where it is."

"Are you sure the inspector's boat hasn't got radar?"

"Absolutely. I've heard him gripe about that for a long time."

"Then—if she *is* tailing us—she's doing it by sight alone. Our radio sure isn't putting out any signal they could take a bearing on because it isn't putting out—period. And with the engine not running we're not making any kind of sound their underwater gear could pick up." Garth looked aft as the last rays of the sun threw an orange sheet across the sea. "That's the only way they can follow us—by watching us." He motioned for Steve to take the wheel and went below.

The sextant had been dumped out of its case and lay in a pool of oily water. Finding a piece of dry sheet he cleaned the mirrors and lenses and checked the penlight. The big chronometer had been ripped off the wall but the small navigating chronometer was still dry and running.

In the cockpit he asked, "Ever done any navigating, Steve?"

"Just enough to keep from hitting *big* things."

"The secret is time," Garth told him. "All you have to do is look at this clock and when I say 'Mark' write down *exactly* the hour, minute and second. You do all that with one hand while you hold the ship as steady as you can with the other."

Picking out the first of the three stars he caught the reflection in the sextant's mirror and then swung the alidade until he could see the horizon through the unsilvered half of the alidade mirror and the star in both mirrors.

"Stand by," he said as he brought the star down. When it was exactly on the horizon he said, "Mark!"

"Got it," Steve told him.

Garth took sights on two more stars. Taking the gear from Steve he said, "I'll work these out below."

"And then what, Garth?" Steve asked, his voice weak in the dark.

"If he's been following us for any length of time—all day, perhaps—by just keeping our topmasts in sight there's no reason for him to think we'll change the course we've been on all day. No reason and actually no way for him to tell. He also knows our speed, and I doubt if we've been averaging four knots. So wouldn't the logical thing be for him to hold his course on our northerly course and hold his speed to our speed since he knows we can't go any faster on a beat to windward?"

Steve sounded defeated. "The guy's so *tricky*. I knew he'd show up."

"Maybe we are, too. If we've come as far as I think we have then we can make a 90° turn and sail due east. That'll put the wind abeam and this old boat can really travel when she doesn't have to knock herself out. We'll make close to eight knots. By dawn, if he holds on our old course and speed, we'll be better than sixty miles away—and out of sight."

Below, with the light of the emergency lantern showing not a gleam above decks, Garth worked out his star sights and grinned as he plotted the little triangle on the chart. He could turn east right now and come abeam of Molahve at a distance of better than twenty miles. Perfect!

Going on deck he took over from Steve and turned the boat 90°. She eased immediately, the pounding stopped and

with the sails set for the beam wind she felt as though she
were flying through the water.

"Good-bye, inspector," Garth said. "Bye bye . . . Let's
have some chow, Steve. And mix up anything you can find
because we're heading home where there's plenty more."

"Where's home?"

Garth looked at him in the starlight and suddenly decided
that there was no reason not to trust him for Steve was
now as much hunted as he was. "Molahve."

Steve said gloomily, "The inspector will dope that out.
When he can't find us in the morning he'll figure that's
where we went."

"Let him. Our course will put us twenty miles north of
the island. He'll head directly toward it so, no matter how
fast he goes, he'll still be moving away from us."

"I hope so."

Steve fixed a good, cold meal and as they sat in the cockpit Garth explained his plan and then they arranged their
watches, each man to sleep for four hours, sail for four,
with Garth to be on the wheel at dawn.

Just before dawn, with Steve still asleep below, Garth
hove to and lowered the sails. He was sure that the inspector
could not have followed him but just in case he was out
there in the darkness waiting for the sunrise to show him a
cloud of white sail Garth was going to give him nothing but
the slim masts.

At the first glow of sunrise he climbed the mast and settled down on the crosstree. With no sail on to steady her
the movement up there was violent.

As though by magic the ocean below him turned a deep,
green-blue and the wave crests looked as soft as long ropes
of cotton.

Nowhere on that ocean was there any sign or mark of
man. No sail, no ship, no wake, no stain of oil, no floating
mess of garbage.

He sat up there swaying across the sky for half an hour

enjoying himself, welcoming the warm sun on his unshaven face.

As he started down he saw the fore hatch open and Steve's head and shoulders appear. Later, Garth remembered as he looked down at this wondering what the man was doing in the forecastle. There was nothing up there to interest Steve—no food, no water, no place to sleep. Why was he there?

On deck again Garth raised the sails and set her on course. As she began to move Steve came out of the companionway. "Good morning, *mon capitaine*. How goes the ship?"

"Just right. We lost him."

Steve stood looking slowly around. "Just knowing he's in the same ocean scares me."

"I'll get some chow," Garth said, moving aside.

In the galley he noticed that Steve had left the fore hatch open and as he went into the forecastle to close it he saw the ping locator headphones lying on top of a pile of fittings that had been dumped out of the lockers.

As he picked up the locator he couldn't remember seeing it there before, but the ship was in such a mess he couldn't be sure.

With the headphones in his hands he suddenly wondered whether they could pick up anything beside the sound of the beacon they were designed to hear. Could they, he wondered, pick up the sound from a ship? The thrash of propellers, perhaps, or some sound created by the ignition system?

He put the phones on.

The sound in the phones felt like spikes driving through his skull and he snatched the phones off and shook his head.

Garth stood there staring at the phones hanging in his hand. Now, even without them on, he could hear the steady *ping-ping-ping* coming through them.

Coming from where . . . ?

Turning the locator volume to low he held one phone to his ear. The pinging, much lower in volume, was steady.

He put the headphones on again and swung the locator slowly from side to side, zeroing in on the source of the sound.

It was not coming from somewhere astern, but dead ahead.

The big, thirty-day, battery-operated 100-mile pinger beacon was lying under a piece of spare canvas.

The switch was on.

Garth turned it off, put the headphones down and walked aft through the ship.

In the cockpit he went to the wheel, slapped the beckets on the spokes and at last said to Steve, "Get up and come with me."

"What's the trouble, boss?"

Garth didn't answer as he went below, Steve following.

In the forecastle Garth stood to one side as Steve came in. "What's up?" Steve asked, his voice anxious.

"I saw you in here this morning. What were you doing?"

"Me? Nothing."

"Why were you in here?"

Steve looked at him with frightened eyes. "I don't know, Garth. I just came in here—to open the hatch, I guess. That's what I did . . . Is that wrong? Did I do something wrong?"

Garth had a hard time controlling himself. He slowly stooped and picked up the beacon. Holding it out toward Steve he said, "When did you turn this on?"

"Turn it on, Garth? What's the trouble? What did I do?" He looked at the beacon. "I don't even know what that thing is."

"You must have done it yesterday," Garth said slowly. "Yes . . . He couldn't get lucky enough to spot us in that storm. Somebody had to lead him to us . . . 'I'm cold,' you said, yesterday. Remember? 'Can I go below?' you said. That was yesterday. Ever since then we've been telling him —with this!" He shoved the beacon into Steve's gut and then put it down. "I wanted to drop you overboard when you came crawling out of that hatch. I should have done it." With his arm he pushed Steve aside and went aft.

Coming out of the companionway Garth realized that he was not really even surprised.

A mile astern and coming fast was the Coast Guard cutter he had seen moored at Monique.

22

The chain locked to the handcuffs on Garth's wrists had just enough scope to let him stand up on the lab bench. There, by straining against the chain and pushing his head up, he could open the skylight an inch or so.

He stood there now looking out through the narrow slit. The sky was dark, with broken clouds, and there was no moon. Although the typhoon had changed many landmarks he could still make out the old, familiar things of his Molahve lagoon. The cloud-shrouded volcanoes, the curve of the peninsula, the three tall trees he had so often used for bearings.

Only now his lagoon was not empty. The Monique cutter lay at anchor, lights glowing, and Smith's copra boat, with only a dim yellow light showing from the wheelhouse, was a few hundred yards away.

Standing in the darkness, his wrists aching from the pull of the chain, Garth couldn't help admiring the efficiency of his enemies. The cutter had swept in on him, machine guns and the one-pounder making it clear that the inspector was serious. Within fifteen minutes after Garth had first seen the cutter close aboard, the *Uldra* had been put in tow, at high speed. The inspector had handcuffed and chained

Garth to the wheelbox and had chained Steve, badly hurt and bleeding, to the mainmast. One of the inspector's men stood guard over them with a shotgun.

The *Uldra* had not been designed for high speed towing so the trip to Molahve had ruined her. Every shroud was now slack, every chainplate hanging from bent bolts. Her fore and aft stays hung in sad curves and Garth marveled that her masts had not whipped themselves clean out of the steps.

He had had all that day to look at Steve lying hurt and chained in the broiling sun. There had been nothing phony about the inspector's attitude when he had first come aboard. And the pistol whipping he had given Steve had been no act as, with each swing of the gun barrel, he had commanded Steve to tell him where the jewels were hidden.

They had arrived at Molahve late in the afternoon and, as though at a signal, Smith's old copra boat had come steaming around the peninsula with Sam at the wheel and Jake handling the anchor. The cutter's powerboat had picked up Smith, wearing his big hat, and the inspector had greeted him at the top of the gangplank.

Garth had been surprised that Smith had not come over to the *Uldra* with the inspector.

If there had been any doubt left in Garth's mind that Steve had been telling him the truth all along there was none left after the inspector drove him across the deck, beating him with the chain, and drove him down into the powerboat.

Garth had expected the same treatment and sat waiting for it but the inspector had not touched him as he directed the guard to take him below. In the lab they had chained him to the thick steel leg of the lab bench. And then, without a word, the inspector had left the boat.

That had puzzled Garth. Why, he wondered, were the inspector and Smith wasting time on Steve? Why not start working over the man who knew?

There had been no sign of the guard as Garth waited

for darkness. Now a little squall of rain was sweeping down on Molahve and Garth waited for it, reasoning that if the guard was still aboard he would certainly come below when the rain hit him.

Garth waited, watching the squall sweep over the jungle to the north, and heard the sharp crack of thunder.

The thunder cracked again and this time he saw a bright, yellowish explosion on the bow of the cutter.

For a second he didn't understand it, but then the one-pounder fired again and in the glow from the muzzle blast he could see the gun crew.

He heard the shell strike—a short, crunching noise—and then saw the deck of Smith's boat rise straight up in the air.

The gun fired again and this time hit the fuel tanks and Smith's boat was instantly afire, huge, ugly flames bursting out of her and flowing all over her.

The gun kept on firing as Smith's boat, now just an ugly target of flame, drifted seaward.

Garth closed his eyes and let the skylight down.

They had been spies; they had informed on him, lied to him, but he could not help remembering Sam and Jake at other times. They had been good people . . .

For a moment he wondered why and then that was clear, too. Smith must now be destroying all evidence that could connect him with the subchaser and its mute story of theft and murder. By sinking his ship it would be established that he had put out from Efrahte on a routine copra pick up trip and had just disappeared at sea, with all hands.

This deliberate destruction of his ship, this murder of Sam and Jake brought everything into sharp and fearful focus.

There were others Smith would have to murder. He could, perhaps, let the inspector live. Just pay him off and dismiss him.

Steve didn't have a chance.

But, at the top of Smith's list, there had to be—Garth Larson.

For a moment he stood on the bench looking at the dim rectangle of the door and listening to the drumming of rain on the deck. Then he climbed down and got the gas fueled Bunsen burner but did not light it until he had it under the bench where the glow of the flame wouldn't shine directly up through the skylight.

Now he could see. One end of the chain was locked to the link between the handcuffs, the other end to the bench leg. Pulling the chain taut just above the sharp angle iron of the leg brace he held it in position with his feet as he turned the flame of the burner on one link and held it steady until the link began to glow a dull red. While it was still glowing he brought it down on the brace, picked up the ten pound stainless-steel rod of the Phleger corer and slammed it down on the hot link.

His swelling wrists stabbed him with pain.

As the glow of the link died he lifted it and heated it again, listening for any sound of a guard.

No one came to stop him, nothing moved.

He heated the link, struck it, heated it, struck it . . .

At last the link gave way.

He was free of the bench leg but his wrists were still handcuffed together.

The sight of them in the light of the burner shocked him. The swelling had grown so great that a heavy fold of almost purple flesh flowed completely over the metal band of the handcuffs. Dull red streaks were already sprouting from the purple swelling and he knew that in a little while gangrene would start and those streaks would advance up his arms.

Lifting the chain over his shoulder he started aft to the engine room when a sound he knew could not be of the boat itself stopped him in his tracks.

Something—perhaps a floating log—had struck the side of the *Uldra*.

Garth knew that it had not been a log. Turning back he

stooped and put out the Bunsen burner, moving it back to the bench. Then, as he heard voices on deck, he wrapped an end of the chain back around the brace to make it appear as though he were still chained to it.

A light appeared at the head of the companion hatch and he saw figures moving down the ladder.

Four men were carrying the body of another one.

Steve? It must be, Garth thought. They were through with him and now it's my turn.

The men turned at the foot of the ladder and carried the body into the after cabin where Garth heard them dump it on the bare springs of the bunk.

Garth stooped in the dark, felt around until he found the corer rod and then put it on the bench. He could whirl, pick it up, throw it in one movement and then he could use the chain locked to his wrists as a lethal whip . . .

A strong light moved into the main cabin and he watched the beam of it playing on the ruined walls and deck. Then the light beam was at the lab door.

Garth stood facing it, waiting for the light to stop blinding him before he made his move. "Good evening, Inspector."

A voice behind the light gave a short order and the light swung away so that Garth could see the silhouette of the man who held it. He was short, slight; not as tall as the inspector or Smith. . . .

Garth watched the four of them go up the ladder. None were tall, none bald-headed or bearded.

This sudden, silent departure confused him until he realized suddenly that Smith and the inspector must now be convinced that the jewels were no longer in the *Uldra*—if they had ever been in her. They must think now, he reasoned, that they were still in the subchaser or that he had hidden them in the lagoon or the jungle.

Were they waiting until daylight to start on him?

If they were they were making a serious mistake.

He was sure that he could, still handcuffed, make it to the beach. It was only a mile or so. But as he felt the stabbing pain shooting up from his wrists he knew that the gangrene wasn't going to let him get much farther than the beach.

Before he could go anywhere he had to get the handcuffs off. No matter how long it took, he had to do that first. Or nothing else would matter.

In the engine room he got the hacksaw and sat down, holding the frame of it between his knees.

He was ashamed of himself. He could not bear the pain and the movement of his hands across the saw blade hurt so much that his knees went weak and the saw fell into the bilge water.

He tried again and the saw fell again.

Picking it up he got over to the door where he put the frame of the saw between the hinge side and the jamb. Holding the door open with his foot he looped the chain around the knob and then around his waist so that, when he leaned against it, the door jammed the saw frame in the crack.

As he pushed the tongue half of the handcuff against the upright blade and began sawing up and down he felt pain so deep and so acute that he didn't think he could endure it. At each movement a black wave of pain seemed on the verge of sweeping over his mind.

Added to this deep pain was a sharp surface pain when, at times, the dizziness made him careless and his swollen flesh raked across the saw teeth.

The blood helped a little for it ran down his hand and, by twisting a little, he could make it run into the trench the blade was cutting and that helped cool the metal.

When the blade at last went through, the pressure of the swelling snapped the thing away from his wrist and there was a sudden easing of pain and a slow feeling of life coming into his hand.

But that was only the hinged side of it. The other half
Garth had to dig out of his flesh, slowly and painfully.

And then he had it all to do over again on the other hand.

When at last the other band parted he slumped down,
his face rubbing down the edge of the door, his hands
dangling into the bilge water.

It took all his strength to get up on his knees and start
looking in the main cabin for some swim fins.

And as he crawled around he suddenly remembered
Steve . . .

I have to go! Garth said to himself. I can't wait! I haven't
got enough time! I've got to go *now!*

Perhaps Steve was dead . . .

Someone had been kind enough to throw a blanket over
Steve. Garth felt under it with his wet, bloody hand. The
skin was warm. Steve was breathing. "Steve! Steve!" he
said, slapping the warm flesh. There was no reaction, just
the slow breathing.

Garth tried then to lift him but something held his body
to the bed.

With his numb fingers he found that Steve was handcuffed as he had been and chained to the frame of the
bunk.

Garth was feeling around for the hacksaw when he
noticed the moving, dim glow of light and heard voices.

For a second he felt cheated. It wasn't daylight yet—
they had no right to come back . . .

If he ran up the ladder? . . .

The light was brightening at the hatch opening.

Grabbing up his chain he pressed the sawed links of
the handcuffs back around his swollen wrists as he went
forward to the lab. At the bench he wrapped the end of
the chain around the brace again. But, even as he did
and stood up to face them, he knew that it was all useless.
He might hit one of them with the corer bitt, lash another
with the chain—what good would it do in the end?

The inspector came in followed by two of the uniformed

guards carrying flashlights and a Coleman lantern. They were all armed with the big-butted guns.

As the lights held on Garth the inspector was a dark, menacing shadow.

23.

Garth studied the tall figure and thought of the weapons he had as the guard pumped up the Coleman lantern. It was a short list. He was physically free although the inspector thought that he was chained and handcuffed. One weapon, but what good was it against the guns? His second weapon was that he, and he alone, knew where the jewels were.

"I hold no animosity toward you," the inspector said in the dark shadow. "I expect a man in jail to try to escape and respect him if he's successful."

The guard lit the lantern, the mantel glowing softly for a moment and then producing that hard, bright, white glow. When the guard hung it from the skylight it threw a distinct cone of light down on him and the inspector.

The inspector motioned for the guards to leave and stood waiting until they had gone, closing the door behind them.

"I even admire the way you drugged me," the inspector said, half sitting down on the lab bench. "What was that, by the way?"

"Tranquilizer. For sharks." Garth studied the distance between him and the inspector and tried to visualize the sequence of movements if he suddenly yanked the chain

free and with both hands still manacled struck upward . . .
The gun could be moved much faster.

"I want you to cooperate with me, for your own sake,"
the inspector said, taking a small plastic box out of his
tunic pocket and putting it on the bench. "You *will* cooperate eventually so if you do it now you'll save yourself
some rather unpleasant things. Also, if you cooperate without what might be called coercion I will drop all my government's very serious charges against you and will see to
it that you are never identified to the government of the
Philippines."

In his mind's eye Garth saw Steve's bloody head as he
was being whipped across the deck.

"In the subchaser," the inspector went on, "you found,
in the crew's compartment, a galvanized iron washtub with
'Made in USA' on the bottom of it. This tub contained
jewels stolen from the Philippines. They were—and still
are—the property of the Republic of the Philippines and
I want to return them to their rightful owners."

Garth wondered what sort of deal Smith had made with
this man. Wondered why Smith had decided it was necessary to give him so many details which only Smith could
know. It seemed to Garth a dangerous, foolish, and incriminating thing for Smith to have done.

And then Garth wondered if, perhaps it was entirely
the other way around. If all this accurate information had
come from some other source then it would be the inspector,
not Smith, who would be in control.

Suddenly Garth remembered that day a long time ago
when Smith had threatened to kill him and Garth had
warned him not to. He remembered the way Smith had said
it; as though talking to himself—"I had to do it once. And
now I think I may have to do it again."

That could be the answer. During the theft perhaps this
man, this inspector, had seen Smith and the others carrying
the washtub away. He could have followed them and seen
them put it aboard the subchaser. Perhaps this man had

been watching Smith during all that time on Efrahte—watching and waiting.

"I know that you took the jewels, Larson," the inspector said, taking a hypodermic needle out of the little box. "Tell me where they are and you will be a free man, all charges dropped and in the clear with the Filipinos."

The cone of light fell on the dull stainless steel of the Phleger corer rod. And it fell on a few of the tanks, the red warning signs bright in the hard light.

The inspector finished filling the glass cylinder from a glass phial in the box. "This is a very effective truth serum," he said, holding the needle up to the light. "Unfortunately, it has rather disastrous side effects." He lowered the needle and looked at Garth. "If you force me to use this to make you tell me then it will be an entirely different story. I will have to report that a criminal, charged with narcotic smuggling, drugged an official and escaped from the Monique jail. Setting out to sea in the face of a storm he and his ship—perished."

The mollusk tank was the closest one to Garth. There were some butterfly fish in it he used to feed the specimens and some pretty cowries, mantles out, moving around on the surface of the sand. All the *Conus* were buried and out of sight, their presence just under the surface marked only by small, smooth mounds of sand.

Garth leaned forward and read the label on the serum. "Hmm," he said. "That's a *very* potent serum." He looked over at the inspector. "I'm sure you've already found out that it can often be fatal."

"Not immediately."

Garth moved back, this time closer to the mollusk tank so that his body now concealed it from the inspector. "But fatal. So, since you've already torn my boat apart looking for the jewels you know they are not here, don't you? Why don't you look for them in the subchaser before taking a chance with that serum? I can't tell you much dead."

The inspector smiled at him. "I have to admire you,

Larson, but time isn't going to buy you anything and there are two good reasons why I'm not going to waste time in that subchaser. First, the jewels are not in it. You're too intelligent to have left them there where we would be free to spend any amount of time looking for them. Unless, of course, another storm came up and covered the ship with sand again." He smiled again. "And, second, to prevent you from pulling that old smuggler's trick of hiding things in places that have already been searched—and I assure you Smith has spent a week searching—Smith has booby-trapped the subchaser. He has very cleverly rigged it with its own depth charges so that anyone going near it . . . Well, it will be a very big explosion."

"How do you know Smith didn't find them?" Garth asked. "That many jewels can put a strain on a friendship."

"He didn't," the inspector said flatly.

"If you believe him then we're right back where we started." Garth turned sideways and held his upper arm out a little. "Go ahead. But remember, that serum can be a one-shot deal. After you hit me with it I might tell you truthfully that I hid them in some cave in a coral reef or under a tree in the jungle. But I may not be able, truthfully, to remember *exactly* where. I might have to go to that area to recognize a particular piece of coral, a particular tree. But I won't be able to go anywhere if that stuff kills me so you end up with a thousand caves, a million trees to search." Garth leaned back against the mollusk tank. "There's a better way, Inspector."

"Convince me."

"You let me go. In this boat. You give me five days before you go get the jewels from where I've hidden them. Five days without following me. For that you get *all* the jewels. I want nothing but this boat."

Garth watched his face, watched his eyes narrow.

Then the inspector smiled slowly. "Do you really expect me to believe that after five days I could go and find a washtub full of jewels where you told me they would be?"

"If you don't," Garth said, "all you have to do is tell your story to the Philippine authorities and I'm another Ord Smith hiding for the rest of my life on some God-forsaken island. So—take your choice. Let me sail my boat out of here or—go ahead with your serum."

The inspector stood studying him for a long time and then said pleasantly, "It's a pleasure to do business with you, Larson, because you always surprise me . . . All you want out of the deal is this boat? An old, wrecked schooner. Don't you know the masts are about to fall out?"

"That can be fixed and the hull's okay—outside."

The inspector studied him a moment longer and then looked slowly around the lab.

Garth watched him, waiting.

Smiling, the inspector began walking slowly along, occasionally stopping at one of the tanks. He would push the warning sign aside and peer into the dim interior and then walk on. "Nothing but this boat . . . ?"

Garth waited.

At one tank he looked in and said, "Your pretty little fish are dying."

"Thanks to you."

The inspector came back into the cone of bright light. "I apologize," he said. "I've been stupid."

Garth moved so that his body still concealed the mollusk tank.

"With your little red signs . . ." the inspector said, stopping in front of him. "Stand aside, please."

Garth did not move.

The inspector let his hand drop to the butt of the gun. "Stand aside, please."

Slowly Garth moved away from the tank.

The inspector unhooked the warning sign and laid it on the bench. Then he stood a moment watching the butterfly fish darting around inside the tank. "Well done," he said, looking around on the lab bench and spotting the corer bitt.

Picking it up he hefted it, letting it fall into his free hand and then, smiling at Garth, he turned and struck the Plexiglas front of the tank.

Garth stopped breathing.

The gimbals the tank was mounted in absorbed most of the blow, the tank swinging, but staying level.

"Very modern," the inspector said, taking a firmer grip on the bitt.

"When it breaks be careful none of the water splashes on you," Garth told him. "It may be poisonous."

"Good try," the inspector said, striking the tank again.

This time Garth saw a definite dent in the Plexiglas. The fish inside the tank flew around in a panic.

Frowning with irritation the inspector dropped the bitt and looked around for something else. Suddenly he unbuttoned his sleeve and started rolling it up his arm.

"I wouldn't do that," Garth said quietly. "These tanks have extremely venomous animals in them."

The inspector continued to roll up his sleeve. "Cowries?" he asked. "Butterfly fish?"

Garth watched him open the lid of the tank and stick his hand slowly down into the water.

The beautiful little butterfly fish scurried around half afraid, half curious, but the cowries, sensing danger with their delicate filaments, pulled in their mantles, the multicolored flesh moving over the glass-smooth shell and disappearing inside it.

Garth noticed that the hairs on the arm and hand were magnified by the water.

The inspector, in an awkward position, watched his fingers in the tank carefully and guided them down so that they reached the surface of the white sand without touching any of the now motionless cowries.

Holding his five fingers as though to pick up a marble, the inspector pushed them slowly down into the sand.

The hand stopped moving downward and Garth saw the

upper knuckles begin sticking out as the invisible fingers clutched something.

Without withdrawing his fingers from the sand the inspector turned his head so Garth could see his eyes.

There was such triumph in them, such concentrated greed that Garth felt it almost as a physical force and looked away, watching two butterfly fish now investigating the fingers sticking down into their sand.

"Don't look so sad, Mr. Larson," the inspector said. "You couldn't have gotten away with it and now you've spared yourself the—er—side effects of the serum."

Garth was waiting to see the hard flash of a diamond or the soft red glow of a ruby or the green of emerald.

"I can't take all the credit for this," the inspector said. "After all, you practically told me where to look."

There was no flash of diamond, nor ruby glow, nor green, nor blue. Garth could see in the fingers only the shining surface of ivory white and pale browns whose beautiful patterns always reminded him of old maps.

The inspector should have looked through the Plexiglas to see what fabulous jewel he was holding but, instead, he stood on tiptoe and tried to look down through the water whose surface he was disturbing with his movements.

Garth saw the fleshy snout oozing out of the shell and wished that, for once, the thing would get a move on. But it only oozed along, spreading out, tentative, growing longer.

When it happened it was so fast that Garth would not have noticed if he had not been expecting it. For only a split second the snout dropped down on the flesh of the inspector's forefinger and then withdrew into the shell.

Inside the snout, Garth knew, were a number of modified *radula* teeth, tiny things the *Conus* used for rasping its food.

The teeth, however, were hollow and connected by a gland to the poison sac behind the *Conus*' head.

The sting is no more painful than a pin prick.

Jerking his hand up, the inspector dropped the shell and Garth watched it tumble back to the sand.

The inspector ran his dry hand down the bare, wet arm and looked at his finger. "What was that?"

"One of the jewels of the sea," Garth told him. "*Conus geographus.*" Then he smiled and said, "But don't worry, Inspector, only twenty percent of the people who get stung by them die."

The inspector was still looking at his finger, squeezing it hard as though to force the poison out.

Garth leaned back against the bench. "You have about eighteen to twenty hours now."

"To do what?"

Garth sounded surprised. "To save your life, Inspector. Let me read to you about cone shells."

Now the fear showed. "*Was that a cone shell?*"

"One of the prettiest." Garth reached down into one of the cartons where he had put his books and got one out. "This is a book called *Poisonous and Venomous Marine Animals of the World* . . . Here we are: 'Conus . . . the pain,'" he read, "'is excruciating . . . paralysis of the muscles is initiated early . . . and followed by complete generalized muscular paralysis . . . Aphonia and dysphagia may become very marked . . . blurring of vision and diplopia are commonly present . . . death is said to be the result of cardiac failure . . .'"

The inspector was staring down at his hand, his face now gray.

"In a little while, Inspector, your hands and feet and face will start turning purple—or violet, if you prefer. . . ."

"You're lying!" the inspector said. "It's nothing!"

"You'd better hurry because pretty soon you won't be able to talk and, even if you can, you won't be able to understand what you say or what anyone else says. That's what aphonia and dysphagia mean. And you'll begin to see double—that's diplopia. You'd better hurry."

The pain had started. Garth could see it in the man's straining muscles and the shivering of his eyelids.

"You're lying!"

"No," Garth said. "See the nice picture?" He held the book's illustration, in color, out for him to see.

The inspector grabbed the book and whirled to the tank where the cone shell was already burrowing its way back into the sand.

"You haven't got much time, Inspector. Eighteen hours, perhaps twenty. Although some people have died within four hours. You'd better move while you *can* move. In a little while you'll hardly be able to breathe, Inspector."

The inspector let the book fall out of his hands and stumbled toward the cabin door, clinging to his wrist with his good hand. He swayed as he walked and his face was ashy and drawn. Without turning to look at Garth he said in a weak, quavering voice, "I'll kill you."

Garth called after him, "If you reach a doctor—and can still talk—tell him you need neostigmine. He'll *know* you need artificial respiration."

Garth watched him as he staggered through the dark cabin and hauled himself up the ladder, crying out to someone as he went.

There were sounds of feet and excited voices from top-side and then the sound of a boat bumping against something and fading voices and at last silence.

Garth pulled the handcuff bands out of his swollen flesh and put them down so that the chain did not make a sound.

Picking up the corer bitt he left the lab, closing the door so that the main cabin was pitch dark.

For a second he stood at the foot of the ladder listening and then moved up it, sliding along the wall and watching the topside opening.

The cockpit was empty.

Raising his head above the hatch he could see no one on deck. It surprised him that the inspector had left no one to guard him until he realized that that man had been too panicked to think of anything except his own life.

He could see the powerboat drawing alongside the cutter and then the men helping the inspector up the ladder.

The cutter was underway before the powerboat had been lifted completely out of the water.

Garth listened to the thrum of her diesels reaching full speed and watched her get up on the step and move out, due west.

Going down the ladder Garth worked out some details.

Right now the inspector was in an hysterical panic, racing to save his life. But Garth was sure that, in a few hours, the man would realize that he wasn't dying after all. And then he would turn around and come back just as fast as he had left. A cone shell sting on the finger is frighteningly painful but there was no record of a finger bite being fatal except in the case of very young children. In a few hours the pain and sickness would diminish and the inspector would have nothing more than a badly swollen hand.

He'd be back. Even if he didn't want to come back, Smith would force him to.

But they were giving him time he had not even hoped to get.

Scuttling the *Uldra* or setting her adrift to make them think he had left would not work. Smith was too good a seaman to believe she could be sailed in the condition she was in.

It didn't matter. His plan was simple and good. First, get the jewels out of the tanks. Then, if Steve was still alive, Garth decided to take him along to shore. With the jewels and supplies from the cache of food they would move up into the rain forest, leaving no tracks, no trace in that gloomy place.

Up near the eternal clouds they could find a spot where they could scan the sea as they waited.

If that stupid operator in Guam had at last given José Morales the message about the washtub it would not be much longer before someone—the Navy, the Filipinos, *some-one*—would get here.

If the operator had not it still wasn't hopeless. After all, Garth thought, it had been a week since Guam had heard from him and no one had answered any calls Guam might have made to him. They must be getting a little worried by now. And when those Scripps people got to Monique they'd be asking awkward questions. Someone would come and, until they did, he and Steve would be safe in the rain forest.

Garth got the Coleman out of the lab and carried it into the after cabin. Then he got the saw and went over to the bunk where Steve still lay motionless, face down under the blanket.

As Garth lifted the blanket away the hard white light from the Coleman shimmered on the wet-looking perfectly hairless skin.

As the head turned slowly the red of the beard seemed pale.

Ord Smith looked up at him with a steady, calm stare.

24.

Garth backed away from the man and stood looking down at him in silence. He was confused now and angry and did not know what to do.

Smith continued to stare at him, his eyes slowly moving and then at last said, "You look all right."

"I am all right."

"I didn't think he could break you without that drug."

"I'm leaving."

For some reason Smith looked sad, disappointed. "With him?"

"Without him." He would lock the cabin door to make doubly sure Smith could not get at him. Then, in an hour, he could get the live specimens back into the sea, empty the tanks and go ashore.

"That's what he wants you to do," Smith said as Garth turned toward the door. "He can say you were trying to escape and he had to kill you."

Garth looked back at him and Smith said quietly, "He *has* to do that, Garth."

Garth didn't care about any of this. Perhaps, he thought, the two thieves had had a falling out—what did it matter?

He went back and got the hacksaw from where he had left it on the bunk.

"He's already arranged everything so that he can kill me any time he wants to," Smith said. "Did you know he sank my boat?"

"I saw that."

"Sam and Jake were in her. He didn't even give them a chance to get off. He killed them."

Garth looked down at him. "You killed them. The way you killed the others. The way you're planning to kill me. This time it isn't going to work because I'm leaving."

"He'll track you down," Smith said. "As soon as he gets the jewels he's going to kill us both. He *has* to, don't you understand that?"

"He isn't going to get them. Neither are you."

Smith stared at him with a look of disbelief. Then he began to laugh. "Oh, that's great!" he said. "Great! What did you do, throw them overboard where no one can ever find them?"

"Let's just say you and your friend will never find them." Garth moved a little closer to him and watched his face as he said, "If there's any reward for returning them I think I'll look up a family named Barrett and give them some of it."

Garth was surprised by how well it worked. Smith's eyes widened and his mouth almost fell open. "Barrett?" He almost whispered the name.

Garth went forward to the lab, picking up the sextant's penlight as he went. In the lab he found the subchaser's log with the *Natural History of Mammals* jacket still on it. Opening to one of the pages where the code groups were scattered through the navigation he took it back to the after cabin.

Holding it so Smith could see only the one page, he said, "Here's a story that needs telling. All about you."

Smith studied the page for a moment and then looked up at him. "A story?"

"See that little group of letters?" Garth asked, pointing out one of the code groups.

For a long time Smith studied the letters in silence and then raised his head. "Where did you find this, Garth?"

"I found it. And I'm going to show it to a lot of people."

"In an ammo box?" Smith asked.

It took Garth a few seconds to begin wondering how Smith knew a detail like that.

"It's a code," Smith said. "The key word is 'barrett.' No. 'Wm barrett.'"

Garth stared at him. "How do you know that?"

"It's mine," Smith said. "William S. Barrett, Quartermaster Third Class, U. S. Navy."

It had to be another one of Smith's tricks.

"You're Barrett?" Garth asked incredulously.

Smith nodded. "He knows who I am, too."

"How did he find out? Did you tell him when he hit you with the truth serum?"

"He knew," Smith said. "That's why—even if he never gets the jewels—we haven't got a chance, Garth."

Garth stood there studying him, confused now and yet with a growing feeling of hope.

"I should've known him, too," Smith said quietly. "He kept coming back to Molahve, time after time. After every typhoon, after every big storm he came back to look for the wreck. I should have known it was him."

"Who?"

"If I hadn't been so stupid I could have finished what I started. I could have been here waiting for him."

"For who?"

"Schloss. An Army man who stole the jewels . . . It happened a long time ago, in the Philippines . . ." Smith's tone suddenly changed, growing anxious. "Why's he taking so long? What's he doing?"

"He's gone. But he'll be back."

Smith looked at him with an odd, gentle expression. "Don't be ashamed because you told him, Garth. Why should you let him hurt you for some jewels you had nothing to do with?"

"*I* hurt *him*," Garth said. "A cone shell stung him and now he's heading for Monique and a doctor. But he'll recover in an hour or so. Then he'll turn around and come back . . ."

"He's not here?" Smith asked, excited. "Where's the guard?" He lowered his voice to a whisper. "Cut me loose and we can jump him."

"There's no guard . . . Are you really Barrett?"

"No guard! Nobody? Sure, I'm Barrett. Cut me loose, Garth! We've got a chance!"

In Garth's mind everything seemed to be in broken, jagged pieces, nothing fitting together. He wanted to believe this man and yet he needed proof. "Who was Skippy?"

"Skippy?" Smith said in a low voice. "Skippy was my brother."

"What happened to him?"

"Schloss killed him."

Garth picked up the hacksaw. "There are a lot of reasons for me not to believe you, Smith, but I'm going to take a chance that, this time, you're telling the truth."

As he began sawing at one of the handcuffs Smith asked, "How much time do you think we've got?"

"Enough."

"Your ship's in bad shape. Can we sail her?"

"No. But I don't think he can find us once we get over on the island."

"Good. It won't take long before my people start looking for me."

"A lot of people ought to show up here pretty soon." Garth suddenly stopped the saw and looked at Smith. "How did he know I found the subchaser? Did you tell him?"

"Are you crazy?"

"How did he find out?"

"Did you say anything about it when you radioed your people in Guam?"

"Of course not! Come on, Smith, there's something phony here. You . . ." He stopped and lowered his voice. "Washtub," he said. "I sent a message to a Filipino in Guam saying I had found his washtub."

"That would be all Schloss needed to hear. He's spent his life looking for that washtub."

"No!" Garth said. "There're a million radio transmissions a day. How could he have picked out just by chance the one in a million he wanted to hear?"

"I don't know, but how else could he find out? What else did you say?"

As the knowledge hit him, Garth felt weak and sick—and afraid. "What does Schloss look like? An old, shriveled up man with bushy hair. A sarcastic-looking face . . ."

"And real cold, milky-colored eyes," Smith said.

Schloss. Wasn't that the German word for 'castle'?

"I know him," Garth said. "He calls himself Professor Castle." Then everything fell apart again. "But how do you know what he looks like now. I thought you never saw the man who kept coming back here."

"What do you mean?" Smith asked. "I saw him *today*. With that customs inspector."

That dumb radio operator had delivered his message all right—to the one man in the world who should not have received it. "Oh, man!" Garth said. "How wrong can I get? It's been Castle all along—getting me to Monique, the opium, everything." He started sawing again. "I apologize to you, Ord. I have been *so* wrong."

"So have I," Smith said. "But I've lived with that fear for so many years I just couldn't see you as anything but a threat. I was afraid you'd tear down my little world."

"What happened? Who sank her?"

"We sank her," Smith said. "We had to . . . How much do you know about the jewels?"

"That there are a lot of them."

"Yeah. They came from the Philippines. A long time ago. Have you ever seen the island of Corregidor in Manila Bay?"

"I've seen it."

"It was terrible then. The Japs had guns set up all around the bay and were just—*pounding* Corregidor. Day and night, never stopping. It was horrible, Garth. All hands —Army, Navy, Filipinos—all hands were on Corregidor, thousands of 'em, living like rats in some tunnels they had dug into a mountain there. They were sick, they were starving, they didn't have anything left to fight with.

"All the big Navy ships had been sunk or scuttled so nothing was left except the little stuff—like the 206. We were tied up at the town there on Corregidor . . . just waiting because the word was out that we were going to surrender soon.

"And then—I guess it was just about the last night before the surrender—these four Army guys came aboard and told the skipper that some admiral had said get out if we could.

"It was better than sitting there, waiting, so the skipper decided to make a run for it."

Smith looked at him and smiled. "It was like rain, Garth. Except the stuff falling down was bombs and shells and bullets and—just stuff, concrete, dirt, trees . . . Those Army guys stayed under the mess table all the time, I mean, *scared*. I was, too.

"You know, we went through it all. Not a thing hit us.

"For a week or so we sneaked down through the islands, hiding the ship in the mangroves in the daytime and pushing the diesels at flank all night. We'd get food and water and sometimes fuel from the little *barrios* on the coast . . .

"Well, anyway, the four Army guys—I've forgotten their names, but the big shot was named Schloss—began to take charge after we got clear of the Philippines. The skipper wanted to head south to Australia but they wanted to go east toward the States—and they argued about it. One night—I was on the bridge and they were arguing—Schloss just shot the captain. Just shot him, like that. Then, when the exec came running in, he shot him, too. That left only enlisted men. We didn't argue."

Smith was silent for a moment and then said, quietly, "We didn't argue with them but we talked about it among ourselves because it looked like they wanted to kill us all and we couldn't figure out why.

"We found out, though, when we came to a little island called Sonsorol and got some food and fuel. In the Philippines nobody had charged us for anything but at Sonsorol they wanted to get paid. They were. With diamonds.

"Well, it didn't take long for us to find out that those guys had a whole washtub full of jewels. They must've stolen them from Corregidor because I'd heard that in one of the tunnels there were millions of dollars and Filipino pesos and gold and jewels.

"That changed everything—for us, anyway.

"They had all the guns and they stood watches, one or two of them on watch all the time. So we figured out a way to get rid of them—before they got rid of us. We were going to rush them and push them overboard." Smith stopped and took a deep breath.

"It didn't work. The night we planned to do it Schloss called us all into the compartment. All of them were there, and all of us. When they got through shooting there were only two of us left."

The saw went through the link and freed one of Smith's hands. "One more," Garth said. "Hold it out away from your skin."

Smith pushed the handcuff up with his free hand.

"Why didn't they shoot you, too?" Garth asked.

"Because they needed us, me and Skippy. He could make the diesels run and I could navigate. But it didn't take a genius to figure that as soon as we got out of enemy water and got near some civilized island they wouldn't need us any more. So we rigged it for the ship to go aground on Molahve and, just in case she didn't hit hard enough, we fixed it so the water intake would sink her anyway."

Smith smiled as though remembering something pleasant. "We were just kids. I remember the nights we used to sneak around the ship getting ready. Snitching food, getting bottles to hold water, siphoning gas for the life boat's motor. We even rigged the davit falls so that when the ship struck the boat would break clear of the davits and just drop into the water—with us in her. We figured that in all the darkness and confusion we could sneak away and they'd be left with a sinking ship."

"Weren't there two life boats?" Garth asked.

"We pulled the distributor out of the other one . . . We were just dumb kids. Schloss wasn't." Smith looked up at him. "We came close though, Garth. In another minute we'd have made it.

"I had the helm—we'd arranged that—and it was a beautiful dark rainy night. We couldn't have asked for a better night. You couldn't see *anything*. I wasn't even worried when Schloss came up on the bridge and stood around. All I was worried about was that we were supposed to hit something and I couldn't even *see* anything to hit. It was just black and we kept on going. Skippy was back in the engine room and he must've been really sweating because we figured we'd hit the island at no later than one-thirty in the morning and it was already past that.

"And then it happened," Smith said. "I never saw anything like it. Like day. Just one great big bolt of lightning came down on those volcanoes and there was Molahve dead ahead.

"Schloss made a grab for the wheel and I made a grab for the enunciator. I rang for Skippy to open 'em up flank and then tried to fight off Schloss.

"It was a close thing and if he hadn't shot me I think I could have piled it up on the beach."

Smith looked over at him. "You know, Garth, when you get shot you don't even feel it. I mean, it doesn't hurt. Just one minute I was holding the wheel steady for the island with Schloss behind me and choking me, pulling me away and the next I was flat on my back, not knowing what had hit me.

"Schloss managed to turn her away from the island and get her headed out to sea again but then—and it must have been Skippy—the engines stopped. I guess he just shifted from flank ahead straight back into reverse and took the gears out of her like shelling corn.

"By the time I got up on my hands and knees there was nobody on the bridge and the ship was already at anchor. The best I could do was to crawl along on hands and knees and I went aft to get Skippy.

"Schloss had already shot him. He was lying over the gear box, dead."

Garth thought of the skeleton lying so strangely pitiful over the gear box.

Smith went on. "Our life boat was on the other side of the ship so I started crawling toward the stern but when I heard somebody forward and saw Schloss coming I got into the galley.

"He must have seen me because I heard him at the door so I went on into the crew's compartment."

Smith looked up. "They were all dead. One was in his bunk, shot through the head. There was a gun there, too, and I got it and when Schloss came in from the galley I shot him.

"From then on, Garth, it's dim. I remember getting into the boat and getting it down to the water and it seems to me I tried to start the engine but I don't think I did."

"Where did you want to go?" Garth asked.

"Efrahte. I knew there were people on it."

"You must have made it."

"No. I don't know how long it was before they found me, but they found me here."

"Who?"

"A fishing party from Efrahte. They came over just looking around after the typhoon."

"When did the typhoon hit?"

"I don't know. I don't remember it at all but it must

have been within a day or so after I left the ship because I couldn't have lived much longer than that."

"You just drifted ashore in the lifeboat?"

"I must have because they found that. The typhoon had shoved it way up into the jungle . . . They only found one. One lifeboat, Garth. And no ship."

"Both boats are gone," Garth said.

"I know it. *Now.* And he must have taken it but I didn't know anything then. It was almost a year before I could really think again . . . Those are good people, Garth. You wouldn't believe what they did for me, day and night, for weeks, *months.* I don't know what they did—I only remember them using leaves and roots and berries and mud. They took care of me and fed me and kept me clean and all I could do was lie there. They know a lot of magic we don't know."

Smith winced as Garth accidently let the blade saw across the base of his thumb. "Sorry," Garth said.

"Chop it off, just let's get out of here."

"You've stayed at Efrahte ever since?"

"At first I had to, after that I chose to. Because by the time I got well enough to move around a little the enemy had taken over the whole area. Their planes and ships were all over the place so no one could move. It was suicide even to go out fishing in an outrigger.

"And then the war ended. I know it was a great thing for the world but it was terrible for me."

"What do you mean?"

"I was happy at Efrahte, Garth. For the first time in my life I was really happy. I had friends on Efrahte—and no enemies. I'd gotten a little accomplished. You know, Garth, out here everything's so big, the sea's so huge that a little island gets to be the whole thing, the whole world. Efrahte was my world and I didn't want to lose it."

"I don't follow," Garth said.

"You don't know the Navy. As soon as I heard the war was over I knew the Navy would come looking for its ship.

They have to. They have a list of ships they own and they've got to account to somebody for them. They can't just let them wander off. Some day some Navy ship would sail into that lagoon and some seaman deuce would look down and see an old subchaser. And then they'd find out that it belonged to them and start looking for the crew.

"Then they'd find me, Bill Barrett. AWOL for nine hundred years. It's hard to explain things to the Navy. Can't you see me sitting in some courtroom in San Diego explaining how I just happened to like living at Efrahte and so I didn't bother mentioning their ship to the Navy?

"As soon as it was safe I went over to Molahve. I figured that the depth charges would still be okay and maybe I could blow the old tub up. Get rid of her so the Navy'd *never* find her—or me.

"She was gone. There wasn't a trace of her."

"Didn't you figure that storms had buried her?"

"I hoped so. Or that the typhoon had blown her out to sea and she'd sunk in deep water. But I never was sure. For all those years I've been sort of waiting to hear that an old subchaser has been found—maybe still drifting around, maybe on some beach."

"Now you know," Garth said.

"And if I'd had only a few more hours today there wouldn't have been a trace of her. Like everything else in the ship the depth charges are as good as the day she went down and I've rigged them all over her so that all I had to do was give one yank and there wouldn't have been a piece of that ship as big as your hand left."

"Why didn't you?"

"I ran out of rope. Everything's rigged aboard but I had to have enough rope so I could get well clear of her when I pulled the pins. I went over to Efrahte to get some and when I got back—there he was."

"You knew the jewels weren't in her?"

Smith turned his head slowly and looked at Garth. "I

haven't thought about those things for years. I couldn't care less, Garth."

Garth studied his face and believed him. "So that taboo was only to keep people from finding the ship? When did you start setting it up?"

"The head man did that to protect me. He and his sons, Sam and Jake, set it up and in a few years it was working. Occasionally we'd hear that some mainlander had dropped in at Molahve but I didn't pay any attention. After every storm I'd go over there just to be sure the old bucket of bolts hadn't been uncovered. That's how stupid I was."

"You didn't suspect that someone else might be doing the same thing?" Garth asked.

"I had no reason to because I thought I'd killed the only other man who knew where the 206 went down. Schloss is smart. He always came in a different ship—sometimes a yacht, or a freighter, even in a Navy boat once—so I never even thought that it was the same man every time." Smith suddenly laughed. "Schloss must have had one wild ride in that lifeboat in a typhoon."

"We'll get him to tell us about it sometime. After we get the jewels back to the Philippines . . . There, all done."

"Good! Let's get out of here," Smith said, rubbing his wrists.

Garth didn't know exactly what warned him—whether it was a sound, or a movement of the boat or, simply, instinct—but he suddenly *knew* that someone had come aboard the *Uldra*. He could feel their presence and it seemed to him that they were very close, motionless and listening.

"Once we get ashore . . ." Smith said as Garth leaned close to him. Whispering, Garth said, "Keep talking. Out loud. Someone's aboard."

Smith stared at him as he went on talking, "Once we get up in the rain forest . . ."

"They're listening," Garth whispered.

". . . they can't track us," Smith went on.

"We've got to get off the boat," Garth whispered.

As Smith nodded he said, out loud, "You've got some food stashed on the beach, haven't you?"

"Plenty," Garth said out loud and whispered, "And get them off, too."

"So we'll pick up some chow on our way and vanish," Smith said. "We can sit it out in the jungle forever if we have to."

Garth glanced up at where the wreckers had torn the screen off the fresh air vent in the cabin ceiling. Anyone on deck could hear everything they said through the vent hood.

"How long before daylight?" Garth asked out loud.

"Less than an hour so we'd better get moving."

As Smith spoke Garth whispered to him, "We'll go up the companion ladder and make a dive for it. Straight aft and over the stern."

"We've got to wait for daylight," Garth said loudly.

"Why?" Smith asked.

Garth tried to make his laugh sound natural. "I've got some rock collecting to do."

"Rock collecting!" Smith said, his eyes questioning. "I thought you had 'em."

"They're still in the subchaser," Garth said, winking at him.

Smith nodded and said, "You're kidding! They can't be. I searched every inch of that ship."

Garth tried to laugh again. "I know you did and that's how I tricked you, Smitty. I hid them in the Charlie Noble." He motioned for Smith to stand up.

"You're lying," Smith said, making it sound genuine. "I looked in there."

"I know you did," Garth said, walking carefully toward the door. "And as soon as you got through looking I slipped 'em in there and put the screen back on. So we've got to wait here until daylight." Then he leaned close to Smith. "Keep talking. I'm going to take a look."

As Garth moved silently into the main cabin Smith said,

"Well, buddy, there aren't going to be any more tricks because if you try going after 'em by yourself you're going to get blown to kingdom come. I've rigged that ship so that if you try to get into her every depth charge aboard will explode."

Garth worked his way carefully along the wall until he could see up the companion ladder. Nothing moved in the rectangle of starlit sky framed by the hatch.

Smith was still talking. "So if you want to see those jewels again you'll have to take me with you because I know how to get in there without blowing myself up."

Garth motioned for Smith to join him.

As Smith left the cabin he said, "But I sure can't do it in the dark, so we'll just have to wait here until daylight."

Smith joined him and Garth whispered, "Follow me up then straight aft. As fast as you can go."

His bare feet didn't make a sound as he lunged up the treads of the ladder toward the clean night sky above him. Behind him he could hear Smith coming almost silently.

Garth crashed head on into the hatch cover as it slammed shut across the open rectangle. And then Smith came plowing into him. Both stunned, they rolled together back down the ladder and into the bilge water at the foot of it.

25.

Garth had seen so many of these lovely dawns in this lagoon. The early morning sunlight glittered on the clear water making the Monique cutter look as though it lay in a bed of jewels. The wake of the powerboat coming over from the cutter spread away in a gleaming triangle and the only sound was of its motor echoing from the green jungle.

Professor Castle sat on the companion hatch with a shotgun across his knees. Smith, handcuffed and chained again, sat on the starboard side of the cockpit. Garth was chained to the wheel.

"As they say in the Military Code of Justice," Castle was saying, "you made a fatal error, Barrett. You thought you had killed me. It was a close thing, at that. I almost died in the lifeboat."

Garth stood up as far as his chain would let him and looked at the approaching boat. He expected to see the tall figure of the inspector but he was not aboard. "How's the inspector?" he asked.

"The inspector?" Castle said. "I'm sorry to say that he died—as a result of being stung by a cone shell."

Garth looked at the man. "With a lot of help from you."

Castle shrugged and turned to look at the powerboat. "A

beautiful morning," he said. "Those jewels will sparkle in this sunshine."

"Not for you, they won't," Smith said.

Castle turned and looked at him with those cold and faded eyes. "Let's try to understand each other," he said. "All I want is the jewels. You're no doubt convinced that as soon as I get them I'll be forced to murder you. That's not my intention. To kill you, Barrett, would cause no trouble but with Larson it's a different story. His death could create problems for me—after all there are six Monique sailors over on that cutter who might talk—to someone like José Morales for instance. So you see, I don't need problems."

Smith started to say something but Castle held up his hand. "Wait. You think I'll have to kill you to keep you from exposing me. That just isn't true, my friend. Don't you realize that no one will believe such a fantastic tale which, of course, you won't be able to prove?" He leaned forward, looking at them. "Believe me, I want no trouble. I can use your help getting the jewels, but I can get them without it. However, that will only delay your freedom."

"You don't even know where they are, Schloss," Smith said.

Castle smiled at him. "What, exactly, is a Charlie Noble, Barrett? . . . Now, gentlemen, I'll explain to you what I want you to do. I want you to go down and fix those depth charges so they won't explode. Naturally, you'll be careful not to blow yourselves up in the process."

"We haven't got any air," Garth told him. "They emptied all my tanks and we can't skin dive to sixty feet."

"You'll have all the air you need," Castle said. Then he smiled at them again. "After you make the ship safe for me I'll go down and retrieve the jewels. That done, I will sail away, leaving you with your little paradise. So, talk it over. If you don't choose to cooperate you can see that it will only delay my departure."

Castle stood up and started forward. At the hatch he

stopped and turned, smiling again. "And don't plan to set up any small surprises for me in that ship because when I go down for the jewels you two are going with me. You'll probably sink faster than I do because of the weight of the chains binding you."

Smith and Garth sat in silence watching Castle as he walked forward and sat down in the bow, his back to them.

Smith turned slowly and looked at Garth. "He's lying. We'll never come up."

Garth nodded.

Smith lowered his voice. "Are they really in the Charlie Noble?"

Garth shook his head. "Are the depth charges still rigged to go off?"

"Just pull the plug," Smith said.

"Can you get in her?"

"*I* can. There're wires and ropes all over the place."

The powerboat came alongside and they watched Hal King unloading scuba gear and wet suits.

"I never liked that clown," Garth said. "He's got Professional Coward printed on his calling cards."

Smith stared away at the clouds. "You know something, Garth, if I could figure a way I'm about ready to go— if I could take Schloss with me."

"I'm not," Garth said. "Was rope all you needed?"

Smith looked puzzled. "For what? Oh—yeah. Just rope. But a lot of it. A hundred fath . . ."

"Belay it!" Garth said in a low voice, sitting back on the wheelbox as Castle and King came aft.

"All right, gentlemen, what's your decision?" Castle asked.

"The sooner you get out of here, the better," Garth said. "Splendid."

With King standing guard with the shotgun Castle unchained them. "Let's go to work," he said.

As Garth walked past King he looked at him and said, "How'd you get in on this deal, you ding-a-ling?"

King laughed at him. "That's my uncle, chum."

Garth glanced at Castle. "Lucky you."

With the suits and scuba gear on they got down into the boat, Castle in the bow with the gun, Garth and Smith amidships, and King on the helm with a pistol in one hand.

Garth checked the landmarks and pointed out the direction. As the boat moved out into the lagoon he leaned over the side, staring down through the water which was as clear as he remembered it.

"Don't look so gloomy, Barrett," Castle said. "I promise you that as soon as I have those jewels I'll leave you and Larson here—unharmed."

"Oh, I believe you, Schloss. All I have to do is see those skeletons in the subchaser again to know that you wouldn't hurt a fly," Smith told him.

"There she is," Garth said.

King stopped the engine and Castle carefully dropped the anchor straight down. Garth watched it hit the bottom well clear of the subchaser.

"Now, gentlemen, don't be foolish. I can see you down there. If you try to swim away all I have to do is follow you. I might simply keep you under water until your air runs out or shoot you when you come up. Do we understand each other?"

Garth said, "Why don't I slip down there, get them and bring them back?"

Castle smiled at him. "It's been a long time. I've forgotten what they look like. How many there were." His voice changed. "I want them *all*, Larson. You make the ship safe and then *I* will go get them."

As Garth prepared to go over the side he looked at Castle and grinned. "Charlie Noble is the galley smoke pipe, professor."

They went down together and at about ten feet above the ship Smith motioned to stop.

He had done a tremendous job. Depth charges were lashed all along the rails, one was wedged up on top of the bridge, another was strapped to the smoke pipe. Smith had used everything he could find to connect them—steering cable, electric cord, ignition wires, rope. The topside was spiderwebbed with it.

Garth touched his arm and pointed to the engine room, making a motion of entering with his hands. Smith nodded but held up his hand in caution.

Swimming slowly with Smith ahead, they approached the ship. At the door to the engine room Smith pointed down at two wires running along the deck, warning him not to touch them as he opened the door carefully and carefully closed it after they got inside.

The only light now came through the portholes so that they moved in a world of dim green. Garth swam over to the starter motor on the port diesel and studied the case for a moment and then pointed at the bolts holding the bearing block and made a motion of unscrewing them. Smith looked puzzled but pointed toward the tool rack.

The tools lay in orderly rows in the trays and as Garth picked out the end wrench he needed he glanced at the skeleton of Smith's brother still lying across the gear box. Skippy had been a good, neat mechanic.

Garth had no difficulty getting the bearing block off the back end and pulling the armature out of the motor. Smith watched him, evidently not understanding what he was doing.

Getting a hammer and small chisel he had Smith hold the armature firmly on the deck by the shaft ends. Setting the chisel just at the edge of the winding he struck it lightly and then scrubbed away the sea slime, exposing the copper wire coiled around the iron core.

With his fingernail Garth pried the end of the wire out of the varnish and uncoiled a little of it.

As Smith saw the thin wire smile lines showed around his eyes.

Garth held the wire in both hands and yanked at it but the wire did not break.

They went out, again being careful not to foul the door edge in the wires on deck.

Garth held the armature in close to his body so Castle couldn't see it and then looked up at the bottom of the boat breaking the smooth surface of the water.

Smith touched his arm and pointed forward.

At the bow of the subchaser he had gathered together the ends of all his exploder wires and ropes and had knotted them around a cleat. Floating now above it Smith made a motion as though taking the bundle in his hands. Then he jerked his arm back and then, using both hands, made an upward, exploding gesture.

Garth nodded and Smith swam down to the cleat. Carefully so as not to put any strain on the bundle Smith held it while Garth wrapped the armature wire around it and knotted it tightly. Then, motioning for Smith to hold fast, he swam away from the bow, uncoiling wire from the armature as he went. Clear of the ship he stopped and peeled off the wire, letting it drop to the bottom. When he was sure that he had enough slack to take care of any accidents he moved back to Smith.

Tapping Smith on the head he pointed away toward the east and then tapped Smith's chest. Next Garth tapped his own chest and pointed to the west. Then he made a swimming movement with his free hand.

Smith nodded and held out his hands for the armature. Garth moved it away, shaking his head.

Smith scowled at him and made a jerking motion with his hands. Again Garth shook his head and gently pushed Smith away, and moved away himself.

Floating down until he was only a few feet from the rough bottom Garth held the armature by the shaft ends and began swimming toward the beach. Looking up he saw Smith above him, watching him, but at last Smith turned and started swimming away in the opposite direction.

Garth had not gone far before he heard the rattle of the motor starting. Turning to look up he saw the surface suddenly shattered by a white coil of water spinning off the propeller blades.

What would Castle do? he wondered as he swam along, reeling off the wire. Would he chase Smith who was now much farther away? Or would he suspect that Garth, because he was moving so slowly, was doing something that threatened him?

He paused a second and watched the hull of the boat swing around and then move until it was directly above him.

The copper wire looked very bright, almost golden but Garth doubted if Castle could see it among the rocks and pieces of coral. Even if he could, he argued, there wasn't anything he could do about it.

He was wrong.

There was a sudden explosion, the concussion of it slamming against him.

Looking up he saw a funnel shaped roil of white foam beside the boat, a funnel which plunged straight down toward him.

And then from the bottom of the funnel a little black object came down through the water.

Garth watched it as it went past him, going slowly, and turning end for end. The nose of the bullet had been a little flattened by the impact but otherwise it was in good shape.

He swam on, the armature unreeling the wire. Above him now the boat moved and they continued to shoot at him, the concussions jarring him and making his head ache a little.

Garth felt a fine sense of power now. They couldn't stop the process. Not with bullets. And if either one, or both of them, came into the water he was sure he could handle them.

Only the wire could stop him and already the coil was thin, the wrappings very near the core.

Garth looked back and was shocked by how close the

subchaser seemed. It didn't look as though he had gone more than a hundred feet. At that distance one depth charge would tear him all to pieces—and there were a dozen.

He swam on, over sandy bottom now, watching the bright wire reeling off the core. He could hear the boat's motor and see the shadow of it moving along with him but that did not concern him.

The shaft ends turned easily in his cupped fingers and the wire peeled off, yard after yard, exposing more bright layers. And then at last the dark iron core appeared.

Garth swam very slowly as the last coils unwound and when he felt a slight pull on the wire he stopped.

He could see the bow of the subchaser, he could read the number on it. He could see the frame of the bridge window. He could see the depth charge on the roof.

It was so *close!*

He floated there.

Turning his head slowly he looked for Smith but could not see him anywhere.

Above him the sound of the motor grew louder and when he looked up he saw a great boil of water around the stern and then the boat began to move.

Castle had figured it out, Garth decided, and was running.

With the wire still attached to the armature he wrapped it twice around his left wrist and then began swimming.

He drove the fins against the water, powering them from his hips and could feel the water flowing past him.

And then the wire yanked his arm, slewing him around.

26

Brilliant little sparks of light flashed on the deck of the subchaser and then Garth heard a series of sharp, hard clicking sounds.

Grabbing himself, he flattened out face down on the sandy bottom.

The shock wave of the explosion was enormous. It struck him like an immense hammer, compressing him until he felt as though all the bones in his body were broken and then it passed on, leaving him suddenly in a profound silence where nothing seemed to move.

Not sure that he was alive he was just beginning to move his arms and legs when the water around him which had been so still and silent went insane.

It literally grabbed him and hurled him at the beach, beating him against the bottom, throwing him to the surface, dragging him down again. It tore off his mask, ripped the breather out of his mouth; it beat him with the tanks on his back while the straps tried to break the bones of his chest.

Blinded by the sand, his mouth and nose full of it, he could do nothing to save himself. He did not even know which way was up.

Floundering, in pain, breathless, he suddenly felt less pressure around his face and, in desperate hope, opened his mouth to breathe. . . .

Thick, sandy foam flowed into his throat and when he reached up with his hands he could not find the top of the stuff.

Drowning in foam as the sea still threw him bodily toward the shore a new attack began on him. Something began snatching at him, dragging him, then letting go, only to snatch and grab again. At last, whatever it was caught him around the throat and began to strangle him as it lifted him up.

He could tell that his head was out of the foam by the change of light around his blinded eyes and whatever had him loosened its grip but did not let him go.

Feeling sand grinding in his eyes he opened them and could tell that there was sunlight around him and, close to him, something huge and black, something that writhed in the water, coming close to him and then moving away.

But he could breathe now and he fought against the black thing, trying to free himself from it, as small, but sand-free waves slapped him in the face.

The waves cleared his eyes and he could see that two black men were holding him, swimming him toward the beach.

His dragging feet touched bottom and he pushed them down, pushing against the men.

And then he was standing up, chest deep, with Sam and Jake looking at him anxiously.

They helped him as he stumbled on toward shore and eased him down at last on the sand. And then, suddenly, they were gone.

Garth lifted his head slowly and saw them running together down the beach toward Smith who was wading out of the water.

Garth turned and looked out across the lagoon where an immense disc of dirty water spread against the clean blue.

The powerboat lay capsized in the dying waves, her bottom paint the color of blood in the sunshine. Near her two bodies floated, drifting apart, striking each other, drifting apart again.

Beyond them the old *Uldra* lay calm and dignified on an even keel. Her mainmast lay like a broken arm across her and her foremast leaned at a sick angle to port.

On the other side of the lagoon the Monique cutter seemed unharmed, her crew lining the rail and staring silently.

Garth released the harness buckles and let the tanks fall into the sand. Without their weight he got slowly to his feet and began peeling off what was left of the wet suit. Free of it, but hurting all over, he walked slowly along the beach toward Sam and Jake and Smith.

He stumbled as he reached them and Smith caught him by the shoulders and held him, staring at him.

"How are you?" Garth said.

"Okay . . . Sit down, sit down . . . you're bleeding everywhere."

"I'm all right," Garth said, sitting down on the warm sand.

"Your ears, nose, everywhere," Smith said, worried.

"I'm all right," Garth told him. "Just full of sand. How're you?"

"Shook," Smith said.

Garth looked out across the lagoon. "She really went up," he said.

The two bodies were drifting apart now, moving slowly out to sea. "I think they're dead," Garth said.

"Yeah."

Garth started to get up and Smith helped him. "I thought they'd get away," he said in a dull voice.

"The water must've fallen on the boat," Smith said. "Half the lagoon must have been up in the air. How far away did you get?"

Garth tried to smile. "Far enough."

Jake started talking to Smith.

"How'd *they* get here?" Garth asked.

"Jumped overboard when the first shot struck. Now Jake says they caught somebody last night and tied him to a tree."

"Here?" Garth asked. "What tree?"

"Somebody off the cutter."

Garth followed Sam and Jake, the effort of walking in the sand almost more than he could put out. He felt numb and sick, as though his brains had been beaten into mush and would not work any more, and his whole body ached.

They were into the first low jungle growth when Garth heard the sound of a diesel. Somehow he expected to see the whole U. S. Navy steaming into the lagoon but when he turned and looked seaward there was nothing. Then movement caught his eye and he saw the Monique cutter moving out, her speed increasing, the thrum of her diesels beating against the jungle. Her wake rocked the *Uldra*, the broken mainmast beating at her rail and the foremast swaying in a sickening arc.

The wake also washed over the capsized powerboat and, although he could no longer see them, he knew that it was rolling the bodies of Castle and King.

Getting through the low undergrowth and up into a grove of palms Garth looked ahead and saw the man, his head slumped forward, tied to the trunk of a tree with vines.

It was Steve Osborn. As they approached him he raised his battered face and tried to smile but his lips were too swollen. "Sure is noisy around here," he said.

"Where did you come from?" Garth asked, staring at him.

"You don't look so good yourself," Steve said. "Are these two cannibals friends of yours?"

"Good friends," Garth said, untying the vines. "What happened?"

"What happened? Well, I just got tired of hitting the barrel of that pistol with my face, so I went over the side. What happened to you, you're blood all over."

"Got caught in the noise," Garth said.

Free of the vines Steve stretched his arms and back. "Oh, ouch!" he said. "Where's that professor pal of yours?" he asked, craning to see over the underbrush.

"Dead."

"Well, I don't know how good a friend he was, but for my money he deserves it. He killed the inspector when the guy was lying there, passed out from that poison you gave him. Just killed him. Like that. I think he was going to kill me, too. Only I took a walk. Ker-plunk," Steve said. "And then I ran into a couple of guys who wanted to eat me."

Garth laughed. "They wouldn't eat the best part of you, Steve."

27

Garth hadn't been this peaceful since the early days at Molahve. Sitting on the veranda of Smith's house at Efrahte with his feet up on the rail he looked down at the attractive little village with its people moving about now, getting ready for the evening meal. Kids were playing around in toy outriggers or just paddling logs in the shallow water. The dogs, expectant, had stopped barking and were lying beside the cook fires.

Out in the lagoon one lonesome man sailing in the soft, evening wind made his way between the ships at anchor. The *Uldra* was there, her white hull shining and giving no hint of the wreckage inside. The Philippine Navy destroyer escort was there with her crew in white moving around on the gray decks. Compared to the DE's slim, menacing hull, the Institute's fat-bellied oceanographic research ship looked old and motherly.

Only Smith's copra boat was missing. Maybe, Garth thought, she's still afloat somewhere, a ship burned to the waterline. Or perhaps the diesel in her was too heavy for the buoyant wood and, alone, she sank.

Smith had brought out a long wooden table and covered

it with a blanket and then, on top of that, a white table cloth.

The jewels were spread out on the cloth in groups—diamonds here, rubies there, sapphires, pearls, opals, emeralds. As the gentle wind moved the leaves of a banana tree beside the veranda the waving leaves changed the light on the jewels so that they glowed brightly at times or faded into lovely low gleams of light.

Garth's boss sat beside him, his feet also on the rail. Jenkins, a Ph.D. not an M.D. doctor, looked like a blocking back on a good professional football team because he had earned his way through school being a blocking back on a good professional football team.

"It's discouraging, Garth," Jenkins was saying, "but persuading the young graduates to go to work with you at Molahve isn't easy. No girls. No gold. And, I'm afraid, no glamor." He looked over at the jewels and laughed. "At least, not any more, since you seem to have gotten it all."

"If that's the kind of glamor they want they can have it," Garth said.

"The trouble is," Jenkins said, "this ship they're building down in Palau is a lot more boat than the *Uldra*. She's a beauty, really. But a lot of boat; a huge lab, wonderful equipment. But not a one-man deal by a long shot."

Garth turned and grinned at him. "The project has *got* to have that boat, Doctor. Look, I was working the *Uldra* with one hand. But in a boat like that I'd use both hands!"

Jenkins chuckled and said, "You might change your mind when you see her. She's *big*, Garth." Then he was serious. "No, she's too much boat, too much equipment and, anyway, your project needs more people."

"Two men?" Garth asked.

"I don't think so, Garth," Jenkins said slowly. "Three men at the least, the very least. Believe me, we've tried to persuade every marine biologist or ecologist in the country to take this on—I mean, hundreds of young guys. We've got . . . one. A Scripps man who doesn't seem to want to get rich and famous his first year out of school. But one more isn't enough. On your supply trips to Beaufort or even your disposal runs she's too big for only two men and I'm not sure the man we've got even knows how to sail a boat."

"Three?" Garth asked.

"Three would be okay once your project was set up and running."

"How much will the Institute pay a man?"

"Depends on his degree. A bachelor in marine biology or ecology—six hundred a month. A Master, eight-fifty. A Ph.D.—I think I could talk them into a thousand for a good Ph.D. Only there aren't any who want to take it on."

Garth looked over his shoulder at Steve. He had been half listening to, and enjoying, Steve's efforts to con José Morales into appointing Steve to some important position in the Philippine Government. As far as Garth could tell José wasn't buying the idea. "Hey, Steve," he called.

As Steve came past the table he picked up a handful of diamonds.

The Filipino sailors guarding the table moved in fast, rifles at the ready.

Steve held out his hand and let the jewels fall back into the pile. "Gravel," he said and came on over to Garth.

"What sort of degrees have you got, Steve?" Garth asked him.

"Degrees?" Steve asked. "Oh, yeah, degrees. Well, let's see. After I dropped out of grammar school I took a short course at CYA . . ."

"CYA?" Jenkins asked.

"California Youth Authority—a kind of, well, jail. I got a degree there in pigeon drop and Mexican trunk . . ." Steve broke himself up ". . . and then I went to UCLA and got an LSD . . ."

"Okay, okay," Garth said. "You want a job?"

Steve stopped laughing and stood a moment looking at Garth. "A job? Doing what?"

"Working at Molahve."

"With you?"

"Yes."

"On your project?"

"Yes." He looked at Jenkins. "Five hundred a month?"
Steve said slowly, "I'd like that, Garth."

"You've got it."

Steve's face lit up and he grinned. "How *about* that!
Hey, José. Forget the deal—I don't need it!"

Garth turned to Jenkins. "Okay?"

"It's your crew," Jenkins said.

Smith came out with Sam and Jake following him. When
José Morales spotted him he went over and took Smith by the
arm and led him to where Garth was sitting.

"Big speech time," José said. "My government wants to
thank you cats. And not just 'thanks.'" He reached over and
pushed his hand through a pile of rubies. My government
wants you to be rewarded for returning this property. . . ."

"Wait a minute, José," Smith said. Then he looked at
Garth. "You remember, Garth, I told you I didn't want
those things? I guess that's hard to believe . . ." He turned
to José. "You see the Men's House in the village?"

"Very handsome."

"See the little pieces of glass?"

They were gleaming in the late afternoon sunlight, a
shimmering, sparkling light.

"They're not all glass," Smith said. "For the last week
or so on the old 206 my brother and I would swipe a
diamond or a ruby every chance we got. Just pick one or
two out of that washtub and swing with it. We stole almost
a coffee can full . . ." Smith looked again at the Men's
House. "They belong to you, too, José. Most of them are
still there because the only time we ever used any of them
was when we needed a pump for the well or a generator
for some lights, or a tractor. And the hospital. Well—and
I hocked four of them for the copra boat."

José stood on the veranda looking down at the Men's

House, the jewels shining wonderfully in the now soft light. "They look like glass to me," José said. Then he went over to the table and picked out a huge, cut ruby. Holding it out to Smith, he said, "You'll need this for a new copra boat."

"Thanks, no," Smith said. "We were making pretty good money with the old one and we saved it all. It's enough, but thanks anyway."

"As you wish," José said, turning to Garth and holding out the ruby. "Garth—to repair the *Uldra*."

Garth took the ruby and looked at it in the palm of his hand. Then he reached over to the table and put it gently down among the others. "José, no hard feelings, but I don't want to see any of those rocks again. *Ever*."

The little party ended as the Filipinos began gathering up their stones and Jenkins said good night. Soon everyone had gone except Garth and Steve and Smith.

Garth sat down and put his feet on the rail again. He was thinking about the collection of specimens he and Steve had so carefully transferred from the *Uldra's* aquariums back to their sea.

And he was thinking about the lagoon. On the day they had left for Efrahte he had looked down at where the subchaser had been and there was no sign of her. Torn apart, obliterated by the depth charges, there were, he knew, bits and pieces of her scattered all over that rocky ocean floor but the white sand was coming back, covering everything.

Still, the new lagoon he and Jenkins and Steve had found appealed to him more now. So beautiful, so calm, so protected. He could work much better there.

"When are we leaving for Guam?" Steve asked.

"Guam?" Garth said, not having thought about that. "Oh, whenever Dr. Jenkins wants to go. Then I guess we'll go down to Palau and help get the new ship ready."

"When do you figure we'll get back to Molahve?"

"Three months, more or less. Whenever the ship's ready. And by that time Molahve will be pure again."

"What are they going to do with the *Uldra?*" Smith asked.

Garth looked down at the lagoon where she lay mastless and forlorn in the starlight. "Fit her out again. Fit her out for some young marine biologist so he can get rich and famous."

For a long time none of them said anything but at last Smith asked in a low voice, "Will you let me know when you get back, Garth?"

Garth began to laugh. "You know it! I don't want to meet you—and Sam and Jake—again the way I did the first time." Then he looked at Smith. "What do I call you now? Bill Barrett or Ord Smith?"

"I guess—Smith. Ord Smith. I'm used to that."

"What's that 'Ord'? I never heard a name like Ord," Steve said.

"A long time ago," Smith said, "I needed a new name. A good, simple name so I just picked Smith. Ordinary Smith."

Robb White has actually lived the adventurous life most people only dream of. He was born in the Philippine Islands where his father was a missionary, and almost got killed there as a naval officer aboard an aircraft carrier during the Battle of Leyte Gulf. Determined to be a writer since he was thirteen, he attended the Episcopal High School in Alexandria, Virginia, and was graduated from the U. S. Naval Academy at Annapolis. After resigning his commission in the Navy, he began the adventurous wanderings which have taken him from the mountains of Kurdistan to the beach of Eniwetok Island. He has flown as a pilot and served in submarines, carriers, sailboats, and—once—a rubber life raft. He has written a great many short stories and over twenty books, including *The Survivor* and *Silent Ship, Silent Sea,* as well as *Up Periscope* and *Our Virgin Island,* which were made into movies. Now a retired captain in the Naval Reserve, he and his wife live at Lake Havasu City beside the Colorado River in Arizona, where Mr. White spends his time writing books and motion picture and television scripts.